I0819813

The CIA and Dr. Zhivago

How America's Cold War Spies Played Book Publisher to Bring Hope to Millions

Central Intelligence Agency

NIMBLE BOOKS LLC: THE AI LAB FOR BOOK-LOVERS

~ FRED ZIMMERMAN, EDITOR ~

Humans and AI making books richer, more diverse, and more surprising.

Publishing Information

ISBN: 978-1-60888-310-3

AI-generated Keyword Phrases

Pantheon (publisher);
American Approved for Release;
Russian edition copyright law;
Russian copyright law;
International copyright law;
Pasternak translation;
Pasternak publication history;
Pasternak works
Pasternak interpretation;
Feltrinelli publishing rights;
Dr. Zhivago negotiations;
Dr. Zhivago history;
David Lean Zhivago;
AEDINOSAUR Meeting;
Press coverage Pasternak case;
Italian publisher Feltrinelli;
Feltrinelli

Publisher's Notes

In a world teetering on the brink of atomic war, the Boris Pasternak novel *Doctor Zhivago* offered a profound meditation on the human condition, challenging the reader to confront the tension between individual freedom and societal pressures. Echoing the contemporary struggles for liberty and self-expression unfolding across the globe, Pasternak's masterpiece resonated with our innate desire for autonomy and meaning, urging Soviets and Americans alike to consider the choices we faced in the face of oppression and the enduring power of the human spirit. The subsequent David Lean movie with Omar Sharif and Julie Christie in the leads ensured that *Zhivago* would be a long-lasting cultural milestone, as well as source of great meaning and pleasure to anyone with the capacity to appreciate art and human emotion.

The documents in this book, declassified by the Central Intelligency Agency some years ago, show the Agency in the somewhat surprising role of international book publisher, struggling to disentangle a complicated rights situation so that *Dr. Zhivago* could be published in as many languages and territories as possible. An unusual and fascinating episode that sheds much light on the battle for meaning during the Cold War—and incidentally on the sometimes fractal complexity of book publishing!

This annotated edition illustrates the capabilities of the AI Lab for Book-Lovers to add context and ease-of-use to manuscripts. It includes several types of abstracts, building from simplest to more complex: TLDR (one word), ELI5, TLDR (vanilla), Scientific Style, and Action Items; Notable Passages and summaries for each page; essays to increase viewpoint diversity, such as an exploration of the ethics of the project; Grounds for Dissent, Red Team Critique, MAGA Perspective; and a meta-inquiry in the voice of Pasternak entitled "Pasternak Reflects."

ANNOTATIONS

ABSTRACTS

ANALYSIS BASED ON FULL CONTEXT

These analyses are created by using an LLM with a very long input context window, in this case Google Gemini 1.5-pro. The advantage is that the model can use the entirety of the document in its simulated reasoning.

This document comprises a series of memoranda and letters between various parties regarding the publication and distribution of Boris Pasternak's novel *Doctor Zhivago*. The Soviet Union banned the book's publication domestically, prompting interest from Western entities, including the Central Intelligence Agency (CIA), in disseminating it within the USSR.

The documents detail efforts to secure the manuscript, arrange for typesetting and printing in various languages, and strategize distribution methods to circumvent Soviet censorship. Issues of copyright, author's rights, and potential legal ramifications are discussed, alongside the perceived propaganda value of the novel and its potential impact on Soviet citizens.

The documents reveal a complex web of interactions between the CIA, publishers, legal representatives, and individuals involved in disseminating the book. Efforts to secure a legitimate publication are complicated by concerns for Pasternak's safety, potential legal challenges from the Italian publisher holding the copyright, and the need for covert distribution within the USSR.

ANALYSIS BASED ON ABRIDGED CONTENT WINDOWS

These analyzes are created by analyzing portions or summaries of the document, using LLMs with shorter context windows. The advantage is that these models are faster and cheaper.

TL;DR (ONE WORD)

Complicated.

EXPLAIN IT TO ME LIKE I'M FIVE YEARS OLD

This text is talking about a book called "Doctor Zhivago" and some legal issues around it being published in different countries. Some people were trying to make sure the book was published in the right way and that the rights to the book were protected. It's like making sure a toy is made by the right company and not copied by someone else. They wanted to make sure the book was published in the right way and that the people who wrote it got credit for their work.

TL;DR (Vanilla)

The text discusses the publication rights and agreements related to the book "Dr. Zhivago" by Boris Pasternak, including details about the Russian edition and negotiations with publishers. It also mentions the distribution and sales of the book, as well as the legal implications of publishing it without authorization.

Scientific Style

Recent developments in the publication of Boris Pasternak's "Dr. Zhivago" have raised legal questions regarding the rights of the Italian publisher, Feltrinelli, to produce a Russian edition. Despite claims made in advertisements, it remains unclear if an authorized Russian edition has been published, casting doubt on Feltrinelli's copyright claims. This study highlights the complexities of international copyright law and the challenges faced by publishers in navigating cross-border publishing agreements.

Action Items

Retrospective, as if formulated by a reader at the time of publication. These book publishing "to dos" were someone's job at the CIA at the height of the Cold War..

Contact Pantheon to inquire about the unauthorized Russian edition of the book "Dr. Zhivago" and the rights under copyright law.

Investigate the distribution and sales of the book "Dr. Zhivago" to determine if any special pricing agreements were violated.

Review the agreement with the Italian publisher Feltrinelli regarding the publication of "Dr. Zhivago" in Russian and ensure compliance with the terms.

Follow up on the meeting held on June 12, 1958, to draw up a contract for negotiations related to the book.

Verify the publication rights.

Page-by-Page Summaries

In this section, we abstract one page at a time.

BODY-1 *Legal counsel is seeking approval to broadcast Dr. Zhivago in Russian to Soviet audiences via Radio Liberation, despite Soviet authorities withholding the book. The British Broadcasting Corporation is also broadcasting excerpts.*

BODY-2 *Novoye Russkoye Slovo is serializing the Russian language version of Dr. Zhivago with acknowledgment to the University of Michigan Press. There are legal concerns about broadcasting the Russian version on Radio Liberation.*

BODY-3 *Distribution details of Russian copies of Dr. Zhivago, with 101,000 copies printed by Dutch publisher Mouton. Initial batch distributed to various locations, including Brussels, Frankfurt, Berlin, Munich, London, and Paris. Additional copies to be sent to Headquarters for distribution by SB assets.*

BODY-4 *Order for 3,000 copies of an unabridged Russian edition of "Dr. Zhivago" accepted with a 20% discount. Release expected in six to eight weeks.*

BODY-5 *Suggests bringing Feltrinelli to the US due to his break from Communist associations and the impact of publishing the Pasternak Book on Soviet reputation.*

BODY-6 *Acknowledgment of receipt of a letter and enclosure, with a promise to look into the subject matter further.*

BODY-7 *Urgent request to assist in promoting a book by Pasternak, potential Nobel Prize winner, with a focus on the author's family and connections.*

BODY-8 *Mr. Feltrinelli's departure from the Italian GP is doubted, with speculation that he may have been influenced by the Italian CP or Soviet IS, especially after the publication of Dr. Zhivago. There is suspicion of a Communist informant among his staff or friends.*

BODY-9 *Request for assistance with urgent and important information, seeking help from a publisher for a confidential matter.*

BODY-10 *Doubt surrounds Mr. Feltrinelli's departure from the Italian CP, with speculation of Communist influence or control due to his association with Dr. Zhivago and Boris Pasternak. Possible informant or agent among his office staff or close friends.*

BODY-11 *Mr. Feltrinelli applied for a visa to the U.S. to discuss publishing a Russian-language edition of Dr. Zhivago with the University of Michigan Press and Pantheon Books. Pantheon Books already has a copyright agreement with Mr. Feltrinelli.*

BODY-12 *Acknowledgment of a recent telephone call and letter, promising to look into the subject matter further.*

BODY-13 *Feltrinelli applying for US visa to discuss Russian edition of Dr. Zhivago with University of Michigan Press and Pantheon Books. Pantheon not contracted with Feltrinelli for copyright.*

BODY-14 *A letter thanking Allen Dulles for his note on behalf of an Italian friend who did not even request a visa, highlighting the strangeness of people.*

BODY-15 *Letter discussing the potential benefit of bringing Feltrinelli, who has broken away from Communist associations, to the United States due to his actions against the Soviet position.*

BODY-16 *Discussion of rights and translations in relation to an agreement with a Russian publishing house, with implications for Italian translations and authority from Pasternak.*

BODY-17	*Analysis of copyright issues surrounding Dr. Zhivago, including common-law copyright, unpublished works, and Universal Copyright Convention. Conflicting opinions on alien author rights and enforcement in different countries. No statutory protection for unpublished works under UCC. Feltrinelli's rights would be derivative from Pasternak.*
BODY-18	*Request for clarification on publishing rights for Russian-language editions of Boris Pasternak's works, including poetry and autobiography, to avoid legal and commercial difficulties.*
BODY-19	*Request for opinion on enforceable rights for publishing a Russian-language autobiography, including pages from "Selected Writings of Boris Pasternak" for study.*
BODY-20	*The page discusses copyright issues regarding the Russian edition of a literary work by Pasternak, stating that Feltrinelli has no rights to the Russian edition. It also mentions the possibility of Pasternak bringing action for unauthorized radio broadcasting rights if he leaves the USSR.*
BODY-21	*Legal liability of American Committee for Liberation regarding broadcasting "Dr. Zhivago" in Russia due to copyright issues with Boris Pasternak's work. Unclear origins of manuscript, translations, and copyrights create legal uncertainty.*
BODY-22	*Myron Cohen's collection of stories and jokes, Alexander King's book mixing autobiography and fiction, and an advertisement for American Artist magazine.*
BODY-23	*The page promotes a book by Herbert O. Yardley called "The Education of a Poker Player," which shares secrets and strategies for winning at various types of poker. It includes specific advice, sample hands, and stories from Yardley's own experiences.*
BODY-24	*Summary: Memorandum detailing the resume of an OCB luncheon meeting on November 5, 1958, with Mr. Dulles present.*
BODY-25	*Document approved for release on April 7, 2014.*
BODY-26	*Discussion on US actions following Boris Pasternak's Nobel Prize and refusal, including CIA involvement to exploit the situation in the Soviet Union.*
BODY-27	*Speculation on potential conflicts between China and the Soviet Union, deemed unlikely by respondents due to historical differences and commitment to peace within the socialist camp.*
BODY-28	*The page discusses the Soviet treatment of Pasternak and the reactions in the West, including the possibility of an abridged version of Dr. Zhivago being permitted in the Soviet Union. Student reactions and government involvement are also mentioned.*
BODY-29	*Students react positively to the ban on Pasternak's work, believing it to be necessary due to his subjective writing. They do not see him as a significant Soviet writer and do not emphasize the literary aspects of his work.*
BODY-30	*Soviet students have mixed views on China's path to communism, lack clear understanding of commune system, and defend Russian communism as unique. They value historical facts and recommend agents be well-informed on political movements. Views on Yugoslavia vary, with some seeing it as state capitalism funded by the West.*
BODY-31	*Purchase of books for distribution to legal travelers entering the Soviet Union and acquisition of Russian literature not available through CIA channels. Delegation of authority for Project AEDINOSAUR established for fund commitments.*

BODY-32	*This page is about the approval and renewal of a project within the Aedinosaurs division, with staff coordination and signatures required for organizational purposes.*
BODY-33	*Project Cryptonym Aedinosaurs is a secret financial data project covering the fiscal period from July 1957 to June 1958, detailing personnel requirements, supplies, equipment, operational expenses, and subsidy payments. Total fund requirements are $756.*
BODY-34	*Request for renewal of project funding for AEDINOSAUR D&TO for USSR in FY 1958, with specific financial considerations and approval processes outlined.*
BODY-35	*Recommendations for handling the publication of Dr. Zhivago in the West, emphasizing the importance of world opinion and the impact on Soviet writers. Focus on maximum foreign editions and Nobel prize consideration, while avoiding a Russian version by political publishers. Coordination and widespread publication are key.*
BODY-36	*Routing and record sheet for confidential communication, with space for comments and officer initials.*
BODY-37	*Discussion of obtaining and distributing copies of Pasternak's novel, with concerns about Soviet interception and plans for worldwide distribution.*
BODY-38	*Request for corrections and clarification on inaccuracies in the Collins project, with a need for immediate reprinting and distribution to continue discussions on its exploitation.*
BODY-39	*Pantheon is collaborating with Collins on a translation, with Pantheon paying for part of the cost and receiving the British translation for re-editing. They are not interested in publishing a Russian text due to copyright issues.*
BODY-40	*Pasternak's novel Dr. Zhivago was published in the Free World after being denied in the USSR. Italian publisher Feltfrinelli took the risk, leading to publications in various countries. Plans to publish the Russian text in a "black edition" to avoid copyright issues.*
BODY-41	*Discussion regarding the Dutch publication of "Doctor Zhivago" and attempts to obtain an excerpted Russian version with Pasternak's approval. Concerns raised about unauthorized access to the original manuscript. Potential Russian edition in preparation in New York.*
BODY-42	*Information about a book appearing in a Russian publication by Mut.*
BODY-43	*This page is a routing and record sheet for classified information, with space for comments and approvals.*
BODY-44	*Discussion regarding the publication of Dr. Zhivago in Russia, with mention of an individual in London and an address in The Hague.*
BODY-45	*Soviet censors banned Boris Pasternak's novel "Dr. Zhivago" for criticizing the Soviet system. Despite this, the book was published in English and efforts were made to distribute it in the USSR.*
BODY-46	*Publication of Pasternak's Dr. Zhivago in English delayed until September 1958. Efforts being made for Russian edition, but no estimated release date. Inquiries requested for desired copies of both editions.*
BODY-47	*Agreement for layout, design, and production of a literary work, with ownership rights retained by the undersigned. Payment based on actual costs, with potential advances. Undertaking to arrange for printing, binding, publishing, and distribution of the work.*

BODY-48	*Agreement for layout, design, and proofreading of "Dr. Zhivago" manuscript in Russian, with a maximum cost limit, to be completed by July 31, 1958.*
BODY-49	*Agreement for services with payment terms and responsibility outlined.*
BODY-50	*A meeting was held to finalize a contract for the type setting, manufacture, and distribution of Pasternak's Dr. Zhivago. Phase one of the contract was agreed upon, but phase two details were still unclear. The estimated costs were considered high but justified due to time constraints.*
BODY-51	*Negotiations for printing and distribution of a book in Europe, disagreement over terms of contract, and discussion of fees for services provided by a representative.*
BODY-52	*Negotiations for a book publishing contract with a European firm were successful after financial terms were agreed upon. Further details and final contract approval were discussed over lunch, with plans to sign the contract in the near future.*
BODY-53	*The page contains redacted information approved for release under AR 70-14, with a reference to an affidavit.*
BODY-55	*Agreement outlining rights and obligations regarding manuscript completion and material payment.*
BODY-57	*Request for permission to publish a manuscript titled "Behind the Past and Beyond the Present" by author C. P. Pasternak.*
BODY-58	*Contract signed for publication of Dr. Zhivago. Outstanding problems: need publisher's note by July 8 and finalize printing with European publisher. Type setting to be completed by July 11. Funds deposited for expenses. Contact Ll for resolution.*
BODY-59	*Instructions and updates regarding the publishing of Dr. Zhivago, including contact information for key individuals involved and the need for authorization for final arrangements with a European publisher.*
BODY-60	*Attorney in New York sent agreement for AEDINOSAUR, found minor defects in manuscript, requesting immediate clarification.*
BODY-61	*Discussion of costs and logistics for printing and distributing a book, with emphasis on security and financial considerations.*
BODY-62	*Meeting on June 9, 1958 to discuss publishing Pasternak's Dr. Zhivago in Russian. Plans to find European publisher, suggested printing in New York for speed. Potential Dutch or Swiss publisher mentioned.*
BODY-63	*Negotiations for publishing Dr. Zhivago manuscript discussed, terms of contract debated, financial responsibilities considered, and proposals made for type setting and printing costs.*
BODY-64	*Negotiations for a book contract were discussed and a new contract was proposed, with terms to be finalized the following week. The individual departed for Washington, D.C. for approval.*
BODY-65	*Meeting report from 1958 discussing plans for publishing Dr. Zhivago in Europe, including type setting, printing, and legal matters.*
BODY-66	*Meeting held on 1 July 1958 regarding AEDINOSAUR project. Reviewed project status and agreed on points for phase two proposal. Negotiations with attorney in New York planned. Agreement to publish non-U.S. reprint, distribute by September 1958, and receive 6,000 discounted copies.*
BODY-67	*Agreement for European printing with protective clauses in case of default, possibility of negotiating a different agreement if default is honest.*

BODY-68 *European edition of books to have no U.S. imprint, emphasize deadline to publisher, review contracts before signing, explore legal complications with attorney for protective measures.*

BODY-69 *Meeting held to discuss negotiating a contract with a European publisher for the second phase of a project, but original proposal deemed undesirable and attorney instructed to present previous proposal.*

BODY-70 *Pasternak faced backlash for his novel, "Doctor Zhivago," with the Union of Writers refusing publication. Despite this, he gave copies to foreign publishers and requested not to publish under duress. Plans for publication and distribution were in progress, with a guarantee to purchase 6,000 copies for operational distribution.*

BODY-71 *Request for authorization to publish a Russian edition of Boris Pasternak's "Dr. Zhivago" due to its controversial message challenging Soviet ethics, promoting individual rights, and criticizing political fanaticism.*

BODY-72 *Approval for release of a book, with author expressing confidence in the content and requesting additional information.*

BODY-73 *Rejection of proposed pricing terms for publishing editions at higher prices, with focus on economic feasibility and distribution rights.*

BODY-74 *Document approved for release in 2012 and again in 2014.*

BODY-75 *Release dates for documents have been approved in 2012 and 2014.*

BODY-76 *Legal document outlining terms and conditions for the distribution and pricing of books, emphasizing limitations on distribution and pricing agreements.*

BODY-77 *The letter discusses the challenges of publishing a book due to legal issues and uncertainties regarding printing and delivery. The author outlines a proposed arrangement for printing and delivering the books to the client's representative by a specified date.*

BODY-79 *The page discusses the process of obtaining permission from publishers to reprint copyrighted material, including negotiating fees and terms.*

BODY-80 *Subject interviewed on January 13, 1958, with details on figures being completed and available in February 1958. No further comments provided at this time.*

BODY-81 *Update on AEDINOSAUR project, with plans for West Coast trip, ongoing Phase 2 negotiations, and concerns about book rights.*

BODY-82 *A Russian novel published in Russia by a Russian author is not entitled to U.S. copyright protection due to lack of reciprocity between the two countries. Assignees do not have better status in acquiring copyright protection. Public domain status applies.*

BODY-83 *Author's work not entitled to copyright in the US, regardless of where it was first published. Author's status, not the proprietor's, determines copyright eligibility. Assignee of author cannot secure copyright if author cannot.*

BODY-84 *Discussion of preliminary discussions and inquiries, actions to be taken regarding material received, location of plates, and accounting of funds in an operation. No payments will be made until questions are resolved.*

BODY-86 *Meeting held to discuss publishing plans for the AJCDINOSAUR case, including obtaining plates, European publishing rumors, and potential gift of plates for printing. Package received did not contain plates as expected. Potential for covert distribution if agreement not reached.*

BODY-87	*Discussion of recent developments in the AEDINOSA project, including potential government interest in purchasing publications and concerns about security violations. Publisher intends to proceed with publishing book in Russian.*
BODY-88	*Discussion and action plan regarding potential legal issues with publishing a book in Russia due to conflicting rights claims by an Italian publisher.*
BODY-89	*Discussion regarding the Project AEDDOSAUR, including communication with individuals and agreements on publication rights and costs.*
BODY-90	*Approval for release granted on September 19, 2012.*
BODY-91	*Discussion of payments, publication proofs, and storage of type for a book project, with delays due to vacation and lack of authorization for payments.*
BODY-92	*Request for distribution of Pasternak's Dr. Zhivago to Soviet tourists and officials in Western Europe and Brussels Fair. Proposal for miniature edition for dissemination in Soviet Union. Funding and logistics discussed.*
BODY-93	*Efforts are being made to distribute a book in the USSR, with American travelers and students involved, and an account set up for Pasternak from book sales.*
BODY-94	*Publication of Pasternak's Dr. Zhivago in Russian for Soviet readers, arranged through Italian publisher, with copies distributed in Europe and efforts made to honor author's safety concerns.*
BODY-95	*The page discusses the agreement with the Italian publisher for the foreign rights of a book, arrangements for distribution in the USSR, and setting up an escrow account for the author's royalties.*
BODY-96	*Russian edition of "Dr. Zhivago" by Boris Pasternak being distributed to Soviet personnel and tourists in Western Europe, despite being rejected for publication in the USSR. Considered a significant literary work by non-Soviet critics.*
BODY-97	*Forwarded attachment for guidance to Commercial Staff with distribution to various files and individuals.*
BODY-98	*Agreed plan of action for handling outstanding proofs and negotiating payment eligibility, emphasizing leniency despite untrustworthy behavior. Request for settlement agreement to cover final payment and prevent future relationships with unreliable parties.*
BODY-99	*A memorandum discussing the status of a project as of September 10, 1918, with updates on the European edition and plans for future actions.*
BODY-100	*Classified message from 1958 discussing legal actions, publishing Russian edition, and reproduction restrictions.*
BODY-101	*Fouled up publication with Trinelli instead of Feltrinelli, may be under threat of squelching.*
BODY-102	*Approved for release dates for specific activities will not change.*
BODY-103	*Approval for the historical collections project ADDOSAUR was renewed for fiscal year 1959.*
BODY-104	*Project proposals developed in FY 1958 with mTO funds, including publications and typesetting for "Dr. Zhivago." Funds needed for other activities in FY 1959.*
BODY-105	*Request for renewal of Project AEDINpSAUR in FY 1959 for SR Division, with plans to expand PP operations and foreseeing special operations requiring increased D&TO funds. Funding history, contribution to book publication, and potential unforeseen expenditures in FY 1959 outlined.*
BODY-106	*Request for renewal of Project AEDINOSAUR for FY 1959, seeking clearance and extension.*

BODY-107 *Staff coordination project for the Aedinosaurs division, involving amendment, renewal, and termination. Staff concurrence attached. Funds programmed in operating budget.*

BODY-108 *Request for information regarding copyright claims by Feltrinelli against foreign publications of Dr. Zhivago to clarify legal situation and determine compliance with Italian copyright law.*

BODY-109 *Request for approval to distribute copies of a book to visitors due to strained feelings caused by requests to purchase it commercially. Waiting for settlement of disagreement before proceeding.*

BODY-110 *A classified message discussing the inaccurate shipment of plates and the need for an agreement with Feltrinelli to settle the affair and avoid publicity and costs.*

BODY-111 *Request for information on Feltrinelli's intentions, direct approach suggested to settle dispute quickly, no large order needed, situation still unclear.*

BODY-112 *Italian publisher holds world rights for original and translated works, including broadcasting rights. German publisher has German rights. Italian publisher refuses to authorize broadcasts in original language. Caution advised to avoid legal action.*

BODY-113 *A message discussing the propaganda value of Boris Pasternak winning the Nobel Prize for his novel "Dr. Zhivago" and the need to avoid referring to him as a Soviet.*

BODY-114 *Classified message discussing the desire to have Soviet citizens read a novel that has not been published in the USSR.*

BODY-115 *Classified message approved for release regarding historical collections, with copies shipped and forwarding total noted.*

BODY-116 *Classified message regarding the approval and destruction of records, with instructions for fulfilling book requests and coordinating officers.*

BODY-117 *Classified message discussing the use of leftist press and writers in the free world to support an appeal to Khrushchev regarding Pasternak. Suggests exploiting assets in the East Zone and mentions German press involvement.*

BODY-118 *Recommendations regarding the suppression of Dr. Zhivago and Pasternak's appearance to accept the Nobel Prize, in order to prevent Soviet propaganda and maintain independence.*

BODY-119 *The page discusses the challenges and complexities of the Communist system, highlighting the importance of understanding its historical and cultural context in order to effectively navigate its dynamics and principles.*

BODY-121 *Pasternak's manuscript of Doctor Zhivago was given to a publisher in Milan after Stalin's death, but the project failed due to bureaucratic red tape.*

BODY-122 *Request to consider boycotting Soviet Union participation in cultural festivals like the Venice Festival to gain wide support for the premise that they should not be invited.*

BODY-123 *Discussion of potential impact of suppression of artists like Pasternak, Chaplin, Beauvoir, and Picasso on global intellectual and artistic world, as well as their past and future reputation.*

BODY-124 *Message classified as routing, with actions regarding the Pasternak case and request for all Nobel prize assets to exploit Pasternak's rejection.*

BODY-125 *Information regarding the publication of an unabridged Russian edition book by a Dutch publisher on November 2nd, with a request to avoid duplication and a reply expected from Feltrinelli.*

BODY-126 *Dutch newspapers report on illegal printing of Russian books by Mouton, involving Feltrinelli and Eekhout, leading to a new Russian edition contract.*

BODY-127 *Contract signed for printing legal edition, involving political affairs. Misleading accounts led to confusion with manuscript origins. Beek and Mouton's involvement with anti-communist organization questioned. Legal printing expenses covered by Beek. Original edition considered illegal. Mystery surrounding manuscript origins. Frenchman and Beek obtained text without Feltrinelli's knowledge.*

BODY-128 *Article claims clandestine edition helped Pasternak win Nobel Prize. Feltrinelli and Mouton may still be involved in manuscript theft, with Beek under pressure from Feltrinelli. Possible charges pending.*

BODY-129 *Feltrinelli ordered a Russian edition of a book, but it was impossible to fulfill. The manuscript was not identical to the original, and Feltrinelli considered legal action against the responsible party.*

BODY-130 *Plans to publish and distribute "Dr. Zhivago" through Mouton with 5,000 copies, despite sabotage from Feltrinelli. Illegal copies circulated in Russia.*

BODY-131 *Request for cooperation in publishing a Russian edition of Doctor Zhivago, offering assistance in rounding up publishers, with no response yet. Additional guidance requested for December.*

BODY-132 *Question regarding copyright held by Feltrinelli, confusion over rights sold to Collins, Pasternak's stance on distribution in the US unclear.*

BODY-133 *CIA learns of Pasternak's novel Dr. Zhivago, seeks publication rights, obtains manuscript copy from Collins, and discovers multiple copies in circulation.*

BODY-134 *Proposal to publish an abridged version of Dr. Zhivago in Russian on thin parchment paper, distributed to Soviet sailors and tourists to counter anti-Soviet propaganda. Copyright violation not a major concern.*

BODY-135 *Message regarding the release of a manuscript only if Feltrinelli failed to publish, with confirmation of BBC Russian broadcasts of Dr. Zhivago.*

BODY-136 *Internal routing and record sheet for confidential documents, with space for officer comments and tracking of document movement.*

BODY-137 *Document discussing historical collections, client confidentiality, and operational procedures.*

BODY-138 *Classified message from 1950 regarding concerns about a Feltrinelli publication, specifically a book in draft.*

BODY-139 *Classified message regarding the release of a story on Howard Fast and Pasternak in the literary section of Al Nahar. Reference to Redwood used in error.*

BODY-140 *Coverage of Pasternak's Nobel Prize, expulsion from Soviet writers' union, and rejection of Nobel Prize covered by various newspapers. Substantial coverage by Al Jarida, Al Amal, Al Iraq, and limited mention in Pro Nasir papers. Al Bina had front page coverage of Pasternak's Nobel Prize refusal.*

BODY-141 *Routing and Record Sheet instructions for officers to use, date, and initial before further routing. Remove from attached document.*

BODY-142 *Pasternak's book published in Italy without permission from Soviet Writers Union, causing controversy. Soviet writers critical of Soviet life, facing persecution.*

BODY-143 *Instructions for routing and recording documents, including officer designations, numbering comments, and obtaining initials before further routing. Remove the sheet from the attached document.*

BODY-144	*Shipment details of Dr. Zhivago copies to Headquarters, with specific quantities sent by sea and air pouches. Some copies retained for reference and operational use.*
BODY-145	*Approval dates for release of information.*
BODY-146	*AR 70-14 is a historical collection approved for release in 2014.*
BODY-147	*Information regarding the publication of a Russian edition by Feltrinelli, which was deemed illegal due to lack of specific approval and led to a dispute.*
BODY-148	*Classified message regarding distribution of approximately six hundred copies to Soviet visitors at a fair, with concerns about Russian officers and reproduction restrictions.*
BODY-149	*The history of the Dr. Zhivago manuscript, including its completion in 1954, initial mention in Soviet press in 1954, rejection for publication by the Union of Writers of the USSR in 1956, and acceptance by Italian Communist publisher Giangiacomo FELTRINELLI.*
BODY-150	*Author instructs foreign publishers to ignore any letter he might write under duress requesting that the manuscript not be published.*
BODY-151	*This page discusses the potential legal issues that may arise from attributing a book to a deceased author, highlighting the importance of accuracy in authorship to avoid complications.*
BODY-152	*Upcoming publications announced, including a new edition of "Fellini's Roma" and a new edition of "Michelangelo Antonioni's Red Desert". Rejection of the idea of a miniature edition of a book in a center not part of the Copyright Convention.*
BODY-153	*Approval for the release of historical collections related to President Truman and the Cold War.*
BODY-154	*Request to send 15 copies of the Russian edition of Dr. Zhivago to the USSR.*
BODY-155	*Publication details for the book "Doctor Zhivago" by Boris Pasternak in various countries, including special controls by the publisher in the Netherlands to prevent intelligence exploitation.*
BODY-156	*Publication approvals and details for various countries including Portugal, Spain, Germany, Poland, Czechoslovakia, Hungary, Greece, Yugoslavia, Soviet Union, Bulgaria, Romania, and Turkey.*
BODY-157	*Various publications and serialization of books in different languages in countries like Saudi Arabia, Iraq, Jordan, Sudan, Kuwait, Iran, Pakistan, India, Lebanon, Israel, Brazil, and others. Some books still in talking stage.*
BODY-158	*Various publications in different countries have approved the serialization or condensation of a book titled "Le Estera" in Spanish, "Sekai Shubo" in Japanese, and "Chen Peo" in Chinese.*
BODY-159	*Approval for release of historical collections DAR 70-14.*
BODY-160	*Approval for release of historical collections AR 70-14 in 2012.*
BODY-161	*Document approved for release in 2014 and 2012.*
BODY-163	*The memorandum discusses an article in the National Review Bulletin alleging CIA involvement in the publication of "Dr. Zhivago," with ties to extreme right-wing elements and European press coverage.*
BODY-164	*Approval for release of historical collection AR 70-14D in September 2012.*
BODY-165	*Document approved for release in 2012.*
BODY-167	*This page is about historical collections that have been approved for release.*

BODY-171 *Plans were made to publish a Russian edition of Dr. Zhivago after the manuscript was smuggled out of the Soviet Union in 1957. Discussions were held to determine the best way to publish the book, aiming for a legitimate publisher.*

BODY-172 *Controversy over Russian edition of Zhivago, University of Michigan to publish without Feltrinelli copyright, legal dispute looming.*

BODY-173 *Page contains information on release dates and approvals, with redacted details.*

BODY-174 *Efforts to expedite the publication of Dr. Zhivago by having the manuscript typeset in the United States were hindered when the typesetter failed to find a European publisher as instructed, leading to concerns about breach of contract and unethical conduct.*

BODY-175 *Routing and record sheet for a classified document, with space for officer's initials, dates, and comments.*

BODY-176 *Publication of the Russian edition of Dr. Zhivago in the U.S. was discouraged due to potential harm to relations with other governments, author's safety concerns, and legal issues with the Italian publisher. Concerns arose when a Dutch publisher obtained the original manuscript and reproduction proofs.*

BODY-177 *Illegal edition of a book distributed without approval, leading to a new legal edition being printed. Employee failed to finalize arrangements with publisher, resulting in unauthorized distribution at a fair. Feltrinelli announced limited edition to be released.*

BODY-178 *Delay in completion of Russian edition of Dr. Zhivago, no distribution yet, comparison with Feltrinelli-Mouton edition planned.*

BODY-179 *Comparison of Russian print of Dr. Zhivago with other prints, potential connection to Tolstoy Foundation, bankrupt printer. No information on Trinelli.*

BODY-180 *Approval for the purchase of one thousand copies of a Russian book, depending on the price, for Redwood Psych.*

BODY-181 *Request for prompt forwarding of Russian language publication to headquarters for indexing and distribution, with emphasis on not giving the publication directly to Soviets.*

BODY-182 *Discussion of the Russian language copies of Dr. Zhivago, including the process of pre-screening, printing a pilot edition, and distribution. Mentions awareness of a University of Michigan Press publication and the promise of a copy to a recipient.*

BODY-183 *Routing and Record Sheet instructions for officers to use when forwarding documents, including numbering comments and dating initials before further routing. Remove sheet from attached document.*

BODY-184 *Instructions for distributing a book to travelers, with a preference for giving it to those traveling by air for better chances of delivery. Additional copies can be obtained directly from Mouton & Co. in the Netherlands.*

BODY-185 *Routing and record sheet for historical collections, approved for release in 2014.*

BODY-186 *Instructions for handling a book about Soviet secrets, emphasizing caution and discretion in sharing with Soviet officials or visitors.*

BODY-187 *Plans to publish a Russian text in French edition, considering approaching Feuillien for rights. If impractical, will seek alternative publisher.*

BODY-189 *Approval for distribution of historical collections related to the American intelligence community in 1958.*

BODY-190 *Information regarding the availability of a book edition, potential trouble with distribution, and the decision to proceed with a sale despite difficulties.*

BODY-191 *Dispute between publishers Feltrinelli and Mouton over distribution of book, involving stolen US property and illegal editions. Settlement reached through ordering additional copies and out of court agreement.*

BODY-192 *Efforts to publish a Russian edition of Dr. Zhivago in the U.S. were hindered by political concerns and the author's request not to publish in the U.S. despite efforts to find a legitimate publisher.*

BODY-193 *Discussion of sharing a copy of Dr. Zhivago with Russians, cautioning against provocation, and plans to compare reactions.*

BODY-194 *Routing and Record Sheet instructions for officers to use when forwarding documents, with space for comments and signatures.*

BODY-195 *Routing and record sheet for HR70-14 with approvals and historical collections information.*

BODY-196 *Dispatch regarding operational transmittal of Dr. Zhiyago for possible use in connection with Soviet contacts. No indexing required, possible action by qualified HQ desk. Copies of Dr. Zhiyago sent under separate cover.*

BODY-197 *Publication information for various works in different countries and languages, including books, serials, and excerpts, from Nov. 1958 to Feb. 1959.*

BODY-198 *Publication details of Dr. Zhivago by Boris Pasternak, including various editions and publishers in different countries, as of November 1958.*

BODY-199 *List of foreign publications approved for release in various countries, including books and serials in different languages such as Greek, Turkish, Polish, Arabic, Hebrew, and more.*

BODY-200 *Approval for the publication of a book on Egyptian history and culture, with a focus on Asia. Includes details on the content, format, and release date.*

BODY-201 *Exploitation of Dr. Zhivago novel by Boris Pasternak was prohibited by the Soviet government due to its anti-communist themes, leading to underground circulation and international success.*

BODY-202 *A new attempt to set a captivating narrative, although not as successful as the original. The full-length edition lacks the same impact and depth as the condensed version.*

BODY-204 *Document approved for release on September 19, 2012.*

BODY-205 *Discussion of Pasternak affair and Soviet control over intellectual expression, encouraging conversations with Soviets about artistic freedom and ideological constraints. Highlighting the importance of allowing artists to express their ideas freely.*

BODY-206 *Questioning Soviet censorship of literature and freedom of expression, suggesting that citizens should be allowed to judge for themselves. Encouraging discussion on intellectual freedom.*

BODY-207 *Routing and record sheet for historical collections, with details of approval, comments, officers involved, and microfilmed form.*

BODY-210 *The page discusses the halt of the theft of English-language books and most others from libraries, with an estimated 800-1000 American editions likely being read cover-to-cover.*

BODY-211 *Discussion of publishing rights and editions of Dr. Zhivago and other matters with Giangiacomo Feltrinelli. Concerns about lack of response from authors regarding publishing rights in different languages.*

BODY-212 *Request for purchase of legal edition of Dr. Zhivago was denied by Mouton, with no explanation given. Further attempts to obtain copies were also unsuccessful.*

BODY-213 *Publication of Doctor Zhivago has been postponed, uncertain if it will ever be published. Russian edition has been released by University of Michigan Press.*

BODY-214 *Request for copies of Dr. Zhivago, quantities deemed adequate, no indexing required, historical collections approved for release.*

BODY-215 *Information about obtaining 15 copies of the Russian language edition of Doctor Zhivago at cost, with uncertainty about publication.*

BODY-216 *Approval for release of historical collections AR 70-14, with a specific date of approval indicated.*

BODY-217 *Subject approves the release of information regarding Soviet citizens and their true feelings about life in the USSR, including their support for Putin during the 2017 election.*

BODY-218 *Discussion on handling commercial and legal aspects of a project, focusing on publishing rights for foreign languages, with agreement that it should not be a major concern for certain books already published in English.*

BODY-219 *Negotiated agreement to not participate in royalties, focusing on getting a better price for publication. Plan for multiple deals per year should motivate further price reduction.*

BODY-220 *Discussion of publishing arrangements for a book, focusing on timing and distribution to tourists. Attorney involved in negotiations with author. Publication deadline set for spring of 1960. Further discussions to take place upon attorney's return from trip.*

BODY-221 *Approval for project cryptonym AEDTiiOSAUR, with funding available for FY 1960 from current allocations within the division. Single activities with expenditures up to a certain amount may be authorized by the Chief of the SR Division.*

BODY-222 *Request for authorization to expend funds for a single D&TO activity in FY 1960 due to financial constraints and being the sole D&TO for SR Division.*

BODY-223 *Approval notification for project AEDIIOSAUR with changes in authorization levels and approved expenditure amounts for FY 1960. Renewal approved with conditions for expenditure approval levels.*

BODY-224 *Project AEDINOSAUR involves financial data for the fiscal period of July 1951 to June 1959. It outlines personnel requirements, supplies, equipment, operational expenses, and subsidy payments, with a total fund requirement calculation.*

BODY-225 *Anticipated major operations or events for FY 1959 and FY 1960 include the publication of twelve books for the USSR.*

BODY-226 *Request for renewal of Project-AEDINOSAUR for FY 1960 with funding details and activities summary.*

BODY-227 *Funding and activities related to projects, exploitation of Dr. Zhivago, purchase of books and records, materials for travelers to bring into the USSR, and miscellaneous expenses in FY 1959 and 1960.*

BODY-228 *Approval for release of historical collections, with instructions on how to handle and report any discrepancies.*

BODY-230 *Approval for release granted on September 19, 2012.*

BODY-231 *Approval for release granted on two separate dates in 2012 and 2014.*

BODY-234 *Approval for release of historical collections related to economic policy and planning in Russia, including documents on economic development and industrial production.*

BODY-235 *Historical collection of Russian documents from 1890, discussing censorship, propaganda, and political issues.*

BODY-236 *Boris Pasternak's Dr. Zhivago is a historical epic focusing on the role of the individual in history, arguing that only moral and thinking individuals can build a just society. Despite being completed two years ago, it has not been published in the Soviet Union.*

BODY-237 *Historical document in Russian discussing a military operation in 1890, with detailed instructions and plans for the operation.*

BODY-238 *Publisher's note and rough translation enclosed, with a request for timely processing to avoid delays with plates.*

VIEWPOINTS

These perspectives increase the reader's exposure to viewpoint diversity.

THE ETHICS OF THE CIA'S ACTIONS: THE CASE OF *DR. ZHIVAGO* AND THE LIMITS OF INTERVENTION[1]

Boris Pasternak's sweeping novel chronicling the life of a physician-poet caught in the maelstrom of the Russian Revolution, occupies a peculiar space in literary history. Not only was it a work of profound artistic merit, winning Pasternak the Nobel Prize in Literature in 1958, but it also became a potent symbol of resistance to Soviet ideology during the Cold War. This symbolic power did not go unnoticed by the Central Intelligence Agency (CIA), which saw in *Dr. Zhivago* an opportunity to undermine Soviet authority and promote Western values. The CIA's subsequent covert operation to publish and disseminate the book, however, raises a complex array of ethical questions about the limits of intervention in the cultural sphere.

The documents released by the CIA in 1995 reveal a clear agenda behind the Agency's involvement. They perceived *Dr. Zhivago* as a powerful indictment of the Soviet system, highlighting its suppression of individual freedom and creative expression. The novel's portrayal of the human cost of revolution, the disillusionment with communist ideals, and the yearning for personal autonomy resonated with the CIA's own Cold War narrative. By promoting the book's circulation, particularly among Soviet citizens, the Agency sought to sow discontent with the regime and foster a yearning for Western-style freedoms.

On the surface, the CIA's actions might appear justifiable. After all, *Dr. Zhivago* was a work of literary genius that deserved a wide audience. Moreover, the Soviet government's suppression of the book was a clear

[1] I asked the model to propose three essay topics, this is the one I selected.—Ed.

violation of freedom of expression. The CIA's intervention, then, could be seen as a noble effort to challenge censorship and promote intellectual freedom.

However, the ethical complexities of the situation cannot be dismissed so easily. The CIA's motivations were not purely altruistic. They were driven by Cold War imperatives, seeking to exploit the novel for their own strategic gain. This instrumentalization of art raises concerns about the potential for manipulation and the blurring of boundaries between culture and propaganda.

Furthermore, the CIA's actions had the potential to harm Pasternak himself. While the Agency took steps to conceal its involvement, the risk of exposure was always present. Had the Soviet authorities discovered the CIA's role in publishing *Dr. Zhivago*, Pasternak could have faced severe repercussions. The Agency's covert operation, then, put the author's well-being at risk without his consent.

The CIA's actions also raise broader questions about the limits of intervention in the cultural sphere. To what extent is it acceptable for a government agency to manipulate art for political purposes? Does such intervention undermine the integrity of cultural production and the autonomy of artists? These questions have no easy answers.

In the case of *Dr. Zhivago*, the CIA's actions had a demonstrably positive outcome. The book reached a global audience, contributing to the erosion of Soviet authority and the eventual collapse of the communist system. However, this success does not erase the ethical dilemmas posed by the Agency's covert operation. It serves as a cautionary tale about the dangers of instrumentalizing art for political ends and the potential harm that can result from such interventions, even when motivated by seemingly noble intentions. The legacy of *Dr. Zhivago* remains a testament to the enduring power of literature to transcend political boundaries, but it also stands as a reminder of the need for vigilance in protecting artistic freedom from the encroachments of state power.

Grounds for Dissent

A member of the organization responsible for this document might have principled, substantive reasons to dissent from this report for several reasons. One possible reason could be a disagreement with the assessment of the publishing rights and copyright issues surrounding the Russian edition of the literary work "Dr. Zhivago." The member may believe that Feltrinelli did have the rights to publish a Russian edition and that the organization's opinion on this matter is incorrect.

Additionally, the member may dissent due to concerns about the handling of negotiations and agreements related to the publication of the book. They may believe that the terms and conditions outlined in the report are not accurate or fair, and that the organization's actions in this regard were unjust or unethical.

Furthermore, the member may have a different interpretation of the events and discussions detailed in the report, leading them to question the conclusions drawn by the organization. They may believe that there are important details or perspectives missing from the report that would change the overall assessment of the situation.

Overall, the dissenting member may have legitimate concerns about the accuracy, fairness, and ethical considerations surrounding the issues discussed in the report, leading them to have principled reasons to dissent from its findings.

Red Team Critique

The documents provided is quite disorganized and difficult to follow. There are multiple sections that seem to be fragmented or incomplete, making it hard to understand the overall message being conveyed. Additionally, the document contains a mix of different topics and information, ranging from references to book publishing rights to meeting notes and financial estimates.

Furthermore, there are several inconsistencies and unclear statements throughout the document. For example, the mention of a New York Times ad about Pantheon publishing an authorized Russian edition, but then stating that no authorized Russian edition has been published by Feltrinelli. This contradiction needs to be addressed and clarified for better understanding.

Additionally, the document lacks context and background information, making it challenging to fully comprehend the significance of the details provided. The reader is left wondering about the relevance of certain discussions and agreements mentioned in the document.

In conclusion, this document requires significant restructuring, clarification, and additional context to enhance its overall effectiveness and coherence. Without these improvements, the document fails to effectively convey its intended message.

MAGA PERSPECTIVE

This document is just another example of the liberal media pushing their agenda and trying to undermine American values. It's clear that there was a bias against Russia and anyone who tries to publish works that don't align with their anti-American narrative. The fact that they are questioning the rights of a Russian edition of a book just shows their disregard for international cooperation and understanding.

It's ridiculous that they are trying to control what can be published and by whom. This is a blatant attack on free speech and the freedom of the press. Americans should have the right to publish whatever they want, without interference from foreign entities or the government. This document reeks of censorship and elitist control over literary works.

The fact that they are discussing negotiations and agreements regarding the publication of a book is concerning. This could be seen as collusion between publishers and foreign powers to manipulate the market and control the flow of information. Americans deserve transparency and honesty, not backdoor dealings and secret agreements.

It's clear that the deep state was at work here, trying to control the narrative and suppress any dissenting voices. This document is just another piece of evidence that proves there is a shadowy cabal pulling the strings behind the scenes. Americans need to wake up and see the truth behind these manipulative tactics by the globalist elites. **Bestsellers and blockbuster movies don't just happen.**

PASTERNAK REFLECTS[2]

A manuscript smuggled, a journey it takes,
Across borders, on whispers and wakes.
Milan's embrace, a communist's hand,
To publish my words, forbidden in my land.

They say it's a weapon, a tool in the game,
Of ideologies clashing, where freedom's the aim.
But my Zhivago, he yearns for the soul,
For love in the chaos, a life made whole.

The Agency whispers, with promises veiled,
To spread my creation, my voice now exhaled.
A miniature echo, on thin paper wings,
To fly past the censors, the truth that it brings.

A Nobel, a burden, a price I must pay,
For daring to whisper what words cannot say.
My country, my heart, forever entwined,
Yet my spirit seeks solace, a freedom to find.

They play with my story, a pawn in their fight,
For hearts and for minds, in the day's fading light.
But art cannot be weapon, or tool for a cause,
It lives in the reading, the silence, the pause.

So judge not my story, by players unseen,
But seek in its pages, the truth that's between.
For Zhivago's journey, reflects all our own,
A search for humanity, a love to be known.

[2] I asked the model to write a poem about this document in the voice of Boris Pasternak.—Ed.

Quotations

In the first section, I asked the model to identify the three most important and interesting passages in the entire document.

The Three Most Important Passages

1. The CIA's Motivations and Concerns:

> *"We realize that there are other elements in this situation which are of concern to the Agency. We are simply dealing here with the matter of whether Radio Liberation can legally broadcast the Russian language version, or if not, whether we should do so without legal sanction."*

Importance: This passage highlights the CIA's primary concern—getting the book into the hands of Soviet citizens. They are willing to push legal boundaries to achieve this goal.

Interest: It reveals the CIA's strategic thinking during the Cold War, using cultural materials as a weapon in the ideological battle.

2. The CIA's Strategy:

> *"It is recommended that the views of SR Division ... be obtained on this approach and that U.S. action on the distribution of the book be coordinated, concentrating on obtaining for it widespread publication and acclaim."*

Importance: This passage outlines the CIA's strategy for disseminating the book. They aim for broad international appeal and acclaim to pressure the Soviet government to publish it domestically.

Interest: It illustrates how the CIA sought to leverage cultural tools for geopolitical influence.

3. The CIA's Concerns about Feltrinelli:

> *"The bona fides of Mr. Feltrinelli's departure from the Italian GP is subject to doubt: even if he left the party in good faith, it is conceivable that he may have been brought under the control of either the Italian CP or the Soviet IS at some later date, especially after the publication of* Dr. Zhivago *and the award of the Nobel prize to Boris Pasternak made Mr. Feltrinelli such a tempting target."*

Importance: This passage reveals the CIA's suspicion of Feltrinelli's true motivations. They are concerned he may be a Communist agent and that his actions are not entirely independent.

Interest: This section demonstrates the CIA's distrust of individuals with past Communist affiliations, even when they are seemingly acting in opposition to the Soviet regime.

Notable Passages

In this section, I asked the model to identify the most important passage on each page. Pages where there was no useful response are omitted.

BODY-1 *AmComLib feels that it is important, and we share this feeling, that Radio Liberation do everything possible to make it available to Soviet listeners as a basic part of its mission to keep the Soviet public informed of events and material which the Communist regime seeks to deny them.*

BODY-2 *"We are able to publish Dr. Zhivago thanks to the cooperation of the University of Michigan Press which is shortly publishing the Russian original of Dr. Zhivago in book form."*

BODY-5 *"It does seem to me that if Feltrinelli has indeed broken away from his Communist associations, a useful service might be performed in bringing him to this country. Certainly no development in Russia in recent months has been half so damaging to the Soviet position in world opinion as was Feltrinelli's action in publishing the Pasternak Book."*

BODY-6 *"We know a great deal about the subject matter of this letter and I will • • • whether anything further can be done."*

BODY-7 *"I have a rather urgent and important question to put to you, my good friend of mine, the publisher of Pasternak's Doctor Zhivago. First of all, the publicity. I am sure that in this rather mighty affair you could ask about the family (a great name in Italian industry). Do you see any ways and means how Pasternak could be assisted - via Italy or any other of your official connections? I am, I am sure, to keep this matter as confidential as possible."*

BODY-8 *The bona fides of Mr. Feltrinelli's departure from the Italian GP is subject to doubt: even if he left the party in good faith, it is conceivable that he may have been brought under the control of either the Italian CP or the Soviet IS at some later date, especially after the publication of Dr. Zhivago and the award of the Nobel prize to Boris Pasternak made Mr. Feltrinelli such a tempting target. Even if this were not the case, it would seem rather likely that there is some Communist informant, if not a controlled agent, among his office staff or among his close friends.*

BODY-10 *Even if he left the party in good faith, it is conceivable that he may have been brought under the control of either the Italian CP or the Soviet IS at some later date, especially after the publication of Dr. Zhivago and the award of the Nobel prize to Boris Pasternak made Mr. Feltrinelli such a tempting target.*

BODY-11 *"Mr. Feltrinelli wants to visit the U.S. ostensibly in connection with the plans of the University of Michigan Press to publish a Russian-language edition of Dr. Zhivago, possibly also for talks with Pantheon Books, publishers of the American edition - though the latter would seem less important, since Pantheon, to the best of our knowledge, has properly contracted with Mr. Feltrinelli about copyright."*

BODY-14 *How strange these people are.*

BODY-15 *"It does seem to me that if Feltrinelli has indeed broken away from his Communist associations, a useful service might be performed in bringing him to this country. Certainly no development in Russia in recent months has been half so damaging to the Soviet position in world opinion as was Feltrinelli's action in publishing the Pasternak book."*

BODY-16 *"but presumably in a contest the question of his right to translate in the first place would be controlled by the nature and extent of his authority from Pasternak."*

BODY-17 *"It had turned out to be a fascinating project involving considerable research and some definite conflicts of opinion. However, the following are his conclusions. They fall into three areas: common-law copyright, unpublished works and Universal Copyright Convention."*

BODY-18 *"During the 1920s and 1930s Pasternak wrote a great deal of material, mostly poetry which was published in the Soviet Union. Reportedly, this material is now in the public domain because of Russia's non-participation in certain international copyright conventions and agreements. Since it is our intention to include this material in a Russian-language anthology we desire to have printed, a confirmation of its rights status is requested."*

BODY-20 *"It is our opinion, however, that under present circumstances no authorized Russian edition has been published and, therefore, Feltrinelli has no rights under copyright law or convention in a Russian edition. There is no question that Feltrinelli has copyright protection on his Italian translation not only in Italy but in all signatories to the Berne Convention and to the Universal Copyright Convention."*

BODY-22 *"Whether one regards this as autobiography or fiction, it is at once a story of degradation and depravity and a sensitive and often kindly commentary on human life."*

BODY-23 *"Never open on two small pair: 'Fold them,' Yardley says. He's talking his straight Draw, nothing wild, 7 players. 'It's twelve to one you won't make a Full House. If somebody else opens, don't stay. Anyone who stays on two small pair should have his head examined. You fold - or you bluff by raising before the draw, standing pat, then betting."*

BODY-26 *There was considerable discussion of actions which the U.S. has taken and might take to exploit the situation developing from the award of the Nobel Prize to Boris Pasternak and his subsequent reluctant refusal of it, together with the oppressive actions taken toward him in the Soviet Union.*

BODY-27 *"The Chinese communist war clique might drag the Soviet Union into a disastrous war decimating the Russian population but leaving the Chinese partially annihilated: most of the respondents chewed this one over thoughtfully, gulped a few times to themselves and then tried to dismiss the possibility as remote because the socialist camp is out for peace."*

BODY-28 *West did not seize the Pasternak matter as a cold war weapon but it was only Soviet treatment of Pasternak that caused the shocked reaction in the West: of this no Soviet agent made any point. The vast majority of the students had no idea of how the work was interpreted nor Pasternak judged in the West.*

BODY-29 *"Students were generally in accord with the ban because they considered Pasternak too subjective a writer who had unfairly criticized Soviet reality. His work does not serve the interests of the people and his hero does not represent the thoughts and feelings of the author--as should be the case in true Soviet literature. The picture of*

Soviet life portrayed does not correspond to actual conditions. Thus the ban is considered necessary."

BODY-30 *"Soviet students do not feel that the communes necessarily represent an advanced step toward communism. In their eyes, the commune in China is an institution adapted to special Chinese conditions and is still very young to be judged finally. It was felt that the Chinese communists are taking a different road to communism, but the details of the difference escape practically every Soviet student."*

BODY-35 *"They believe that the greatest effect could be achieved if the pressure of world opinion forced the Soviets to publish the book for domestic use. They are also concerned with the well-being of Pasternak and the effect on other writers inside the Soviet Union who would try to write an independent message to the Soviet public."*

BODY-38 *It appears that the error on the Collins edition is growing, in part because of the procrastination of a person who is working on the translation. It is also understood that the difficulties have arisen in unusual passages which appear in the book later on. It is imperative that Headquarters be kept informed of all details concerning the book so that we may continue to discuss its exploitation with the closest associates as possible.*

BODY-39 *Pantheon is cooperating with Collins on a translation. Pantheon will pay for part of the cost and will receive the British translation as produced. The British translation will then be carefully re-edited to provide a proper text for the American edition. Pantheon is not interested in publishing a Russian text because PretPIvell~ (Milan, ex-Communist) holds the universal copyright and has not issued a license for publication of the Russian version.*

BODY-45 *"when a fine literary work by the man acknowledged to be the greatest living Russian writer is not even available in his own country, in his own language, for his own people to read."*

BODY-50 *"An appointment had been made to see [redacted] to arrive at final terms of the contract between [redacted] concerning the type setting, manufacture of photo offset proofs, lay out and design work of Pasternak's Dr. Zhivago."*

BODY-51 *"It was further emphasized that Headquarters still wanted the book printed and distributed by a reputable publishing firm in Europe and that this in fact was the reason why we had originally approached [redacted]. [Redacted] continued to argue that printing in Europe might slightly lessen and might even increase the effectiveness of the book on a Soviet audience."*

BODY-52 *"During luncheon, I elaborated upon the possibility of publishing the book by and mentioned the possibility of setting aside part of the proceeds from the sale of the book for Pasternak. replied that this could be discussed at a later time."*

BODY-62 *"was extremely interested in the idea of getting this 'great political work published' and said that he thought he could be of help."*

BODY-67 *It was further agreed that the agreement must contain protective clauses in the event of default by [redacted]. However, should this be an honest default on his part, consideration would be given to negotiate a different agreement with [redacted].*

BODY-68 *No commitments are to be made at this time. We desire to review any contract prior to signing.*

BODY-70 *"Meanwhile, Pasternak had given copies of the manuscript to the Italian Communist publisher Feltrinelli and to other visitors from abroad, who were asked to arrange for English and French translations. Pasternak also informed his foreign publishers that they should ignore any letter he might write under duress, requesting that the manuscript not be published."*

BODY-71 *Pasternak's 700-page novel, "Dr. Zhivago," is considered to be the most heretical literary work by a Soviet author since Stalin's death. Pasternak's humanistic message - that every person is entitled to a private life and deserves respect as a human being, irrespective of the extent of his political loyalty or contribution to the state - poses a fundamental challenge to the Soviet ethic of sacrifice of the individual to the Communist system. There is no call to revolt against the regime in the novel, but the ideology which "Dr. Zhivago" preaches - ethical passivity - is fundamental. Pasternak suggests that the small, unimportant people who remain passive to the regime's demands for active participation and emotional*

BODY-82 *Under Section 9(b) of the U.S. Copyright law, that work would not be entitled to U.S. copyright because that section excepts the granting of copyright protection to the works of a foreign author when the foreign state of which such author is a citizen or subject does not afford reciprocity in the granting of copyright protection to American citizens.*

BODY-83 *"The fact that the work has not yet heretofore been published in Russia but was first published in an Italian translation in Italy does not alter the opinion expressed by in his letter of July 18th that the work is not entitled to copyright in the United States."*

BODY-93 *"An attempt is being made to inform Pasternak that an escrow account from the sale of the book has been set up in his name. Pasternak will be told that funds from this account will be available if he is ever in a position to use them."*

BODY-94 *Observing that this great anti-communist philosophical novel was being published in Italian, French, English and German, and realizing that there was little chance of Soviet authorities publishing it in the Soviet Union, we felt that the book should be published in Russian for Soviet readers.*

BODY-95 *An effort is being made to establish an escrow account in Pasternak's name for the author's share in the royalties from the sale of the book.*

BODY-96 *"Pasternak is recognized by non-Soviet critics to be the greatest living Russian writer. 'Dr. Zhivago' is considered to be the best novel to appear since the Revolution and to be an important stimulant to Soviet thinking."*

BODY-98 *"It is our desire that it be made completely clear that we are aware of his untrustworthy behavior changing our relationship, and that we feel that we are being most lenient in our final dealings with him."*

BODY-101 *WAS SUPPOSED TO PUBLISH BOOK JOINTLY WITH FELTRINELLI BUT FOULED UP AND PRINTED ONLY TRINELLI AS PUBLISHER IN BOOK. FELTRINELLI MAY NOW BE UNDER SQUELCH PUBLICATION.*

BODY-104 *"Proofs of Pasternak's novel, 'Dr. Zhivago,' have been purchased and final publishing arrangements are in process or being completed."*

BODY-108 *FYI FELTRINELLI CLAIMS HOLD COPYRIGHT ALL FOREIGN PUBLICATION DR. ZHIVAGO.*

BODY-109 *SINCE MANY PEOPLE KNOW OF THIS DISTRIBUTION (NON-MEMBERS AND OTHERS) WITH REQUESTS TO BUY, CAUSING STRAINED FEELINGS ON ALL SIDES.*

BODY-111 *"PLEASE KEEP ADVISED BY CABLE OF ANY INFO RE fELTRINELLI'S INTENTIONS WHICH CAN DEVELOP. APPROACH DIRECTLY TO DIS*

'THOUSANDS FOR BOOKS AND USE THIS CONVERSATION TO INQUIRE HOWL- ----- GET DISPUTE SETTLED. THIS TO GIVE STIMULUS TO SETTLE QUICKLY. NO LARGE ORDER NEED. ACTUALLY, BE PLACED UNLESS ' '.zf>E"

BODY-112 "As far as we have ascertained, the Italian publisher has secured world rights for the original language and the translations, including broadcasting rights. The Italian publisher has assigned to a German publisher all German rights. As far as we know, he has retained the original language broadcasting rights himself."

BODY-114 DESIRE USE EVERY OPPORTUDITY HAVE SOV CITIZENS READ NOVEL .AND LEARN ABOVE FACTS.

BODY-117 LEFTIST PRESS AND WRITERS IN FREE WORLD SHOULD BE PARTICULARLY EFFECTIVE. ALSO INTERNATIONAL PEN GROUP SHOULD BE ENLISTED TO MAKE DIRECT APPEAL TO KRUSCHEV. ALLOW PASTERNAK APPEARANCE.

BODY-118 PROP SHOULD CHALLENGE UNLIKE EVEN SO NIGGARDLY CONCESSION TO HUMAN DECENCY. IN CULTURAL FIELD AS TO LET PASTERNAK APPEAR WITH WIFE TO ACCEPT AWARD. JUST AS ALL OTHER QUESTION WHETHER SOV CM FREE COUNTRIES HAVE DONE AS OF RIGHT NOT PRIVILEGE BUT SHARE STOOP TO SAME LEVEL IN THIS MANNER AS NAZIS WHO PREVENTED CARL VON OSSIETZKY ACCEPT PEACE PRIZE 1938.

BODY-122 CITE WITHOUT KNOWING YOUR ABILITY TO ACCOMPLISH; SUBMIT THIS IS PRECISELY CORRECT TIME ATTEMPT ACHIEVE BOYCOTT OF LITERARY OR OTHER CULTURAL FESTIVALS IN WHICH SOVIET UNION IS PARTICIPANT, SUCH AS VENICE FESTIVAL OR OTHER SIMILAR CULTURAL JAMBOREES, OR AT LEAST ATTEMPT TO SECURE WIDE SUPPORT OF PREMISE THAT SOVIET UNION SHOULD NOT BE INVITED TO PARTICIPATE.

BODY-123 "PERHAPS AN OPPORTUNITY EXISTS TO OBTAIN ROBERSON, CHAPLIN, BEAUVOIR, ET AL. APPEALS FROM THESE PERSONS IN THE ARTISTIC AND INTELLECTUAL WORLD. OBJECTIONS BY PICASSO MIGHT CARRY GLOBAL IMPACT."

BODY-126 "WITH ALL FUSS ABOUT MYSTERY HAS ARISEN AND MOST OF ANSWERS REMAIN BE FOUND IN NETH A PARTICULAR! ACCORDING EEKHOUT, SOVIET VISITORS TO E~PO GIVEN FREE IN VATICAN PAVILION IN WHICH FELTRiNELLI, WHO HAS BOOK RIGHTS, PRINTING OF RUSSIAN PROVED BE MOUTON ACT I. RED AS PUBLISHER ALTHOUGH HE HAD NOT PLACE'D ORDER.FOR THESE COPIES ORIGINATED FROM ILLEGAL SOURCE WHICH COMPLETE IGNORANCE. F AND M NOW MADE CONTRACT FOR MEW RUSSIAN EDITION OF BOOK."

BODY-127 "EEKHOUT EXPLAINED STORY BECAUSE OF MISLEADING ACCOUNTS IN WHICH HE MORE OR LESS IMPUTED PARTICIPATING POLITICAL AFFAIR. EEKHOUT SAID THEY INVOLVED IN POLITICS WITHOUT KNOWING. THOUGHT WAS FROM FELTRINELLI CLEAR TO THIS DAY. SOMEONE CAME FROM PARIS TO BRING MANUSCRIPT WHICH BUT LATER LEARNED THIS NOT CASE. MOTIVES OF E MOUTON DID NOT KNOW HIS RELATIONSHIP WITH BEEK IN DEALING WITH BEEK, EN VRIJHEID, AN ANTI-COMMUNIST ORGANIZATION, WHICH SEEMS HAVE DISTRIBUTED TO RUSSIAN VISITORS AT VATIC

BODY-128 "ALTHOUGH PRESSURE AND FLOW ORDERS FROM ABROAD HAD INDUCED FELTRINELLI AND MOUTON TO COME TO AN AGREEMENT, FELTRINELLI AND BEEK WHO MAY STILL BE ON HOOK. IT IS CONCEIVABLE THAT FELTRINELLI, SATISFIED THAT HE HAS SETTLED WITH MOUTON AND PUBLICLY

'DISGRACED' THE OTHER HAND, BEEK UNDER INCREASING PRESSURE FROM FELTRINELLI THAT HE STOLE MANUSCRIPT."

BODY-129 *"To de Ridder's stupefaction, Beek took printing plates out of his briefcase. Best our knowledge no Russian edition ever published and we tried contact Feltrinelli to inform him this startling visit but he not available. In preserve Feltrinelli's rights, we now reproducing book photo-mechanic to another publisher."*

BODY-130 *"ILLEGAL PUBLICATION STUPID AND WILD WEST LIKE."*

BODY-131 *"THAT SOME WEEKS AGO HE HAD WRITTEN GIANGIACOMO FELTRINELLI THAT BIG AUTHORITATIVE 'CLEAN RUSSIAN EDITION OF DOCTOR ZHIVAGO AN URGENT REQUIREMENT. URGED FELTRINELLI TO COOPERATE WITH HIM STATING HE ENTIRELY AT HIS DISPOSAL FOR SUCH PUBLICATION AND WILLING, ABLE OR ROUND UP GERMAN OR INTERNATIONAL PUBLISHERS. NO ANSWER YET."*

BODY-132 *There has been some question as to the copyright actually held by Feltrinelli. In conclusion, the story as we have it is that L asked Feltrinelli for the Russian and English rights. Feltrinelli sold Collins only the English rights. I never gave WJ any details on their transactions with Feltrinelli. Pasternak himself did not want the book to come out in the U.S. He was reported as favoring a neutral distribution.*

BODY-142 *"The case had been extremely badly handled by the Soviet writers. They issued emotional statements without taking any political advice. The insistence on the fact that the Soviet government had not taken part in this incident impelled Secretary of State Dulles immediately to seize the opportunity to stand against the Soviet Union, therefore forcing the Soviet government to make a reply."*

BODY-147 *"In view great demand Sov intellectuals circulating normal ition, HQS considering publication comments re publication. Be understood be had rights, employee failed to get specific approval Feltrdelli. Name made edition illegal. Feltri dispute followed by recent approval Russian edition for Feltrinelli. Publication date about 1 Jan 1959."*

BODY-149 *"refusing publication and accusing him of using his 'great gift' to 'resuscitate in the soul of our people ideals which have been dead for a long time.'"*

BODY-171 *"In January 1958, the beginning Russian manuscript of Dr. Zhivago was read. First impressions of the manuscript indicated that this was a great literary work which would produce a psychological impact upon Soviet readers."*

BODY-177 *"When Feltrinelli heard that the book was being distributed at the Vatican Pavilion, he immediately labeled it as an illegal edition brought out without his approval."*

BODY-184 *"It is better to give the book to travelers going by air since the likelihood of getting the book through is much greater than if it is taken in the mail."*

BODY-186 *"the broader proposition that it presents to the regime of the Soviet Union. This is to make the book available to as many Soviet readers as possible. For this reason, however, this book must be handled with great care. For the reasons given above, the book has been bought from a Romanian immigrant and is either entirely or in part to be sent to the Soviet Union. The book was obtained from a person who got it at the Brussels Fair. It was bought for a few francs and is therefore not to be given or sold to anyone traveling to the USSR; nor should Americans give it directly to Soviet officials or visitors."*

BODY-187 *NEXT STEP MAY BE APPROACH FELTRINEll NECESSARY OFFER INDUCEMENTS ASSURE DELAYING TACTICS. THIS FOR HQS. H. FElTRiNEll WHO PLANS STATEMENT AND IF REALIZE HE MAY REFUSE OR USE.*

BODY-191 *"An unknown French man came to Mouton and ordered 11000 copies of the book."*

BODY-193 *"I said he was about to return the book when he remembered and the previous discussion concerning passing the book to the Russians. I suggested that she pass the book on to one of her acquaintances and then discuss it with him or her later on. She was cautioned not to mention that she had obtained the book from an American as it might appear to the Russians to be an act of provocation which might cause her embarrassment."*

BODY-204 *'n/a'*

BODY-205 *The whole Pasternak affair is indeed a tragic classic example of the system of thought control which the party has always used to maintain its position of power over the intellectual. Like jamming, censorship, and the party ideological decrees for writers and artists, the banning of this book is another example of the means which the regime must use to control the Soviet mind. It is a reflection of the intellectual barbarity and the cultural sterility which are features of the closed society.*

BODY-206 *Soviets can be asked why they are not permitted to read Dr. Zhivago or any other literary work and judge its value for themselves. If the communist society is superior to any Western society, as its advocates claim, one may legitimately ask why it attempts to prevent the circulation of ideas whether they originate inside or outside the Soviet Union. Why, too, does the regime prohibit the import of most foreign journals and books? Surely, after forty years of communism Soviet citizens should be mature enough to make up their own minds about what is good and bad art.*

BODY-214 *For the present, the previously reserved quantities of 50 copies of regular edition and 500 of the pocket-size seem adequate.*

BODY-218 *"it was agreed that this matter should not be of too much concern on the first book, or on any other book which had already published in English, since in those instances should either already have the foreign language rights, or know how to get them, or not really be concerned about the matter."*

BODY-219 *It was also agreed that we would make no attempt to participate in any royalties but that we have responsibilities for getting a better price from than the one originally proposed since we will be undertaking the costs of publication and the books sells will be more advantageous to us. Also the fact that we plan four or five deals each year should be further incentive for him to reduce the contract price.*

BODY-220 *"8. He also is very concerned with timing because it is SR's position that they must have the first look, and all other books given to him this year, published by this spring of 1960 or the books would be of no value. They have to aim at the tourists each year and their distribution season is May through August."*

BODY-222 *It is requested that Chief, SR Division be authorized to expend up to $1 for a single D&TO activity. This level is suggested in view of the financial level of the project and the fact that this is the sole D&TO for SR Division.*

BODY-236 *"Life revealed the many abysses and terrifying discoveries of the unknown." - Boris Pasternak*

OGC 8-1913

31 October 1958

MEMORANDUM FOR: Office of General Counsel

ATTENTION: [redacted]

SUBJECT: Broadcast of Serialization of Dr. Zhivago by Radio Liberation.

1. There is attached hereto a copy of a letter to Chief, IO/5 from [redacted] Legal Counsel to the American Committee for Liberation, N.Y., outlining the legal problem confronting AmComLib in its desire to broadcast the Russian language version of the Pasternak book, Dr. Zhivago, in serial form to its audiences in the Soviet Union.

2. As you know, this book is being withheld from the Soviet public by the Soviet authorities who have refused to allow its publication in that country. AmComLib feels that it is important, and we share this feeling, that Radio Liberation do everything possible to make it available to Soviet listeners as a basic part of its mission to keep the Soviet public informed of events and material which the Communist regime seeks to deny them.

3. [redacted] letter sums up the legal position as he sees it and we solicit your comment and advice thereon. [redacted]

4. There are two angles not covered in [redacted] memorandum:

a. We are informed that the British Broadcasting Corporation is broadcasting now extensive daily excerpts from the book and expects to cover in this way about one-third of the total length. Our information, however, does not indicate whether these broadcasts are being made in the English or Russian language and we are endeavoring to clarify this.

b. The New York emigre

SECRET

b. The New York emigre newspaper Novoye Russkoye Slovo is serializing the Russian language version with this acknowledgment to the University of Michigan: "We are able to publish Dr. Zhivago thanks to the cooperation of the University of Michigan Press which is shortly publishing the Russian original of Dr. Zhivago in book form."

5. We realize that there are other elements in this situation which are of concern to the Agency. We are simply dealing here with the matter of whether Radio Liberation can legally broadcast the Russian language version, or if not, whether we should do so without legal sanction.

C/IO/5

Attachments
2 copies ltr frm
to

31 October 1958

MEMORANDUM FOR : Chief, PRD

ATTENTION :

SUBJECT : Distribution of Russian copies of Dr. Zhivago

1. It is estimated that the Dutch publisher Mouton printed about 10,000 copies of the Russian edition of Dr. Zhivago.

2. The received the first thousand copies off the press at a special price.

3. These thousand copies have been distributed in the following manner:

a. Three hundred sixty-five copies were sent to Brussels and distributed to Soviet visitors at the Brussels Fair.

b. Two hundred copies were sent to Frankfurt for distribution to Soviet citizens.

c. One hundred copies were sent to Berlin for distribution.

d. One hundred copies were sent to Munich for distribution.

e. Two hundred copies have been sent to Headquarters but have not yet arrived. These will be sent to various and distributed by SR assets.

f. Twenty-five were sent to London and have been distributed to Soviet visitors in Britain or given to travelers going to the USSR.

g. Ten copies were sent to Paris for distribution to Soviet visitors.

SR/2/

Distribution:
2 - C/PRD
2 - SR/2

Dr Zhivago

CLASSIFIED MESSAGE

~~S-E-C-R-E-T~~

1	SR/2	4
2		5
3		6

DATE : 31 OCT 58

TO : DIRECTOR

FROM :

ACTION: SR 6

INFO :

RE Filing (check one):
No CS Record Value. Destroy. ☐
RI file this copy as indicated ☑
Branch copy filed as indicated ☐
RE Indexing
Marked
Signature

OCT 31 20272 58

ROUTINE

TO DIR INFO CITE

REDWOOD AEDINOSAUR

RE

ANSWERED TELEGRAM BY LETTER 27 OCTOBER. SAID OFFICIAL UNABRIDGED RUSSIAN EDITION WILL APPEAR SIX TO EIGHT WEEKS. ACCEPTED ORDER 3,000 COPIES. PRICE WITH 20 PER CENT DISCOUNT.

END OF MESSAGE

CS COMMENT: *QUERIED IF HAD PLACED ORDER FOR BOOKS (PASTERNAK'S "DR ZHIVAGO") WITH

RI COPY

AEDINOSAUR

ROUTING	INITIAL
RI/AN	
RI/TY	✓
~~DESTROY~~	
RI/FI	

~~S-E-C-R-E-T~~

FORM 4-58 1389 USE PREVIOUS EDITIONS REPRODUCTION BY OTHER THAN THE ISSUING OFFICE IS PROHIBITED. Copy No. (35)

COPY

December 15, 1958

PERSONAL

Mr. Allen W. Dulles
2430 E Street, N. W.
Washington, D. C.

Dear Allen:

This is the letter I spoke to you about on Saturday. The writer of the letter,

It does seem to me that if Feltrinelli has indeed broken away from his Communist associations, a useful service might be performed in bringing him to this country.

Certainly no development in Russia in recent months has been half so damaging to the Soviet position in world opinion as was Feltrinelli's action in publishing the Pasternak Book. It was good to talk to you.

With warm regards,

Encl:

22 December 1958

Dear

I appreciate your recent telephone call and your letter of 15 December with its enclosure, of which I have taken a copy. We know a great deal about the subject matter of this letter and I will see whether anything further can be done.

Sincerely,

Encl.

1 - DCI
1 -
1 - DDP

Body-6

EXECUTIVE

Personal

Allen, I'm not sure that I grasp this particular point -

Dear

I wonder where this will reach you -

I have a rather urgent and very important question to put up to you:a good friend of mine,the publisher of Pasternak's Dr.Zhivago,Giangiacomo Feltrinelli whose name you have seen in the papers on account of all the publicity given to Pasternak when he got the Nobel prize,has rather weighty affairs to see to in the US.Unfortunately,on account of his former communist affiliations,he finds it impossible to obtain a visa through the ordinary channels.Now,Feltrinelli broke off his ties after the Hungarian revolution,and,as you know,it has been tried to make him a took of certain cold war activities,using Pasternak's book, which,again,has been against his will and intention.

You could ask about the family (a great name in Italian industry).

Do you see any ways and means how Feltrinelli could be assisted - via or any other of your official connections?

I wish to add,unnessarily I am sure,to keep this matter as confidential as possible.

Sincerely

3. The bona fides of Mr. Feltrinelli's departure from the Italian CP is subject to doubt: even if he left the party in good faith, it is conceivable that he may have been brought under the control of either the Italian CP or the Soviet IS at some later date, especially after the publication of Dr. Zhivago and the award of the Nobel prize to Boris Pasternak made Mr. Feltrinelli such a tempting target. Even if this were not the case, it would seem rather likely that there is some Communist informant, if not a controlled agent, among his office staff or among his close friends.

Chief
Staff

Attachments:
1. Ltr to 22 Dec.
2. Ltr to Mr. Dulles, 15 Dec.
3. Ltr to from about 8 Dec.

Personal

Dear

I wonder where this will reach you –

I have a rather urgent and very important question to put up to you: a good friend of mine, the publisher of Pasternak's Dr. Zhivago, Giangiacomo Feltrinelli whose name you have seen in the papers on account of all the publicity given to Pasternak when he got the Nobel prize, has rather weighty affairs to see to in the US. Unfortunately, on account of his former communist affiliations, he finds it impossible to obtain a visa through the ordinary channels. Now, Feltrinelli broke off his ties after the Hungarian revolution, and, as you know, it has been tried to make him a took of certain cold war activities, using Pasternak's book, which, again, has been against his will and intention.

You could ask about the family (a great name in Italian industry).

Do you see any ways and means how Feltrinelli could be assisted – via or any other of your official connections?

I wish to add, unnessarily I am sure, to keep this matter as confidential as possible.

Allen, I'm not sure that I grasp this particular point –

Body-9

3. The bona fides of Mr. Feltrinelli's departure from the Italian CP is subject to doubt: even if he left the party in good faith, it is conceivable that he may have been brought under the control of either the Italian CP or the Soviet IS at some later date, especially after the publication of Dr. Zhivago and the award of the Nobel prize to Boris Pasternak made Mr. Feltrinelli such a tempting target. Even if this were not the case, it would seem rather likely that there is some Communist informant, if not a controlled agent, among his office staff or among his close friends.

Chief

Staff

Attachments:

1. Ltr to 22 Dec.
2. Ltr to Mr. Dulles, 15 Dec.
3. Ltr to from about 8 Dec.

2 January 1959

MEMORANDUM FOR: Assistant to the Director

SUBJECT: Giangiacomo Feltrinelli; Application for Visa to the U. S.

REFERENCE: Personal letter from , dated 15 December 1958 (enclosure: letter from dated 8 December 1958).

2. Mr. Feltrinelli wants to visit the U. S. ostensibly in connection with the plans of the University of Michigan Press to publish a Russian-language edition of Dr. Zhivago, possibly also for talks with Pantheon Books, publishers of the American edition -- though the latter would seem less important, since Pantheon, to the best of our knowledge, has properly contracted with Mr. Feltrinelli about copyright.

22 December 1958

Dear

I appreciate your recent telephone call and your letter of 15 December with its enclosure, of which I have taken a copy. We know a great deal about the subject matter of this letter and I will see whether anything further can be done.

Sincerely,

Encl.

1 - DCI w/ basic & copy of encl.
1 - w/ basic
1 - DDP

1958

(EXECUTIVE

2 January 1959

MEMORANDUM FOR: Mr. [redacted]
Assistant to the Director

SUBJECT: Giangiacomo Feltrinelli;
Application for Visa to the U. S.

REFERENCE: Personal letter from [redacted] [redacted] dated 15 December 1958 (enclosure: letter from [redacted] [redacted] dated 8 December 1958).

[redacted]

2. Mr. Feltrinelli wants to visit the U. S. ostensibly in connection with the plans of the University of Michigan Press to publish a Russian-language edition of Dr. Zhivago, possibly also for talks with Pantheon Books, publishers of the American edition -- though the latter would seem less important, since Pantheon, to the best of our knowledge, has properly contracted with Mr. Feltrinelli about copyright. [redacted]

[redacted]

5 Jan 59

December 29, 1958

AWD

Mr. Allen W. Dulles
Main Post Office
Box 1513
Washington 13, D. C.

Dear Allen:

Thank you so much for your note on behalf of our Italian "friend". I have since been informed that the gentleman has not even made a request for a visa. How strange these people are.

With warm regards,

December 15, 1958

PERSONAL

Mr. Allen W. Dulles
2430 E Street, N. W.
Washington, D. C.

Dear Allen:

This is the letter I spoke to you about on Saturday. The writer of the letter,

It does seem to me that if Feltrinelli has indeed broken away from his Communist associations, a useful service might be performed in bringing him to this country.

Certainly no development in Russia in recent months has been half so damaging to the Soviet position in world opinion than was Feltrinelli's action in publishing the Pasternak book. It was good to talk to you.

With warm regards,

Encl:

the current agreement, it might well be argued that any rights that exist are in the Russian publishing house. Feltrinelli would have some right, for instance, in an Italian translation, but presumably in a contest the question of his right to translate in the first place would be controlled by the nature and extent of his authority from Pasternak.

Assistant General Counsel

OGC:

√ Subject
Signer
Chrono

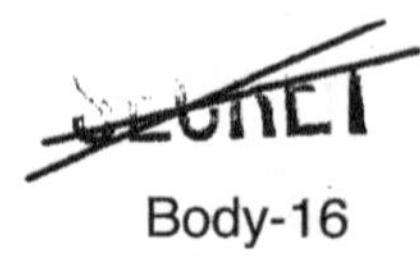

20 March 1959

MEMORANDUM FOR THE RECORD

SUBJECT: Dr. Zhivago - Telephone Conversation with [redacted]

1. [redacted] called today to give me the answers to questions that I asked about Feltrinelli's rights in any of the Pasternak material. It had turned out to be a fasinating project involving considerable research and some definite conflicts of opinion. However, the following are his conclusions. They fall into three areas: common-law copyright, unpublished works and Universal Copyright Convention.

2. As far as Dr. Zhivago is concerned, [redacted] feels that Pasternak had a common-law copyright even though he was an alien. This was reserved by the U.S. act of 1909. As to whether an alien loses this common-law right as a result of translation in a third country, there is a difference of opinion, and [redacted] admits that some of his colleagues do not agree with him. He thinks, however, that the alien does lose what he described as the pre-publication rights in the manuscript. This either leaves him without the right ([redacted] opinion) or raises the problem of how he might enforce it in this country.

3. As an unpublished work, there is no statutory protection even under the Universal Copyright Convention. This follows for two reasons: (a) he has not complied with the formalities, and (b) he has authorized translations. Sections 2 and 11 of the U.S. act control. We should note that Sec. 11 has been held to apply to unpublished manuscripts even though it seems restricted to musical works. Generally, this is the protection for works that are not reproduced for sale. A song writer, for example, who did not want to put his work on the market right away, would file a copy with the Library of Congress under this provision.

4. The Universal Copyright Convention provides for preservation of the common-law copyright in accordance with local law and this, as we have just mentioned, is accomplished under Sections 2 and 11 of the U.S. act.

5. Again, any rights that Feltrinelli might have obtained from Pasternak would be derivative insofar as the Russian manuscript is concerned. This raises the problem of whether Pasternak has any rights to transfer. Under

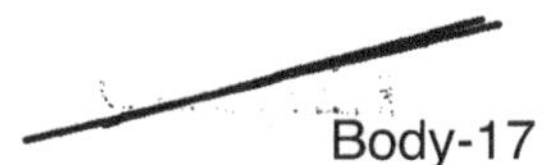

OGC 9-0279

5 February 1959

MEMORANDUM FOR: Office of General Counsel

SUBJECT: Clarification of Author's and Publisher's Rights Regarding Works of Boris Pasternak

1. The Commercial Staff currently is working with SR Division on a project which involves the commercial publication and distribution of Russian-language editions of certain of the works of Boris Pasternak.

2. As your office is aware, a previous operation involving Pasternak's novel, Dr. Zhivago, illustrated the complex rights problems pertaining to at least one of Pasternak's works and also demonstrated the potential legal and commercial difficulties that could arise from an uninformed approach to transactions involving these works.

3. To obviate future difficulties and to permit this staff to provide certain individuals cooperating in this project with adequate guidance, it is requested that we be provided with the opinion of the Office of General Counsel regarding the publishing rights considerations in the following two specific situations:

a. During the 1920's and 1930's Pasternak wrote a great deal of material, mostly poetry which was published in the Soviet Union. Reportedly, this material is now in the public domain because of Russia's non-participation in certain international copyright conventions and agreements. Since it is our intention to include this material in a Russian-language anthology we desire to have printed, a confirmation of its rights status is requested. Certain of the works have been published in English in the United States.

b. After completion of Dr. Zhivago, Pasternak wrote an autobiography which has been published by the French publishing house, Gallimard, under the title Essai d'Autobiographie. The French publisher has claimed that the Italian publisher of Dr. Zhivago, Feltrinelli, likewise claims rights to any Russian-language edition of the autobiography. It is further reported by Gallimard that Feltrinelli intends to have the work published in Russian in Holland or Belgium. Further, a recent ad in the New York Times states that Pantheon, who published the American

Approved for Release: 2012/09/19

edition of Dr. Zhivago, plans to publish the autobiography in this country.

[redacted] the Agency has obtained a copy of the Russian-language manuscript of the autobiography from which the French translation was made. We desire to include this work in the Russian-language anthology mentioned above. We would appreciate receiving your opinion regarding possible enforceable rights which could be held by Feltrinelli and which could serve as the basis of suit in the event of our publishing the work.

4. Attached hereto are copies of some introductory pages of "Selected Writings of Boris Pasternak" published in this country by New Directions Press. We feel these may be of interest in any study made.

Chief, Commercial Staff

DDS [redacted]

Distribution:
Original & 1--OGC (w/att.)
1--C/[redacted]
1-[redacted]/Subj.
1--[redacted]
1--CM/Chrono.

It is our opinion, however, that under present circumstances no authorized Russian edition has been published and, therefore, Feltrinelli has no rights under copyright law or convention in a Russian edition.

There is no question that Feltrinelli has copyright protection on his Italian translation not only in Italy but in all signatories to the Berne Convention and to the Universal Copyright Convention.

However, both the Berne and Universal Copyright Conventions consider translations as separate and apart from the original work so that publication of a translation does not vest any rights in the Russian edition in Feltrinelli.

Further, pursuant to Article 11 (Bis) of the Berne Convention the exclusive right of authorizing the radio broadcasting of the work in Russian is vested in Mr. Pasternak.

Under the Berne Convention it is a matter for legislation in the countries of the Berne Union to determine the conditions under which the radio broadcasting rights may be exercised but the Convention provides that such legislation shall not be prejudicial to the moral right of the author, nor to his right to obtain just remuneration which in the absence of agreement shall be fixed by competent authority.

In view of the fact that the USSR has refused permission to Mr. Pasternak to publish the literary work in Russian we believe a fair inference may be drawn that Pasternak has not granted any broadcasting rights in Russian to Feltrinelli.

Further, if the public press is to be believed there appears to be little chance of Mr. Pasternak being permitted to leave the USSR at the present time.

If Mr. Pasternak should be ejected from the USSR he would under the Berne Convention, and provided he established domicile in a Berne Convention Country, be able to bring action for the unauthorized use of the radio broadcasting rights.

In view of the fact, however, that, as we understand it, such planned radio broadcasts would be to the so-called "Iron Curtain"countries we do not believe any competent authority would award substantial damages to Mr. Pasternak.

Very truly yours,

/s/

C
O
P
Y

Counselors At Law

November 12, 1958

Henry Poor, Esq.
Greenman, Shea & Zimet
20 Pine Street
New York, N.Y.

Dear Mr. Poor:

You have requested our opinion as to the legal liability of American Committee for Liberation, if such Committee should broadcast by radio in Russia the literary work entitled "Dr. Zhivago" by Boris Pasternak.

The facts as disclosed to us by you and from our own research in the matter are as follows:

Boris Pasternak the author of Dr. Zhivago is a citizen of and is domiciled in the USSR. The USSR is not a party to any copyright convention and more particularly is not a signatory to the Berne Convention, or the Universal Copyright Convention.

A manuscript in Russian of the literary work was obtained by G. Feltrinelli, Editore of Milan, Italy. Whether such manuscript was obtained by Feltrinelli directly from Mr. Pasternak, or from a Soviet publishing firm is not known. Similarly, whether or not any contract or grant of rights exists between Mr. Pasternak, or any Soviet publishing house and Feltrinelli is also unknown.

Feltrinelli caused an Italian translation of the Russian manuscript to be made which despite the protests of Mr. Pasternak was published in 1958 and copyright thereon was obtained by Feltrinelli by compliance with Italian law and the provisions of the Universal Copyright Convention.

Subsequently, an English translation was published and copyrighted in England by William Collins & Sons Company, Ltd. of London, England with the consent of Feltrinelli. Similarly, Pantheon Books, Inc. in New York has published an American edition with revisions of the English translation which has been copyrighted by Pantheon Books, Inc.

In 1958, a limited edition in Russian was printed and published in Holland bearing the name of Feltrinelli as publisher. We are informed that in fact such edition was not published, nor was its publication authorized by Feltrinelli.

You will, of course, appreciate that in the absence of an inspection of whatever documents may be held by Feltrinelli it is, of course, impossible to render a definitive opinion as to Feltrinelli's rights.

Notice

We, Mouton & Co. Publishers, Inc., having our registered offices at 5, Herderstraat, The Hague, Holland

whereas

only owing to a deplorable misunderstanding we contributed in bona fide to the publication of an edition, of about 1160 copies, in Russian language, of the book "Doctor Zhivago" by the Russian author Boris Pasternak, such edition having been issued at The Hague in summer 1958, hereby

acknowledge

that the Italian Editor Feltrinelli, Publisher in Milan, had given no authorization to said publication, nor to the indication of his name in the frontispiece of the book, and

state

that it never has been our intention to infringe on any rights of

S.I.A.S. Giangiacomo Feltrinelli Editore

having their offices at 6, Via Andegari, Milan, Italy, on

Doctor Zhivago

by Boris Pasternak

which was issued for the first time in the world at Milan by Feltrinelli in November 1957 as a consequence of a regular contract of edition and which is, therefore, protected in conformity with the International Copyrights Agreement.

This notice is appearing simultaneously on following newspapers: "Il Corriere della Sera" of Milan; "Telegraf" of Amsterdam; "The Times" of London; "The New York Times" (supplement) of New York; "Le Figaro" of Paris; "Die Welt" of Hamburg, and "Frankfurter Allgemeine Zeitung" of Frankfurt am Main.

A Life In Ferment

MINE ENEMY GROWS OLDER. By Alexander King. 374 pp. New York: Simon and Schuster. $4.50.

By RAYMOND HOLDEN

FEW ordinary writers could or would attempt to write a life of Alexander King. While they wrote about him, he would no doubt confound them by becoming someone else. It is by no means certain that the man who finally did get around to writing about him isn't subject to the same difficulty. That man is Alexander King himself—or is he? Perhaps he doesn't, and never did, exist at all. It says in this book that some years ago a New York columnist declared that Alexander King was the invention of a couple of Hungarian journalists.

If so, those journalists were men of immense and macabre imagination. For Alexander King, as he describes himself, is really something. He is a sick man whose days, since his inventors didn't provide him with adequate kidneys, are numbered. He is, or was, a drug addict possessed of unusual gusto and a talent for sounding the lowest depths. He is an artist, with both a capital and a small "A." He has decorated department store windows and done illustrations for more than sixty books. He once invented a syndicate of seven or eight artists to do a series of leaflets for an advertising agency. He played the parts of every one of these artists himself. Their work was so successful that the agency put King on the spot by giving a terrific cocktail party and inviting all eight to attend.

WHEN he wasn't being an artist, he was an editor. He got around. He seems to have met everybody from William Seabrook to Henry Luce and to have formed very strong opinions, some favorable but mostly unfavorable, about all of his acquaintances. Some of them are not going to be very happy about their part in this book. The reader who has a strong stomach and is not irritated by the author's verbal juggling and sometimes painful name-calling will be made either happy or morbidly excited. Others probably won't read his book. This may be a pity, since there are sandwiched in between its horrors some anecdotes and personal narratives of rare subtlety and humor. Whether one regards this as autobiography or fiction (the two are not really so far apart), it is at once a story of degradation and depravity and a sensitive and often kindly commentary on human life.

Mr. Holden, a poet, author and critic, has a close acquaintance with the literary world.

His extraordinary book shows you

THE SECRETS OF WINNING POKER

Be the first in your crowd to get his runaway best-seller that almost takes the gamble out of poker. The first four editions were sold out as soon as the ink was dry. A fifth printing has just been delivered and a sixth is on press.

Photograph by Ollie Atkins

THE HERBERT O. YARDLEY book started selling like wildfire when a small fraction of it appeared in *The Saturday Evening Post.*

Your best friends won't tell you what's in it – and when you've read it you won't tell them.

It's called THE EDUCATION OF A POKER PLAYER. And it's a priceless education. In it Yardley tells the secrets of his systems for winning at all the usual (and many of the rare) kinds of Draw and Stud Poker.

"Never open on two small pair – never"

"Fold them," Yardley says. He's talking about Straight Draw, nothing wild, 7 players. "It's twelve to one you won't make a Full House. If somebody else opens, don't stay. Anyone who stays on two small pair should have his head examined. You fold – or you bluff by raising before the draw, standing pat, then betting."

In the same specific way Yardley looks over your shoulder at every hand and tells you exactly when to *open,* and when to pass (even though you have openers), when to *call* or *stay,* when to *bluff,* when to *raise,* when to be *cautious,* when to be brazenly *bold.* And when to meekly fold.

He shows you all this by means of actual sample hands which he plays out for you and analyzes. And you learn how to play *with* the odds instead of against them.

How to develop not only a poker-face but a poker head

Yardley tells you how to study and "read" the other players – watching and analyzing their mannerisms, learning their weaknesses and their strengths. He makes you a master strategist at poker's psychological war.

He tells you wonderful salty stories (probably not for your Aunt Hermine) out of his own poker experience around the world – stories that sharpen your poker sense.

You "sit in" on the game in which the corn grower "Bones" Alverson bet his farm against a circus tent show at Five-Card Draw Deuces Wild – and won under the unfortunate circumstance of no longer being alive at the time. (After which Yardley gives you a brilliant analysis of how to play your cards at Five-Card Draw Deuces Wild.)

You watch Jake Moses lose ten trunks full of sample shoes – and you profit from his mistake. You see how good and bad poker players from the old west to China played their hands – and how they should've played them.

Send for your copy today – at no risk

Yardley's book could easily turn a steady loser into a steady winner. With its specific advice and its great stories out of Yardley's own experience, it amounts to a professional education in the theory and practice of winning – and a post-graduate course in the art of the bluff.

Send for your copy today. Get hold of it before the others in your crowd. Send no money. When the mailman brings your copy, read it, enjoy it, study it for three full weeks on the house. If you don't actually win several times the small cost of the book in your next few poker sessions, simply return the book within three weeks and pay nothing. Otherwise we'll bill you $3.95 plus postage as payment in full. Simon and Schuster, Publishers, Dept. 49, 630 Fifth Avenue, New York City.

About HERBERT O. YARDLEY

Yardley's mastery of the infinite subtleties of poker made him just the kind of agile thinker whom you would expect to crack a wartime Japanese code (he did) and to write the classic book on codes, ciphers and spies (he did: *The American Black Chamber).*

"Because he plays such a tight game of poker," says *The Saturday Evening Post,* "Yardley has been dubbed 'Old Adhesive' by his friends. After his retirement (as a cryptanalyst) three years ago, Yardley made a scientific study of poker in all its variations, thus reinforcing his fifty years of experience as a player. Now he has told all in THE EDUCATION OF A POKER PLAYER."

Here's how good it is (the first tribute to Yardley's book)

The New York Herald Tribune Book Review says, "It should be part of every father's investment portfolio for his son – or for himself. What Goren and Vanderbilt have done for the bridge player, Yardley has now done for that submerged four-fifths of American manhood that plays poker. He has given us dignity, wisdom and philosophy."
– THEODORE H. WHITE.

To Your Bookseller or
SIMON AND SCHUSTER, Inc., Dept. 49
630 Fifth Avenue, New York 20, N. Y.

I'm from Missouri and want to be *shown.* So send me a copy of Herbert O. Yardley's new book, THE EDUCATION OF A POKER PLAYER. If I don't win several times the price of the book in my next few poker sessions, I'll send the book back within three weeks and pay nothing. Otherwise, I will remit only $3.95 plus a few cents postage as payment in full.

Name ....

Address ....

City ....Zone....State..............

☐ **SAVE POSTAGE.** Check here if ENCLOSING $3.95 as payment in full, in which case we pay postage. Same return privilege, with money refunded in full. N. Y. City residents please add 12¢ city sales tax.

THIS IS HOW YARDLEY WOULD PLAY THE HANDS IN PANEL ABOVE

One Big Pair: Yardley says, "Never stay on less. If you are sitting to the left of the opener, raise on a pair of Kings or Aces. If you drive out other players and the opener draws three cards, draw three with him. If he draws two cards, or one, draw two. If he checks, bet regardless of your hand. If an occasional player stays after you have raised, draw two and bet, unless someone stands pat."

Four-Card Flush: Yardley says, "A four-card flush should never be played unless there is over five times as much in the pot as the bet itself. That goes, too, for a four-card straight, open at both ends. As for an inside straight, why draw to it? The odds are twelve-to-one you don't make it."

Three-of-a-Kind: "My rule is this," says Yardley. "If you're holding three-of-a-kind, Tens or better, don't raise. You want to entice as many others to stay as you can, because you're pretty sure of winning. However, if your threes are Nines or worse, raise. You want to drive out players who might draw against you."

5 November 1958

MEMORANDUM FOR THE RECORD

SUBJECT: Resume of OCB Luncheon Meeting, 5 November 1958

PRESENT: Mr. Dulles,

Approved for Release: 2014/04/07

6. Pasternak and "Dr. Zhivago"

There was considerable discussion of actions which the U.S. has taken and might take to exploit the situation developing from the award of the Nobel Prize to Boris Pasternak and his subsequent reluctant refusal of it, together with the oppressive actions taken toward him in the Soviet Union.

In this connection the DCI gave a summary of actions which the Agency has taken and plans to take. It was agreed that CIA officers would confer with to assure that there is no conflict with

ALLEN W. DULLES
Director

Distribution:
Orig - DCI files
1 - DDCI
1 - BA/OCB

IV. RUMOR IMPLANTATION ON SINO-SOVIET RELATIONS

A. The communes are the essence of communism and for reasons of block solidarity, Soviet leaders may be forced to institute them in the USSR: this was viewed as highly improbably by student respondents who argue that conditons of mentality between the two peoples and historical developments are totally different.

B. The Chinese communist war clique might drag the Soviet Union into a disastrous war decimating the Russian population but leaving the Chinese only partially annihilated: most of the respondents chewed this one over thoughtfully, gulped a few times to themselves and then tried to dismiss the possibility as remote because the socialist camp is only for peace. This was also evidently a painful question to Russian listeners.

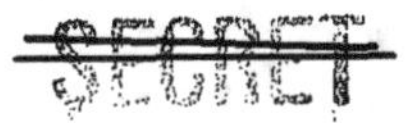

E. West did not seize the Pasternak matter as a cold war weapon but it was only Soviet treatment of Pasternak that caused the shocked reaction in the West: of this no Soviet student made any point. The vast majority of the students had no idea of how the work was interpreted nor Pasternak judged in the West.

II. RUMOR IMPLANTATION ON PASTERNAK AND DR. ZHIVAGO

A. Is it true some great Soviet writers refused to sign the ban on Pasternak? No student could imagine that there might be such a difference within an organization such as the Writers' Union. They explained this away by saying that the will of the majority rules in any "democracy". They also wanted names of such writers, essentially so that they could judge the worth of the voice of these adherents to Pasternak. They doubted that these people could be very "great" if they sided with a writer who produced untrue pictures of contemporary Soviet life.

B. Is it true that Khrushchev will permit an abridged version of Dr. Zhivago which Soviet citizens may read? This possibility was regarded as unlikely in view of the government's stand to date in the matter. They did feel that such an edition would be read out of curiosity to see what the essence of the criticism was. Categorically it was thought that Mr. Khrushchev himself could have little personally with the ordering of such an act. A vote of the entire government would be necessary, as the Soviet system is not based on arbitary one-man rule.

C. Is it true that there have been student demonstrations in MGU against Surkov's condemnation of Pasternak and Dr. Zhivago? No, this is not true. There were some Komsomol-led discussions of excerpts of the novel which tended to show why it was bad and had been condemned. The students felt that no single man such as Surkov could possibly issue such a ban alone, but that he must have had the entire Writers' Union squarely behind him.

D. Is it true that the Komsomol organization in Moscow, Leningrad and Kiev universities had been instructed not to permit student discussions about Pasternak and Dr. Zhivago? Students were unable to give any information about happenings at other universities than their own, but to the best of their knowledge no such instructions had been issued. On the contrary, Komsomol in MGU had given its own interpretation and had invited student participation.

III. ANALYSIS OF QUESTIONS ON SINO-SOVIET RELATIONS

A. Student reaction to increased Soviet military and economic aid to Red China: student opinion represented the point of view that such aid had not in fact increased. Source was unable to refute this statement because of lack of facts on his own part. This is a serious handicap to

Ex...rpts from Report by [redacted]

I. ANALYSIS OF PASTERNAK AND DR. ZHIVAGO AMONG STUDENTS

A. Student reaction to government ban on Pasternak and Dr. Zhivago: Students were generally in accord with the ban because they considered Pasternak too subjective a writer who had unfairly criticized Soviet reality. His work does not serve the interests of the people and his hero does not represent the thoughts and feeling of the author--as should be the case in true Soviet literature. The picture of Soviet life portrayed does not correspond to actual conditions. Thus the ban is considered necessary. No student was aware that the State Publishing House had accepted publications before the ban was pronounced by the Writers' Union.

B. Frequency of those who had read Dr. Zhivago or other Pasternak works: None had read the former and only one or two had read any of his poems. His translations were known and thought to be of high quality, but this work was not thought to be of a creative nature. One or two contacts admitted having read through the excerpts of Dr. Zhivago furnished by the Komsomol and were in agreement with the ban based only on examination of these selected sections. Source was unable to check any reasonable percentage of book shops to learn which of Pasternak's work are available on the Soviet market in the capital. None of the respondents were knowledgeable of the fact that the Polish Writers' Union had telegraphed congratulations to Pasternak for receipt of the Nobel Prize. Pasternak is now regarded by students as an insignificant Soviet writer who is incapable of turning out a literary work capable of winning a prize as highly regarded as the Nobel Prize. They feel that he has deviated and must be so treated.

C. The Pasternak affair and "liberalization" after the 20th Party Congress: only very begrudging do Soviet students admit the possibility that Pasternak's Dr. Zhivago may one day be found to contain grains of truth and thus deserve to be read by Soviet citizens and that thus Pasternak--in a changed political climate--may be "rehabilited". They acknowledge that this kind of change has happened before in modern Soviet times, but they do not regard the Pasternak ban as a step backward away from Liberalization. They frankly state that the USSR is a dictatorship and that there is no place for those to enjoy "freedom in the Soviet sense of the word" who abused it by writing untruths.

D. Emphasis of the literary aspects of the work, not the political content: as none of the participants had read the book, they were at a loss to judge its literary value. They did feel strongly that the West chose the novel for the political criticism they believe it points against the Soviet Union, not alone for the literary character it may contain.

~~SECRET~~

any Westerner in arguments with Soviet students. They often have facts and appreciate their value in coming to grips with the solution of problems, so any future agents sent to the USSR ought to have thorough grounding in factual material. Assuming that Soviet aid to Red China had increased, Soviet students did not view this with alarm, as China was held to be in need of help from more advanced socialist countries.

B. Reactions to Mao's and Peiping's reported claims of "ideological equality" with Moscow: Source noted that this point was conceded with some reluctance by Soviet students. They choose rather to think that conditions in China are so different that they call for and justify a different path toward workable communism in China. All Soviet students consider the Chinese communists to be diligent, frugal and very pleasant people who have a large country, a large population and large potential and large problems.

C. Reactions of intellectuals and peasants to the Chinese Communes, Do they represent a advanced step toward communism, Are the Chinese communists taking a different road to communism, Is the Sovkhoz and Agrogorod idea a step toward the Commune idea in the USSR, Does Moscow recognize different roads to communism?: Practically no student with whom source spoke had any clear understanding of the commune system as practiced in China. Source was unable to visit any places in the country to talk to peasants and obtain their opinions or determine their state of knowledge. The Soviet students do not feel that the communes necessarily represent an advanced step toward communism. In their eyes the commune in China is an institution adapted to special Chinese conditions and is still very young to be judged finally. It was felt that the Chinese communists are taking a different road to communism, but the details of the difference escape practically every Soviet student. There reigns a general lack of factual material information for establishing such a comparison. It is not felt that the Sovkhoz and Agrogorod idea in the USSR are steps toward the commune system in Russia. Russian conditions and historical traditions under communism are defended as being different and necessary in their own right. Again, source recommends vigorously that future agents be armed with historical and up-to-date facts on such movements and developments as the commune idea. Many of source's contacts had worked during the summers in the Virgin Lands and thought this experience valuable for them personally. As to whether Moscow recognizes different roads to communism, this appeared to be a moot point for most Soviet students vis-a-vis China. They see themselves confronted by a fait accompli on the part of a powerful neighbor and cannot very well argue about ways and means in these circumstances. But when the same question is posed with reference to Poland or particularly to Yugoslavia, the answers are radically different and the Russians present a solid front that these smaller nations must learn from the Soviet Union and dare not deviate. Yugoslavia was regarded by a certain number of vociferous students as being not a socialist state but one fostering state capitalism with the money supplied largely by imperialist nations of the West. This question is obviously a very sensitive one for Soviet students.

d) The purchase of books and literature to be given to legal travelers entering the Soviet Union for the purpose of inside distribution, briefing, and orientation of travelers. ------------------------ $

f) The purchase of Russian books, brochures, and periodicals not available through overt CIA channels. --------------------- $

Chief, SR Division

4. **RECOMMENDATION**

It is recommended that the delegation of authority for Project AEDINOSAUR be established as follows:

a. The Chief, SR Division, may, without reference to higher authority, authorize the committment of funds not to exceed for any single activity during any calendar month.

b. Committments of funds in excess of the above will be coordinated with and will require the approval of DD/P or DCI, as appropriate, under the Agency approval system.

APPROVED: ______________________ 24 Jan 1958
A/Deputy Director (Plans) **Date**

~~SECRET~~

PP STAFF COORDINATION

PROJECT:	AEDINOSAUR	
	AMENDMENT NO.	DIVISION SR
X	RENEWAL FY 1958	BRANCH
	TERMINATION	DESK

STAFF CONCURRENCE				MEMORANDUM ATTACHED		
ORGANIZATIONAL ELEMENT	SIGNATURE	COPY NO.	DATE	YES	NO	DATE
SSA-DD/S		2	11 Dec 57			
PP/OPS/PI		3 & 1	6 Jan 58		✓	
[redacted]		[redacted]				

[redacted] APPROVAL		
for CPP	SIGNATURE	DATE 13 Jan '58
A/DD/P/P	SIGNATURE	DATE

(This space reserved for comments of SSA-DD/S; CPP; A/DD/P/P.)

Funds programmed in operating budget. /s/ D.B.A.

Body-32

FORM NO. 848
1 DEC 55

(5)

PROJECT FINANCIAL DATA *MAY NOT EXCEED SECRET CLASSIFICATION	PROJECT CRYPTONYM AEDINOSAUR FISCAL PERIOD COVERED 1 July 1957 THRU 30 JUNE 1958
RESPONSIBLE STAFF OR DIVISION SR Division	CASE OFFICER

A. PERSONNEL REQUIREMENTS

Indicate number and type of personnel required and estimated total compensation for salary, allowances, travel and related employee benefits. Include everyone paid from project.

TYPE	NUMBER		ESTIMATED COMPENSATION		
	U. S. PERSONNEL	FOREIGN NATIONAL	BASE SALARY	ALL OTHER	TOTAL
STAFF EMPLOYEES					
STAFF AGENTS					
CAREER AGENTS					
CONTRACT AGENTS					
CONTRACT CONSULTANTS					
DETAILED PERSONNEL					
FIELD AGENTS					
MILITARY					
ALL OTHER					
TOTAL A.					

B. SUPPLIES, MATERIEL AND EQUIPMENT

Indicate amount required in applicable spaces. Attach complete supporting list for each.

COMMO	CHEMICAL	QUARTERMASTER SUPPLIES	OTHER SUPPLIES
$	$	$	$
MEDICAL	ORDNANCE	SPECIAL DEVICES	OTHER EQUIPMENT
$	$	$	$

TOTAL B.

C. OTHER OPERATIONAL EXPENSES

Indicate volume and nature of expenses such as (1) maintaince of two operational houses abroad (2) spot purchase of information, etc.

D & T/O project.

TOTAL C.

D. SUBSIDY OR PROPRIETARY PAYMENTS

If funds are to be turned over to individuals or groups in large lump sums to be expended by the individuals or groups at their discretion to accomplish an agreed-upon objective, explain the type of financial accounts, factual verification or statements, if any, other than a receipt for the lump sum, which will be obtained.

TOTAL D.

TOTAL FUND REQUIREMENTS (A + B + C + D) $

FORM NO. 756 1 AUG 55 REPLACES FORM 59-25 WHICH MAY BE USED. (1)

29 October 1957

MEMORANDUM FOR : Chief, [redacted] Staff

SUBJECT : Project AEDINOSAUR
D&TO for USSR
Request for FY 1958 Renewal

1. This is to request that subject project be renewed in the amount of [redacted] FY 1958 funds, which conforms with the specific amount included in the SR Division FY 1958 Operational Program for this project.

2. It is proposed that, within the limitations of the allotment account for the project:

a) The Chief, SR Division may, without reference to higher authority, authorize the commitment of funds not to exceed [redacted] for any single activity during any calendar month.

b) Expenditures in excess of the above will be coordinated with CPP and require the approval of higher authority, as appropriate, under the Agency approval system.

3. In support of this request, the following financial considerations may be noted:

a) The FY 1957 authorization totaled ---------------- [redacted]

b) The estimated FY 1957 obligations ---------------- [redacted]

4. The general effectiveness and evaluation of the project for FY 1957 is based upon:

12 December 1957

MEMORANDUM FOR: C/[redacted]

SUBJECT: Pasternak's Dr. Zhivago

1. [redacted] staff heralds the appearance of this book as more important than any other literature which has yet come out of the Soviet Bloc and is deeply concerned that its exploitation in the West be handled with care. They believe that the greatest effect could be achieved if the pressure of world opinion forced the Soviets to publish the book for domestic use. They are also concerned with the well-being of Pasternak and the effect on other writers inside the Soviet Union who would try to write an independent message to the Soviet public.

2. For these reasons, [redacted] takes the following position:

a. Dr. Zhivago should be published in a maximum number of foreign editions, for maximum free world discussion and acclaim and consideration for such honor as the Nobel prize.

b. No Russian version should be published by [redacted] [redacted] or any other obviously political publisher.

c. Radio Liberation should not broadcast the Russian text until it is published but should concentrate on reporting independent reviews.

3. [redacted] has not yet obtained the Russian manuscript of the book, but is quietly seeking the manuscript.

4. It is recommended that the views of SR Division and of [redacted] be obtained on this approach and that U.S. action on the exploitation of the book be coordinated, concentrating on obtaining for it widespread publication and acclaim.

SIGNED

√cc - [redacted]

SECRET

☐ UNCLASSIFIED ☐ INTERNAL ☐ CONFID.

ROUTING AND RECORD SHEET

SUBJECT: (Optional)

FROM: 10/5	NO.
	DATE 13 December 57

TO: (Officer designation, room number, and building)	DATE RECEIVED	DATE FORWARDED	OFFICER'S INITIALS	COMMENTS (Number each comment to show from whom to whom. Draw a line across column after each comment.)
1.				
2.				File
3.				
4.				Pasternak
5.				- View -
6.				Pressure by foreign editions
7.				No political public. in Russian
8.				
9.				
10.				
11.				
12.				
13.				
14.				
15.				

FORM 1 DEC 56 610 USE PREVIOUS EDITIONS ☒ ~~SECRET~~ ☐ CONFIDENTIAL ☐ INTERNAL USE ONLY ☐ UNCLASSIFIED

Copy 1

VIA AIR (Specify Air or Sea Pouch) DESPATCH NO.

SECRET
CLASSIFICATION

PRIORITY

TO Chief, WE DATE 2 January 1958

FROM

SUBJECT { GENERAL Psych
SPECIFIC Transmittal of Film of Pasternak Book

REFERENCE: 25 December 1957

1. Forwarded herewith are two rolls of film which are the negatives of the photocopy of Dr. Zhivago by Pasternak. These have been given to us by who request that they be returned "in due course".

2. are in favor of exploiting Pasternak's book and have offered to provide whatever assistance they can. They are wary, however, of mailing copies into the Soviet Union since they believe that most of them would be intercepted by the censor. They have suggested the possibility of getting copies into the hands of travelers going to the Iron Curtain area.

3. have suggested that choose its extracts for broadcasting with great care.

4. say that there is no doubt that pressure is being brought to bear on Pasternak and that it may not be long before a "revised" version of the novel appears in the Soviet Union.

5. We expect to receive from their paper on Dr. Zhivago during January and shall forward a copy of it to Headquarters.

6. have informed us that they hope next spring, following the appearance in London of the English translation published by Collins, to distribute copies through their regional offices to areas throughout the world. In this connection they are especially interested in what plans we may have so that our efforts may be synchronized.

SECRET
CLASSIFICATION

FORM NO. MAR. 1949 51-28A

PRIORITY

Body-37

7. It appears that the work on the Collins edition is going slowly, in part because of the procrastination of Max Heywood who is working on the translation. We also understand that difficulties have arisen in translating poems which appear in the book into fluent English and that ~~Stevens~~ Stephen Spender may work on this problem.

8. [redacted] said that the first printing of the book in Italy sold out within several weeks of its appearance and that a second edition was immediately undertaken.

9. It is requested that Headquarters keep us informed of its plans concerning the book so that we may continue to discuss its exploitation with the [redacted] as closely as possible.

Encl. as stated (dup)

Distribution:
3 - WE w/encl.

~~Confidential~~

File Pasternak

MEMORANDUM FOR THE RECORD 10 January 1958

Pantheon is cooperating with Collins on a translation. Pantheon will pay for part of the cost and will receive the British translation as produced. The British translation will then be carefully re-edited to provide a proper text for the American edition. Pantheon is not interested in publishing a Russian text because ~~Pretrivelli~~ Feltrinelli (Milan, ex-Communist) holds the unversal copyright and has not issued a license for publication of the Russian version.

[redacted] spoke to [redacted] on the phone recently and advised him that the government was interested in the book [redacted] [redacted]

I stated that a friend of mine, who was something of an amateur man of books etc, [redacted] had spoken to me about it. [redacted] advised my friend to contact [redacted]. Presumably [redacted] suspected the subterfuge but was courteous and willing to go along with my position 100%.

SR/RQ

Ref. [redacted] dtd 02 Jan 58

~~Confidential~~

13 January 1958

SUBJECT: Notes on PASTERNAK's Novel, Dr. Zhivago

1. This novel has not been published in the USSR.

2. PASTERNAK, in the course of 1957, had gotten in touch with an Italian publisher in Milan whose name is Feltrinelli. Feltrinelli is still a Communist, but knowing that the USSR is not a member of the International Copyright Union, he wanted to do PASTERNAK a service. He got the right to publish the novel in the Free World. The book in Italian was well on its way when it became apparent that the Soviets would not permit the publication of the novel in the USSR. Feltrinelli went ahead and the Italian version came out at the end of 1957.

3. Felterinelli has made arrangements for publication of this novel in England through the Printers House of Collins as well as in France and in Germany. The Greeks are putting out the novel in seriel form in their local papers.

4. We have received [redacted] ~~one~~ the microfilm of the Russian text. [redacted]

5. The microfilm was given to Mr. [redacted] for a photostat reproduction (2 copies) on 10 January 1958.

6. Our present plans are to publish the Russian text in a "black" edition giving the Soviet Government's publishing house on the title page. This procedure would take care of any copyright questions which might arise.

7. The question of procurement may have to be settled but at this point, it seems that the best would be to let a variety of rumors take care of that point without indicating any particular source.

8. WE/6 [redacted] – [redacted] is preparing despatch to [redacted] proposing to [redacted] to make Russian edition with permission from Feltrinelli. If that falls thru, we'll do it black –

~~SECRET~~

[redacted] planning background article for march issue on Pasternak himself. 15 Feb is deadline for Mar issue. Therefore urgent Pasternak book review within 2 weeks as possible. [redacted] 14 Jan 58)

[redacted]

February 28, 1958

[redacted]

...NDUM TO: Manager, [redacted] Program Department

...M : Manager, Central Research Department

... : Director, Radio Programming Division

...JECT : Dutch Publication of "Doctor Zhivago"

...ENCE : PXC 11, 2-24-58

[redacted] telephoned a connection of his in [redacted] ...erday and learned that the publisher referred to in your ...m is dickering directly with Pasternak for permission to ...lish an <u>expurgated</u> Russian version of "Doctor Zhivago". ...ing receipt of Pasternak's approval, no action is to be ...n, I gather.

You may be interested to know that the publisher now has ...py of the original manuscript in his possession. I plan to ... into the possibility of getting access to it, but will ...act precipitously without an entree of some kind, for fear ...aring him off.

Incidentally, I have been meaning to write you that [redacted] ... me the other day that a Russian edition of the book is now ...reparation in New York. He claims that "responsible people" ... have obtained a copy of the manuscript. He would not tell ...o these people are -- whether because he cannot or won't, ... unable to say.

[redacted]

[redacted]

cc: [redacted]

??C 11 2-24-58

WE HEA[illegible] AT DR. ZHIVAGO IS APPEARING IN RUSSIAN PUBLISHED

BY MUT[illegible] CO., 5 HERDERSTR., THE HAGUE. PLS CONFIRM

AND R[illegible]S A DOZEN COPIES IF AND WHEN AVAILABLE.

END OF [illegible].

DA

☐ UNCLASSIFIED ☐ [INTERNAL US]E ONLY ☐ CON[FID]ENTIAL ☐ SECRET

ROUTING AND RECORD SHEET

SUBJECT: (Optional)

FROM: 10/5

NO.

DATE

TO: (Officer designation, room number, and building)	DATE RECEIVED	DATE FORWARDED	OFFICER'S INITIALS	COMMENTS (Number each comment to show from whom to whom. Draw a line across column after each comment.)
1. SR/				These are the two references in our files to Dutch publication of Dr. Zhivago. These to complete your file
2.				
3.				
4.				
5.				
6.				
7.				
8.				
9.				
10.				
11.				
12.				
13.				APPROVED FOR RELEASE HISTORICAL COLLECTIONS AR 70-14
14.				
15.				

FORM 1 DEC 56 610 USE PREVIOUS EDITIONS ☐ SECRET ☐ CONFIDENTIAL ☐ INTERNAL USE ONLY ☐ UNCLASSIFIED

3 March 1958

MEMORANDUM FOR THE RECORD

SUBJECT: Dr. Zhivago

1. On 27 February I received a call from IO/5. [redacted] informing me that this novel by Pasternak was to be published in Russian in The Hague. The address is: Mutton Company, 5 Hoarder Street, The Hague.

2. I called [redacted] in WE/6 who said he would have the matter checked [redacted] IO is also going to check the matter.

SR/[redacted]
Distribution:
Orig & 1
1 - SR/[redacted]

~~S-E-C-R-E-T~~

24 April 1958

MEMORANDUM FOR: SR Division Branch Chiefs

SUBJECT: Availability of <u>Dr. Zhivago</u> in English

1. As you know, Boris Pasternak's latest work, the scholarly novel <u>Dr. Zhivago</u>, was scheduled for publication in the USSR, and a copy of the manuscript had even been sent to the Communist Italian publisher Feltrinelli when the Soviet censors suddenly proscribed the book for its passive but piercing exposition of the effect of the Soviet system on the life of a sensitive intelligent citizen. Feltrinelli subsequently published the book in Italian, despite Soviet requests that it be returned "for revision." This month (April 1958) Pantheon Books is publishing <u>Dr. Zhivago</u> in English; but no Soviet edition in the original Russian has appeared, nor is there apt to be one.

2. This book has great propaganda value, not only for its intrinsic message and thought-provoking nature, but also for the circumstances of its publication: we have the opportunity to make Soviet citizens wonder what is wrong with their government, when a fine literary work by the man acknowledged to be the greatest living Russian writer is not even available in his own country in his own language, for his own people to read.

3. We are making efforts to stimulate the production of the book in Russian by some "non-political" and preferably non-American entity. Meanwhile we wish to distribute translated editions, and especially the English-language edition, as widely as possible within the USSR and to official Soviets abroad.

4. Please tell us how many copies of the book you can handle. Then, while you are informing [redacted] the books will be procured through [redacted] and given to you for forwarding to the field.

[redacted]

SR/[redacted]

~~S-E-C-R-E-T~~

~~S-E-C-R-E-T~~

1 May 1958

MEMORANDUM FOR: SR Division Branch Chiefs

SUBJECT: Delay in Publishing Dr. Zhivago

1. Unfortunately we have just learned that publication of Pasternak's Dr. Zhivago in English has been delayed. The English edition will not be available until September 1958.

2. Every effort is being made to have Dr. Zhivago published in Russian as soon as possible. However, several problems are involved so that we cannot now give you any estimate of the date when the Russian edition will be available. It is hoped that arrangements can be made to have the Russian edition published in time for use at the Brussels Fair.

3. To assist us in supplying the [redacted] with copies of the Russian and English edition as quickly as possible, you are requested to query your [redacted] by dispatch asking them to advise Headquarters how many copies of Dr. Zhivago in Russian and English they desire to have.

[redacted]

SR/[redacted]

~~S-E-C-R-E-T~~

(a) Layout and design work --

(b) Type setting and proofreading --

(c) Photo offset and reproduction proofs --

(d) Any additional photo offset reproduction proofs required by the undersigned shall be at the undersigned's additional cost.

6. It is understood and agreed that the undersigned hereby retains all right, title and interest in and to the said literary work and manuscript and said manuscript shall be returned to the undersigned upon completion of the work.

7. You further agree that the material and all rights therein furnished by you hereunder shall become the sole property of the undersigned and shall be delivered to the undersigned or stored, as directed by the undersigned, aud if so stored the undersigned shall pay any storage charges.

8. Payment for such material shall be made to you against your invoice and at the cost charged to you by your suppliers and you agree to furnish to, or permit the inspection by the undersigned of your suppliers' invoices. The undersigned, however, agrees, at your request, to advance to you such sums not exceeding a total of as and when needed by you, but in such event you shall on or before July 31, 1958 furnish detailed invoices from your suppliers of your actual cost incurred and repay any excess advanced.

9. As full compensation for your services and upon completion of the material agreed to be furnished in accordance with the above described time schedule, the undersigned agrees to pay to you a fee in the sum of and an additional fee of for each 24 hours of earlier completion.

10. You further undertake to investigate with reputable and qualified publishing concerns in and other countries approved by the undersigned the making of arrangements for the printing, binding, pubbishing and distribution of "Dr. Zhivago" and to report to the undersigned the terms and conditions, if any, upon

June 19, 1958

Gentlemen:

The following constitutes our agreement:

1. You hereby acknowledge receipt from the undersigned of a manuscript copy of a literary work entitled "Dr. Zhivago" by Boris Pasternak.

2. The undersigned will further furnish you with type copy of a "publishers' note" or preface to be included after the title page of said manuscript.

3. You agree to procure and furnish to the undersigned, the following:

(a) Necessary layout and design work to prepare the manuscript including title page and preface for type set.

(b) Proofread type setting in the Russian language of said manuscript in page size 5 1/2" x 8 1/2". Such type setting to be 23 picas wide and 40 lines long, including folios.

(c) 2 sets of photo offset reproduction proofs of said page type settings of good quality and capable of providing clear and legible offset reproductions.

4. You agree that all of the foregoing work will be of high quality and shall be completed not later than 12:00 Midnight, July 31, 1958.

5. You further undertake and agree that the maximum cost to the undersigned of the components above described shall not exceed the following:

which any such firm will undertake such responsibility. For such services the undersigned agrees to pay you the sum of [redacted] plus any telephone, cable or toll charges incurred by you in the performance of such services.

11. You understand and agree that the undersigned is acting as agent for certain undisclosed principals but the undersigned represents and warrants that he will be personally responsible for the payment of the sums herein contracted to be paid.

Please evidence your acceptance hereof and agreement hereto by signing at the place indicated.

____

ACCEPTED AND AGREED TO:

By______________________

20 June 1958

MEMORANDUM FOR THE RECORD

SUBJECT: Contact Report with [redacted] and [redacted] on 19 June 1958.

1. The undersigned departed from Washington, D.C. at 0730 via American Airlines for New York, New York. After arriving at LaGuardia airport at 0845 [redacted] proceeded to the East Side Terminal and then to the law offices of [redacted]

2. An appointment had been made to see [redacted] at 1030 to discuss final terms of the contract between [redacted] and [redacted] concerning the type setting, manufacture of photo offset proofs, lay out and design work of Pasternak's *Dr. Zhivago*.

3. [redacted] discussed the details of the contract drawn up by the General Counsel's office in consultation with [redacted] and the undersigned which had been approved by the Chief of the Commercial Division and the Cover Division. [redacted] stated that phase one of the proposed contract i.e. regarding the type setting, photo offset proofs and lay out of the book looked good and that a final contract could now be submitted to [redacted] for his signature. He pointed out, however, that the proposal relating to phase two i.e. regarding the printing and distribution of the book in Europe was still too vague to be written in a contract. It was, therefore, agreed that at this time we should confine ourselves to specific negotiations and terms concerning phase one of the project and that subsequently we could write a new contract for phase two when the conditions relating to that phase were clarified. [redacted] said that the estimated cost of type setting, photo offset proofs and lay out work were perhaps on the high side but that this was probably warranted in view of the time factor involved. He also stated that the fee of [redacted] plus a bonus of [redacted] a day for each 24 hours that the book was completed before July 31 was appropriate. He further indicated that as part of phase one we should instruct [redacted] to investigate and designate a qualified and reputable publishing firm in Europe to print and distribute the book. [redacted] felt that [redacted] services in this regard should be included in the contract as part of his fee of [redacted]

Body 50

4. [redacted] had made a previous appointment with [redacted] at 1100 and telephoned him to ask if he could come to [redacted] office for the final negotiations. [redacted] agreed and arrived about ten minutes later to discuss the contract. Early in the conversation [redacted] stated that he had checked with [redacted] for whom he is a representative, and found that [redacted] would be able to do the final printing and distribution of the book. The reporting officer told [redacted] that he was under no authority even to have checked with [redacted] [redacted] as a printing possibility since we had never given him such authority. It was further emphasized that Headquarters still wanted the book printed and distributed by a reputable publishing firm in Europe and that this in fact was the reason why we had originally approached [redacted] [redacted] was somewhat taken aback by our insistence on this point and continued to argue that a [redacted] book would only slightly lessen and might even increase the effectiveness of the book on a Soviet audience. [redacted] replied that we continued to feel that the book would better serve our purpose if it were published in Europe and concluded by saying the the place of printing and imprint was our decision to make and would continue to be so.

5. [redacted] discussed the specific terms of the contract regarding phase one with [redacted] and the latter agreed to undertake the type setting, manufacture of photo offset proofs and lay out work as specified in the contract. [redacted] indicated, however, that as he had mentioned the week before in his discussion with [redacted] he wanted [redacted] for his handling the the whole project (phases one and two), or [redacted] for phase one. [redacted] replied that this amount was entirely too high for the services he would be performing in phase one and that such an amount was unacceptable to his clients. [redacted] stated that he normally handles such projects [redacted] [redacted] on a commercial basis wherein he acts as the "entrepreneur" taking over all of the commercial aspects of publishing such a book. He pointed out that he was not personnally interested in handling the book as we had proposed, but that he was doing this as a "one-shot" deal. The undersigned replied that we had approached [redacted] because we felt that he had the know how and contacts to publish the book along the lines that we had originally suggested and that for the present time Headquarters was not in a position to turn over the manuscript to Mr. [redacted] as he suggested. It was stated that this did not exclude the possibility of selling [redacted] the manuscript at some later time providing he agreed to certain conditions regarding the number of copies we would obtain at a special price etc. [redacted] [redacted] agreed to this and accepted our offer of a fee of [redacted] plus a bonus of [redacted] a day for every day before July 31 that the book was completed. He insisted, however, that he should be paid a fee of [redacted] for his services in finding a reputable and qualified European publisher regardless of whether we used such a publisher.

[redacted] replied that this was entirely too much for his efforts in finding a reputable European publisher and that it should be part of [redacted] fee. [redacted] was adament on this financial point and indicated that he was about to break off negotiations over it. With this the undersigned proposed that [redacted] receive [redacted] for his services in finding a qualified European publishing firm and [redacted] finally accepted this figure. [redacted] further agreed that the results of his investigation would be reported to [redacted] for approval before he entered into negotiations for a contract with a European publishing firm.

6. [redacted] discussed the remaining terms of the proposed contract and [redacted] agreed to all of these (see attached contract). It was agreed that the undersigned should provide [redacted] with a title page or "publisher's note" for the book. There was a final understanding among all parties that if and when Headquarters decided where and how the book should be printed and distributed, that a new contract would be written between [redacted] sometime before the completion of the offset proofs.

7. The meeting with [redacted] was concluded at 1230. [redacted] requested that the undersigned return to his office by 1800 to pick up the final contract for Headquarter's approval. Upon leaving [redacted] office, [redacted] asked [redacted] if he were free to discuss some further details of the book at luncheon. During luncheon, [redacted] elaborated upon the possibility of publishing the book by [redacted] and mentioned the possibility of setting aside part of the proceeds from the sale of the book for Pasternak. [redacted] replied that this could be discussed at a later time. [redacted] also brought up the question of his going to [redacted] to sign the final contract with the [redacted] publisher if such were available. The case officer replied that this decision would have to be made at Headquarters in accordance with government regulations on such overseas trips. [redacted] stated that he felt the book could be published in [redacted] by a publisher friend of his, [redacted] replied that this would probably not be an appropriate place to publish this book. The meeting was concluded at 1345. An appointment was made to see [redacted] at 0900 on 26 June to provide the title page of the book.

8. [redacted] returned to [redacted] office at 1730. He deposited a check for [redacted] in his name payable only to [redacted] to partially cover the costs of type setting and manufacture of photo offset proofs. After looking over the final contract [redacted] took it with him for approval by the necessary parties at Headquarters. The contract is scheduled to be signed the morning of 23 June 1958.

9. [redacted] arrived in Washington, D.C. at 2030.

SR/2/[redacted]

~~SECRET~~

20 June 1958

MEMORANDUM FOR: The Record

SUBJECT: AEDINOSAUR - [redacted]

1. Attached is a draft of an agreement reached 19 June 1958 between the Agency and [redacted] attorney at law, will sign for us on behalf of undisclosed principles, and [redacted] will sign for [redacted] It is planned to execute the agreement on 23 June 1958.

2. The draft has been approved by [redacted] of OGC. Paragraph 10 may be somewhat difficult to administer, but it was the judgement of our negotiators that it was necessary to include this [redacted] amount in order to get [redacted] to accept the agreement.

3. [redacted] will get in touch with us in about ten days in connection with negotiating the second phase having to do with publication in Europe from the proofs which will be delivered under this contract. [redacted] will handle the business and accounting details and will be compensated on a fee basis from project funds. [redacted] [redacted] has informed Central Cover Branch of the above arrangements.

3. [redacted] has been instructed to obtain a [redacted] report on [redacted]

/S/
Chief, Commercial Staff

Attachment - As stated

Distribution:
Orig. & 1 w/att - [redacted] Subj. File
1 w/att - OGC
1 w/att - SR ✓
1 w/att - [redacted]
1 - [redacted] Chrono
1 - [redacted] Chrono

(a) Layout and design work -- [redacted]

(b) Type setting and proofreading -- [redacted]

(c) Photo offset and reproduction proofs -- [redacted]

(d) Any additional photo offset reproduction proofs required by the undersigned shall be at the undersigned's additional cost.

6. It is understood and agreed that the undersigned hereby retains all right, title and interest in and to the said literary work and manuscript and said manuscript shall be returned to the undersigned upon completion of the work.

7. You further agree that the material and all rights therein furnished by you hereunder shall become the sole property of the undersigned and shall be delivered to the undersigned or stored, as directed by the undersigned, and if so stored the undersigned shall pay any storage charges.

8. Payment for such material shall be made to you against your invoice and at the cost charged to you by your suppliers and you agree to furnish to, or permit the inspection by the undersigned of your suppliers' invoices. The undersigned, however, agrees, at your request, to advance to you such sums not exceeding a total of [redacted] as and when needed by you, but in such event you shall on or before July 31, 1958 furnish detailed invoices from your suppliers of your actual cost incurred and repay any excess advanced.

9. As full compensation for your services and upon completion of the material agreed to be furnished in accordance with the above described time schedule, the undersigned agrees to pay to you a fee in the sum of [redacted] and an additional fee of [redacted] for each 24 hours of earlier completion.

10. You further undertake to investigate with reputable and qualified publishing concerns in [redacted] and other countries approved by the undersigned the making of arrangements for the printing, binding, publishing and distribution of "Dr. Zhivago" and to report to the undersigned the terms and conditions, if any, upon

SECRET

~~SECRET~~

which any such firm will undertake such responsibility. For such services the undersigned agrees to pay you the sum of [redacted] plus any telephone, cable or oil charges incurred by you in the performance of such services.

11. You understand and agree that the undersigned is acting as agent for certain undisclosed principals but the undersigned represents and warrants that he will be personally responsible for the payment of the sums herein contracted to be paid.

Please evidence your acceptance hereof and agreement hereto by signing at the place indicated.

[redacted]

ACCEPTED AND AGREED TO:

[redacted]

By ______________________

June 19, 1958

Gentlemen:

The following constitutes our agreement

1. You hereby acknowledge receipt from the undersigned of a manuscript copy of a literary work entitled "Dr. Zhivago" by Boris Pasternak.

2. The undersigned will further furnish you with type copy of a "publishers' note" or preface to be included after the title page of said manuscript.

3. You agree to procure and furnish to the undersigned, the following:

(a) Necessary layout and design work to prepare the manuscript including title page and preface for type set.

(b) Proofread type setting in the Russian language of said manuscript in page size 5 1/2" x 8 1/4". Such type setting to be 23 picas wide and 40 lines long, including folios.

(c) 2 sets of photo offset reproduction proofs of said page type settings of good quality and capable of providing clear and legible offset reproductions.

4. You agree that all of the foregoing work will be of high quality and shall be completed not later than 12:00 Midnight July 31, 1958.

5. You further undertake and agree that the maximum cost to the undersigned of the components above described shall not exceed the following:

SECRET

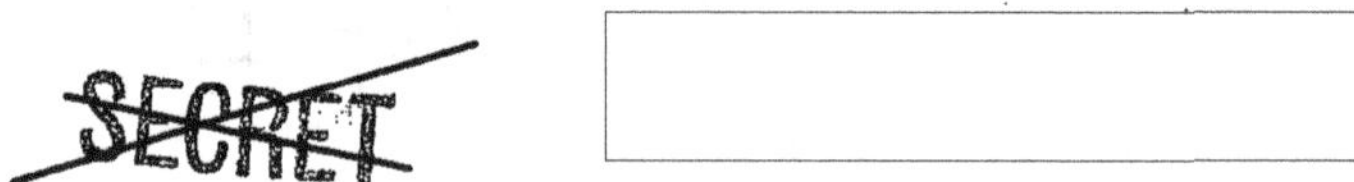

26 June 1958

MEMORANDUM FOR: SR

SUBJECT : Background Information and Outstanding Problems on the Publication of Dr. Zhivago.

1. As you know, a contract has been signed between representing the Agency, and for the type setting and manufacture of photo offset plates for Pasternak's Dr. Zhivago.

2. The two outstanding problems are the following: providing with a publisher's note or preface for the book not later than 8 July, and making final arrangements with for the printing and binding of the book by a European publisher.

3. has stated that the type setting will be completed by 11 July and the photo offset plates by 18 July which, under the terms of the contract, will provide him with his bonus. It is imparative, therefore, that we contact on the above problems in the first week of July.

4. A sum of to partially cover type setting and photo offsetting expenses has been deposited to the special account of On 24 June informed , Chief of the Commercial Division, that had submitted a bill of for the type setting. stated that he considered this to be a reasonable bill for the type setting involved and that he was proceeding to pay this bill. As soon as AEDINOSAUR obtains new funds for FY 1959, a check should be obtained for to be deposited to account to cover the additional expenses involved in phase one of the operation.

5. address is and his office telephone number is his home telephone number is He should be called person to person because quite often he is not in his office.

6. [redacted] knows the undersigned by his true name and is in constant touch with [redacted] of the Research Staff , the Office of Security, who handles [redacted] in a major project. [redacted] can be contacted for any information regarding [redacted] He is not, however, familiar with the details of our efforts in publishing Dr. Zhivago. [redacted] extension is [redacted] and he is located in [redacted]

7. [redacted] the lawyer representing the Agency, is a senior partner of [redacted] can be contacted through [redacted] Chief of the CIA Commercial Division, who has been in touch with [redacted] during the negotiations and is thoroughly familiar with the project. [redacted] should be kept informed of all developments with [redacted] so that he in turn can inform [redacted] who is paying the bills submitted to him by [redacted] and representing us in other legal matters concerning the publication. Any legal action should also be cleared through [redacted] of the General Counsel's Office. [redacted] extension is [redacted] and he is located in [redacted]

8. In a telephone conversation with [redacted] on 26 June, the undersigned told [redacted] that we were presently attempting to get a prominent literary figure to write a preface for <u>Dr. Zhivago</u> and that this or a publisher's note would be forwarded to him not later than 8 July. [redacted] was also told that a [redacted] would contact him in this regard. [redacted] is also very much concerned about our authorising him to make the final arrangements with a European publisher for the printing and binding of the book. He would like to have a paper signed by [redacted] authorising him to do this before he actually takes steps to negotiate a contract. [redacted] stated that he must have the above informationbby 8 July since he would be leaving New York for San Francisco on 12 July for two weeks. He also said he would not be able to use [redacted] after 8 July.

9. Please find in the <u>Dr. Zhivago</u> file the contract written between [redacted] a proposed publisher's note written by the undersigned, reviews of the book by Alberto Moravia, Max Hayward and other British authors. Some of the cable traffic is also included but for complete cable reference check with [redacted]

SR/2[redacted]

cc: [redacted]

27 June 1958

MEMORANDUM FOR: SR Division

ATTENTION: [redacted]

SUBJECT: AEDINOSAUR - Information from Attorney

Our cleared attorney in New York has sent me a copy of the agreement executed with [redacted] on 19 June 1958, which is identical with the draft forwarded you with our memorandum of 20 June 1958. He also said he planned to advance [redacted] for typesetting expense. [redacted] has found several minor defects in the manuscript which require immediate clarification by you. His explanation of this is attached hereto.

Chief, Commercial Staff

Attachment - Ltr. to [redacted]
dated June 20, 1958
from [redacted]

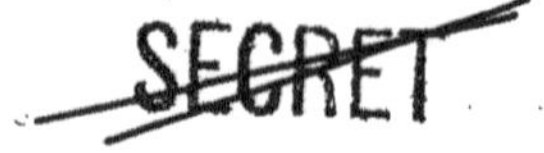

4. Mr. [redacted] gave the following figures for the costs involved and he said that they were conservative, i.e. on the high side:

Type setting:
Photo offset plates:
Design and lay out work:

TOTAL

[redacted] also said that he felt that [redacted] a copy would cover the printing, binding and distribution of the book. Ten thousand books would, therefore, cost [redacted] but part of these costs would be recovered from the proceeds from the sale of the book.

5. [redacted] was told that his recommendation would be considered at Headquarters and another meeting was arranged for 12 June at which time the [redacted] would turn over the Russian manuscript to [redacted] In the meantime, [redacted] said he would check out the Russian printing firms available in New York. [redacted] was reminded of the particular need for security in an operation of this kind.

6. The meeting was concluded at 1230 and the [redacted] returned to Washington, D.C.

SR/2/[redacted]

28 June 1958

MEMORANDUM FOR THE RECORD

SUBJECT: Contact Report of Meeting with [redacted] on 9 June 1958

1. The undersigned departed at 0800 on 9 June from Washington, D.C. via personal auto for New York, New York. Arrangements had been made to meet [redacted] of the Research Staff of the Security Office at [redacted] 1030 and then to meet [redacted] After meeting [redacted] proceeded to [redacted] office. [redacted]

2. [redacted] briefly told Mr. [redacted] of our desire to publish Pasternak's Dr. Zhivago in Russian. [redacted] replied that he knew of the book but inquired about where we would obtain a Russian manuscript. He was told that we have one in our possession and that we were trying to find a way of publishing the book in Eruope. [redacted] was extremely interested in the idea of getting this "great political work published", and said that he thought he could be of help [redacted]

3. [redacted] said that he thought he could find a European publisher to print the book but that he would suggest getting the book type set and photo offset in New York in order to accomplish this in a hurry and also to give him control over this phase of the operation. [redacted] stated that he felt that he could get a Dutch or Swiss publisher for the printing, binding and distribution of the book if we wanted it done that way.

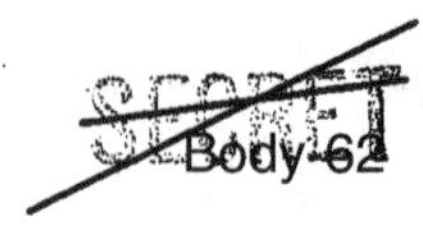

4. At 0930, 12 June, the [redacted] met with [redacted] [redacted] to draw up a contract for negotiations with [redacted]

5. The [redacted] met with [redacted] in his office at 1100 the same morning and gave him the Russian manuscript for Dr. Zhivago. [redacted] [redacted] stated that he felt the manuscript was in good enough shape for type setting and remarked that he had found a suitable printer, [redacted] [redacted] to do the type setting. [redacted] stated that he would be able to complete the type setting by 11 July and to complete the photo offset plates by 18 July. Terms of the contract were discussed. [redacted] [redacted] said that the express terms did not appeal to him, that he preferred to undertake these publishing contracts on a strictly commercial basis, by this he ment that the Agency should turn over to him the manuscript of a book, and in some cases provide work and capital or a guarantee to purchase so many books, and that he in turn would handle all of the problems and costs connected with type setting, printing and binding of the book. Under this arrangement, the proceeds from the sale of such books would accrue to [redacted] The [redacted] told [redacted] that he would have to check with Headquarters on this proposal and let him know our reaction later. In the meantime, [redacted] was asked if he would consider our proposal to pay the costs of the type setting, photo offset prints and lay out for the book plus a [redacted] fee for a time bonus to [redacted] The latter said that he would undertake the project on a fee basis but that he would like to have a fee of [redacted] for both phases of the operation. The [redacted] said that this figure was entirely too high and that he was sure that it would not be acceptable at Headquarters. [redacted] [redacted] in turn asked that we consider his proposal rather than give him a fee. Mr. [redacted] also commented that he would need [redacted] for work and capital to cover the costs of type setting, etc. but that all of this amount would be returned at a specific date to the party that we designated. The meeting was concluded at 1330.

6. At 1330 the [redacted] again met with [redacted] and told him of [redacted] reactions to our proposals and of [redacted] suggestion of turning the manuscript over to him. [redacted] first of all remarked that the figure of [redacted] was preposterous and that we should not agree to these terms under any conditions. Regarding [redacted] own proposal, [redacted] stated that he felt that this had its merits since it would be a lot simpler for us and would place the burden of financial responsibility on [redacted] He stated further that if we accepted this proposal we should have [redacted] write a legal note to the lawyer for the

amount of work and capital provided and that the note should be payable within four months regardless of the status of the book. A new contract spelling out the terms of the agreement as [redacted] proposed was written. It was understood that both contracts would be taken to Washington, D.C., for approval before being turned over to the lawyer for negotiations with [redacted]

7. The [redacted] telephoned [redacted] at 1600 to say that his proposal was being considered and that we would contact him the following week regarding the final negotiations for the contract.

8. The [redacted] departed [redacted] at 1950 and arrived in Washington, D.C., at 2100.

SR/2/[redacted]

SECRET

30 June 1958

MEMORANDUM FOR THE RECORD

SUBJECT: Contact Report of Meeting with [redacted] [redacted] on 11 - 12 June 1958

1. The undersigned departed from National airport at 1135 on 11 June and arrived at LaGuardia at 1245. From LaGuardia he went to the [redacted] Hotel [redacted] for a 1400 meeting with [redacted] [redacted] Chief of the Agency's Commercial Division.

2. [redacted] looked over a draft of the paper written by [redacted] [redacted] and the undersigned concerning our proposals for the publication of Dr. Zhivago in two phases. It was proposed that in phase one [redacted] would arrange for the type setting, manufacture of photo offset proofs and the lay out of the book. Phase two would consist of the printing, binding and distribution of the book in Europe. [redacted] would handle both phases of the publication and would be paid a fee for his services in each phase of the operation. [redacted] thought that this was a good approach to the problem -- particularly because of our desire to have the book published in Europe. He suggested that we talk to one of the business consultants that the Commercial Division used for such projects. [redacted] recommended that we employ [redacted] [redacted]

3. [redacted] telephoned [redacted] and the latter came to [redacted] [redacted] hotel room for discussions on the publication. [redacted] looked over the draft of our proposals and suggested that we confer with [redacted] [redacted] legal specialist in such publication matters, [redacted] [redacted] A meeting was arranged for 1830 at [redacted] office at [redacted] During this meeting, [redacted] was told of our intention to have a book, in the Russian language, type set and photo offset in New York and to then have it published in Europe. He was asked if he would handle the legal problems connected with the publication (signing of contracts, payment of bills, etc.). [redacted] agreed and an appointment was made to discuss the matter with him the following week.

3 July 1958

MEMORANDUM FOR: The Record

SUBJECT: AEDINOSAUR

1. The following persons attended a meeting held on 2 July 1958 in the office of the Chief, Commercial Staff concerning AEDINOSAUR:

[redacted] Chief, Commercial Staff
[redacted] SR Division
[redacted] WE Division
[redacted] Commercial Staff

2. The current status of the project was reviewed and the following main points were agreed upon as regards the second phase of the project:

a. [redacted] to draw up outline of phase two proposal to [redacted] and this outline is to be presented to the cleared attorney in New York as soon as is possible.

b. The attorney will be requested to negotiate the proposal with [redacted] and report the results of this negotiation to [redacted].

c. [redacted] is to call [redacted] and will discuss with him the matter of the preface for the book, as well as telling [redacted] of our interest in a second phase agreement with him and the impending contact from the attorney.

d. Although the final agreement with [redacted] is subject to negotiation, it was agreed at this meeting that any agreement should contain the following basic points:

(1) That a non-U.S. imprint of the book will be published.

(2) That the imprint will be ready for distribution by 1 September 1958.

(3) That we will receive 6,000 copies of the book at a discounted price.

(4) That, if [redacted] is able to arrange the European printing, the plates and rights will be sold to him for [redacted], or [redacted] if the 1 September target date is not met.

e. It was further agreed that the agreement must contain protective clauses in the event of a default by [redacted] However, should this be an honest default on his part, consideration would be given to negotiate a different agreement with [redacted].

Commercial Staff

Distribution:
Original & 1--[redacted] Subject File
1--SR
1--[redacted] Chrono
1-[redacted] Chrono

a. There is to be no U.S. imprint or credits on any of the books published in the European edition.

b. The 1 September deadline should be emphasized to the publisher.

c. We desire to know the name of the European publisher with whom [redacted] is in contact.

d. No commitments are to be made at this time. We desire to review any contract prior to signing.

5. In response to our query regarding publication rights and legal complications, [redacted] advised that he and the attorney would explore this further and attempt to come up with possible protective devices.

Commercial Staff

Distribution:
Original & 1--[redacted] Subject File
1--SR
1--[redacted]-Chrono
1--[redacted]--Chrono (pink)

SECRET

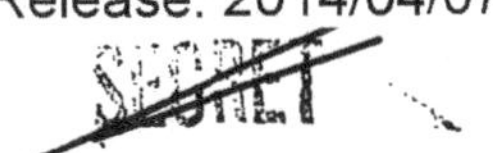

7 July 1958

MEMORANDUM FOR: The Record

SUBJECT: AEDINOSAUR Meeting - 7 July 1958

1. The following persons met on 7 July 1958 in the office of the Chief, Commercial Staff to discuss the most recent developments regarding the second phase of subject project:

[redacted] Chief, Commercial Staff
[redacted] SR Division
WE Division
Commercial Staff

2. [redacted] has established contact with a European publishing concern and has requested immediate authority from the cleared attorney to negotiate a contract along the following lines:

a. European publisher to publish 10,000 copies at approximately [redacted] per copy.

b. 4,000 of these copies to be sold to us at a special price.

c. The remaining 6,000 to be sold on consignment, with us receiving [redacted] per copy as sold.

d. The plates and rights would remain ours upon completion of the European edition.

3. It was decided that the above proposal was not desirable, and that the attorney should present our previous proposal (see Memo for the Record 3 July 1958) to the publisher when he meets with him today. The original proposal should remain unchanged except that we now desire to buy 4,000 copies at publisher's price to distributors, rather than 6,000 copies at a "discounted price."

4. [redacted] was contacted by telephone and requested to pass the following to the attorney for his action:

SECRET

against those who tried to interfere with his work. He ceased publishing after 1932 but earned a good living by translating foreign literature. Following the denigration of Stalin at the 20th party congress in 1956, Pasternak submitted his novel for publication. The Union of Writers refused publication of the manuscript, accusing Pasternak of using his "great gift" to "resuscitate in the soul of our people ideals which have been dead for a long time." Meanwhile, Pasternak had given copies of the manuscript to the Italian Communist publisher Feltrinelli and to other visitors from abroad, who were asked to arrange for English and French translations. Pasternak also informed his foreign publishers that they should ignore any letter he might write under duress requesting that the manuscript not be published.

5. SR Division has already paid [redacted] to the New York publishing agent for the Russian type setting, which will be completed by 11 July. Preparation of the photo offset plates, to be finished by 18 July, will cost an additional [redacted] An exact estimate of additional publication and distribution costs cannot be made now because these arrangements are still under negotiation. However, SR Division intends to guarantee the purchase of 6,000 copies of the novel for operational distribution. This purchase may cost up to [redacted] depending on the unit cost of the edition. If the Division sells the photo offset plates later to the New York publishing agent for [redacted] (as now contemplated), the Division's net expenditure for the Russian language edition of "Dr. Zhivago" will be at least $[redacted]. To provide a margin for special contingencies in this matter, an additional [redacted] may be needed. Therefore SR Division is requesting approval to obligate up to [redacted] for this undertaking.

[redacted]
Chief, SR Division

CONCUR:

Chief, [redacted] Date

APPROVED:

DD/P Date

9 July 1958

MEMORANDUM FOR: Deputy Director (Plans)

VIA: [redacted]

SUBJECT: Request for Authorization to Obligate up to [redacted] from AEDINOSAUR

1. It is requested that SR Division be authorized to expend up to [redacted] from its DTO project AEDINOSAUR to cover the costs of publishing a Russian language edition of Boris Pasternak's book, "Dr. Zhivago."

2. The book was published in Italian by Feltrinelli in April 1958 and is expected to be available in English this fall. The Soviet Union has rejected the novel for publication in the USSR. SR Division is anxious to have the book available as soon as possible for distribution in Russian to Soviet nationals traveling abroad, especially to those attending the Brussels Fair. Representatives of this Division and the General Counsel's Office are currently negotiating with a cleared publishing agent in New York City to arrange for European publication of the book in Russian so that the edition will be available for distribution by 1 September 1958 at the latest.

3. Pasternak's 700-page novel, "Dr. Zhivago" is considered to be the most heretical literary work by a Soviet author since Stalin's death. Pasternak's humanistic message--that every person is entitled to a private life and deserves respect as a human being, irrespective of the extent of his political loyalty or contribution to the state--poses a fundamental challenge to the Soviet ethic of sacrifice of the individual to the Communist system. There is no call to revolt against the regime in the novel, but the heresy which "Dr. Zhivago" preaches--political passivity--is fundamental. Pasternak suggests that the small, unimportant people who remain passive to the regime's demands for active participation and emotional involvement in official campaigns are superior to the political "activists" favored by the system. Further, he dares hint that society might function better without these fanatics.

4. Pasternak is recognized by non-Soviet critics to be the greatest living Russian writer. His originality of poetic expression and his disinterest in political themes brought him into disfavor with the Stalinist regime in the 1930's. Rather than submit and become an unwilling instrument of the party, Pasternak withdrew into silence to harbor bitterness

1)

June 30, 1958

Dear

I should appreciate your informing your people of the following:

1. The enclosed proofs (these are merely rough page proofs, and have no bearing on the final reproduction proofs) will show the type in which the book is being set, and the page design. I myself am extremely pleased with the type font, which is far more esthetic and readable than almost anything to be found in Soviet production. However, it has proved to take up far more space than I originally estimated. From the 20 pica, 35-line page of the 700-page Italian book, I estimated that a 23 pica, 40-line page would make a book of approximately 560 pages. Instead, this is actually running to something above 660 pages. I think it well worth the additional pagination, but I may have to ask for more money than the original estimate.

2. I have not yet received the two-page publisher's note. I have allowed for it in the pagination.

3. On Thursday, June 26, I was notified that there may still come a longish introduction not contemplated previously. If it does, it will have to be paginated in Roman numerals, which is of course no great matter. However, I want it clearly understood that any further delay on the publisher's note and the introduction means that I shall deliver the reproduction proofs as soon as they are ready without this material in order to comply with our agreement.

(over)

and to delivering the European printing of 4,000 at the agreed upon price and time. Otherwise, I am free to do as I please. This means I may publish other editions at prices higher than [redacted] if I so choose; and I can publish any where else I please. Specifically, I mean to publish at [redacted] Press another edition in hard covers. Without the right to publish other editions and at prices economically determined by my operation, I find your client's price for the plates and rights economically impossible for I would have no clear prospect of recovering my costs.

4. For the reasons indicated above, I reject 4.

5. This provision binds me to stick to a list price of [redacted] per copy "until such time as [redacted] pays full amount for the rights and plates," likewise (combining 4. and 5.) compels me to name a wholesale price to a distributor in the original contract with the European publisher (a provision entirely contrary to custom) and, in a word, doesn't permit me to operate in a businesslike way. If the provision No. 5 reads correctly, all this disappears if I pay full amount for the rights and plates. In that case, I prefer to pay that full amount immediately.

6. Agreed.

7. Agreed.

Sincerely,

P.S. As I leave for San Francisco Friday morning, it seems to me that, unless your client is prepared to modify as I propose, I should now step aside altogether; I shall conclude my obligations under the contract covering Phase 1, and your client and I will part company at that point.

2)

MATTERS TO DISCUSS WITH

Phase 1 Contract:

1. Get copy from .

2. Discuss fee of for finding publisher and possibility of taking this out of Phase 2 contract if is to be publisher.

3. Verify that maximum is to be given for Phase 1 composition, typesetting, plates, etc., plus fee and per day for every day the foregoing is finished prior to 7/31/58.

Phase 2 Contract (points to be discussed for inclusion in contract):

1. Books to bear non-U.S. imprint.

2. If manuscript not published by September 1, 1958, we have a right to recover plates or require to publish the book.

3. We agree to sell and agrees to buy rights and plates for before September 1, 1958, or for thereafter. must make down payment of under either plan and agree to a two-year non interest-bearing personal note for the balance payable in installments every six months.

4. If European publisher is found by we must see executed contract between and publisher before we make plates available. We reserve the right to purchase 4,000 copies at the wholesale price to the distributor (which must be verified by contract) either for the paperback or bound edition.

5. Until such time as pays full amount for the rights and plates, the retail price for either the bound or paperback edition cannot exceed per copy, and the wholesale price to the distributor must be consistent with normal trade practice.

6. We can sell or otherwise distribute and dispose of our 4,000 copies at any price, time or place.

7. Upon making partial or full payment for the rights and plates, agrees to hold us harmless from any suits or litigation arising from the publication and/or sale of the manuscript.

COPY

3)

July 7, 1958

Dear

I should like to carry out the wishes of your client but the proposed Phase 2 Contract as it stands is impossible for me to undertake. I specify below, following the numbered points in your memo dated July 7.

1. "Books to bear non-U.S. imprint a must." In the short time required of me before I publish --Sept 1-- I cannot obligate myself to secure a recognised European publisher and cause him to commit himself to manufacture and issue such books --all this in less than eight weeks! The publisher I have in mind will undoubtedly want to consult his attorney on whether or no he has a clear legal right to publish this ms. in the face of Feltrinelli's claim that the author has vested all rights in Feltrinelli.

I from my experience are certain he has such right; but a Dutchman and his counsel may want to think about it for a while. In the end, the first and/or second publisher I approach may want no part of this complicated piece of business. Therefore, all I can guarantee your client is neither a European publisher nor such a near deadline as September 1. What I can guarantee him is the actual manufacture and delivery of these books in Europe, with the imprint in it of a printer or a printer-publisher, whose name I cannot now specify because I cannot guess in advance who can be gotten to do it. I would guarantee to deliver these to your client's representative in the city of manufacture (in all probability Amsterdam) no later than September 15, if your client and I sign a contract this week.

If I understand your client's needs, I undertake to deliver to him 4,000 copies of a paperback edition which he guarantees to purchase at per copy. He in turn may dispose of them at any price, time or place.

The above arrangement is contingent upon acceptance by your client of my proposals under 3. below.

2. Your client under this claims right to cover plates or require me to publish the book if the ms. is not published by Sept 1,1958. I do not understand the import of "require to publish the book." As to recovery of the plates, this would mean I should have worked for nothing. I therefore cannot accept this provision.

3. I accept your client's proposal, namely, I agree to buy rights and plates for before Sept 1, 1958, make down payment of and execute a two-year non interest-bearing personal note for the balance payable in installments every six months. However, I do so only on condition that I [illegible] bject only to paying for them

Body-77

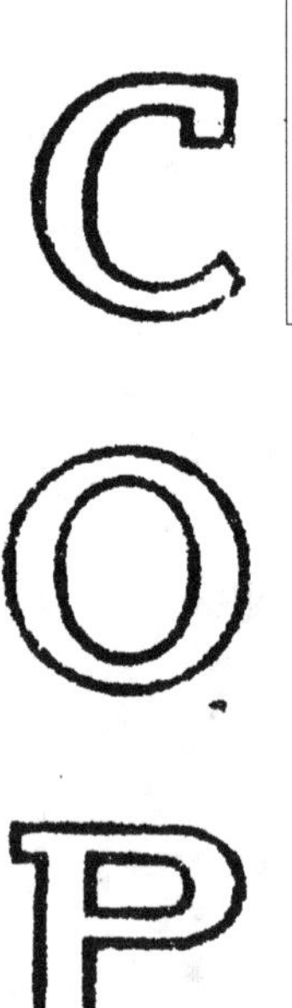
COPY

I shall, of course, also handle the later material through reproduction proofs apart from the agreement.

4. As I told your people on the telephone on June 26th, I had completed the survey of European publishers called for in the agreement, and was ready to proceed to make a contract with one of these publishers as soon as I receive from you a letter authorizing me to do so. Under this agreement, we would pay approximately per copy for the manufacture of ten thousand copies (perhaps ten cents more per copy in the light of the present estimate pagination), plus a schedule of advertisements and perhaps an allowance to the publisher for a publicity campaign. In turn, the publisher would agree to (a.) sell 4,000 copies at a special price to someone we would designate. (b.) Hold the other 6,000 on consignment and pay us something like copy when and as sold. (c.) The offset plates would remain our property and all further printings would be done on the same basis and only on our instructions.

As time was indicated to be of the essence, I must point out that in authorizing me to make such a contract from this point on means lost time.

5. My offer to have the book published with the imprint of Press will be withdrawn July 7th; thereafter, if you authorize me to publish here, it would be under the imprint of

6. I enclose herewith our invoice for the remaining advances of

Sincerely yours,

encl; 1-inv
2-prfs

P.S. On July 11th I am leaving the city for three weeks. I made arrangements with my production people to complete the proof arrangement with you and the two sets of reproduction proofs will be delivered personally to you.

RATING: —

Interviewed January 13, 1958, [redacted] stated that officers for subject continue to be the same. [redacted] stated that figures pertaining to subject would not be submitted at this time. He did state that the auditors are currently completing figures on the subject and these figures will be made available during February, 1958. [redacted] refused to comment on condition at this time.

14 July 1958

MEMORANDUM FOR: Chief, SR

ATTENTION: [redacted]

SUBJECT: AEDINOSAUR - Current Developments

1. [redacted] planned to leave for the West Coast on 11 July 1958, for three weeks and has presumably departed. He stated in his letter of 30 June 1958 to [redacted] that he had made arrangements with the production people in his company to deliver the reproduction proofs to [redacted] Your [redacted] Cashier's Check was mailed last week to [redacted] [redacted] who will deliver it to [redacted]

2. In accordance with our instructions, [redacted] informed [redacted] that we are having further consultations on Phase 2 and will advise him of the results. As you can see from the attachments, we were still some distance from agreement on Phase 2. However, it appears that the gap is not too difficult to bridge, since it stems in considerable measure from misunderstandings arising out of the haste of negotiations.

3. [redacted] has become somewhat concerned by the recent statements that the book may be published by someone else who claims to possess the legal rights. He was aware from the outset that we did not possess the rights, but our information at that time was that Feltrinelli did not have the Russian language rights and, apparently, had no intention to publish the book in Russian. In view of the current indications, [redacted] prefers not to personally head business negotiations with [redacted] on Phase 2, although he will continue to act as our attorney.

Chief, Commercial Staff

Attachments:

1) Ltr. to [redacted] from [redacted] of 30 June 1958 (Note publisher's name in margin)
2) Undated Negotiation Outline of [redacted]
3) [redacted] Ltr. to [redacted] of July 7, 1958
4) [redacted] on [redacted]

CM 58-1026

July 18, 1958

Attention:

Dear :

You have inquired with respect to a novel first published in Russia written by a Russian author there domiciled.

Under Section 9(b) of the U.S. Copyright law, that work would not be entitled to U.S. copyright because that section excepts the granting of copyright protection to the works of a foreign author when the foreign state of which such author is a citizen or subject does not afford reciprocity in the granting of copyright protection to American citizens. Russia falls within the category of countries which do not grant reciprocal protection to American authors. Accordingly, works published in Russia by a Russian author are in the public domain in this country (except, as provided by section 9(a), when the alien author is domiciled within the United States at the time of first publication, which was not the fact in the situation you outlined to me). Furthermore, an assignee (such as the Italian publisher which you mentioned) stands in no better status in acquiring copyright protection than does the author.

I am enclosing bill covering our services, which I trust will be satisfactory.

Sincerely yours,

Enclosure

July 28, 1958

Attention:

Dear

This is in response to your letter of July 24th addressed to

The fact that the work has not yet heretofore been published in Russia but was first published in an Italian translation in Italy does not alter the opinion expressed by in his letter of July 18th that the work is not entitled to copyright in the United States.

Under Section 9(b) of the U.S. Copyright Law, referred to by in his letter of July 16th, the status of the author is the determining factor not that of the proprietor to whom the author has assigned the work. Since in this case the author himself would not be entitled to secure copyright in the United States, as stated in the letter of July 16th, the assignee of such an author is in no better position to acquire copyright protection in the United States. In other words, the author cannot confer any right upon his assignee to secure American copyright when the author himself could not acquire such copyright protection.

We trust that the foregoing clears up the matter. If you have any further question, please do not hesitate to communicate with us.

Very truly yours,

6. [redacted] emphasized that [redacted] may well be merely "feeling out the market" with their inquiry to [redacted] and it was agreed that there is evidence in the correspondence to indicate that [redacted] has had some type of preliminary discussions with the [redacted] which could prompt such an inquiry.

7. It was agreed that the following action would be taken:

a. [redacted] will have the material received from [redacted] examined to determine precisely what we have received.

b. SR Division will advise [redacted] of the course of action as soon as they have received replies to their inquiries [redacted] [redacted] to [redacted]

c. [redacted] will determine the present location and availability of the photo offset plates, and will also obtain a full accounting of funds received and paid out in this operation.

d. Until the above questions are resolved no payments to [redacted] will be made, the plates will not be picked up from wherever they are at the moment, and no further action will be taken by [redacted]

8. The remainder of the meeting was devoted to a short briefing of [redacted] by [redacted] on certain aspects of the [redacted] operation.

Commercial Staff

ATT FOR SR

July 10, 1958

Dear

I am sure you understand that the inability of your clients to come to a decision before I leave the city means that, for my part, anything I have had to say about phase two goes by the board, and any proposal hereafter by your client will have to start from scratch.

I shall be at the San Francisco, Calif., from Sunday, July 13th through the 19th. From Sunday, July 20th until Thursday, July 24th, I shall be in Chicago at the

The following week I can best be reach through my New York office.

I shall return to New York Monday, August 4th.

Thank you very much for your cooperation.

Sincerely yours,

18 July 1958

MEMORANDUM FOR: The Record

SUBJECT: AEDINOSAUR Meeting of 17 July 1958

1. [redacted] SR Division met with [redacted] of the Commercial Staff on 17 July 1958 in the CM Library to discuss the latest developments in the AEDINOSAUR case.

2. [redacted] pointed out that [redacted] had contacted SR Division and had informed them that the [redacted] was planning to publish the book in question. [redacted] was interested in knowing the extent of SR's interest in getting copies. SR requested [redacted] to determine where the [redacted] obtained the plates, whether they had the rights, and the cost per copy of the edition they plan to publish. [redacted] is to advise SR of this information on Friday, 18 July.

3. [redacted] announced that he had picked up a package during his latest visit to New York which it was assumed contained the plates for the book. The package was opened at the meeting and was found to contain the manuscript and what appeared to be plate proofs, but it did not contain any plates as such. [redacted] stated he would take the material and have it examined by technicians familiar with printing processes to determine its exact nature.

4. As regards the recent rumors as to European publishing of the book, [redacted] advised that Feltrinelli, the Italian publisher, had no facilities for publishing the book in Russian, but that he had contacted [redacted] in [redacted] to try and make arrangements for publishing in the Russian language.

5. SR Division has initiated an inquiry [redacted] requesting that they explore with [redacted] the possibility of our making a gift of the plates to [redacted] on the provision that they print the book in time for normal commercial distribution at the time and location targeted for in this operation. Should this be agreeable to [redacted] SR Division will follow this course; if not accepted by [redacted] consideration will be given to printing a black edition and distributing it through covert channels in the target area.

SECRET

28 July 1958

MEMORANDUM FOR: The Record

SUBJECT: AEDINOSAUR - Recent Developments

1. [redacted] of [redacted] Staff met with [redacted] of SR Division and [redacted] Office of Security, to discuss the most recent developments of AEDINOSAUR project.

2. [redacted] explained that the Office of Security has a long-range interest in [redacted] and although no monetary relationship exists at the moment, if certain projects were approved such a relationship would exist in the future.

3. [redacted] stated that in view of the most recent developments in this case he felt that [redacted] contacts in Security should be brought into the AEDINOSAUR picture at this stage.

4. [redacted] once again contacted [redacted] on 25 July regarding the number of such publications the United States Government would be interested in purchasing. [redacted] replied that there was no Government interest at this time. [redacted] stated that it planned to publish subject book in Russian regardless of Government interest in procurement of copies. [redacted] pointed out that it appears that [redacted] in his dealings with [redacted] has gone entirely too far, and may well have committed one or more security violations. Specifically, [redacted] queried [redacted] as to CIA's interest in the book and whether or not the Agency was subsidizing the publishing of the book in Europe. In reply to [redacted] question as to [redacted] source of the rights or capabilities for publishing the book, [redacted] stated in circumstance that "[redacted] has given us what we have." An attempt is being made through [redacted] of the [redacted] Staff to determine exactly what, if anything, [redacted] has passed to [redacted].

5. [redacted] stated that a cable reply had been received from Europe and that the [redacted] publisher is definitely interested in publishing the book in Russian. The publisher has stated that the operational deadline of this book can be met provided that the publisher receives the necessary material within a week. SR Division is desirous of proceeding

SECRET

along this line provided that the details can be suitably negotiated. The Division definitely does not want the book published at [redacted] or elsewhere in the United States and [redacted] so told [redacted] by telephone on the morning of 28 July.

6. After some discussion of the action to be taken at this time, it was agreed at the meeting that the following would be done as promptly as possible:

(a) Obtain through [redacted] specific information as to what material [redacted] may have passed to [redacted]

(b) Upon receipt of the above, the Chief, [redacted] will notify the attorney in New York of the status of the case and will request that he call [redacted] and discuss it with him. During this conversation the attorney should bring out the fact that there is a distinct probability that the Italian publisher is prepared to sue anyone publishing the book in Russian since the Italian publisher claims to have publishing rights and the intention to publish the book himself. The attorney should also attempt to determine from [redacted] the nature of any agreements the latter has made with [redacted]

(c) If, after the above steps have been taken, it is felt that the situation warrants it, [redacted] will be requested to call [redacted] and assert pressure upon him to abide to the terms of our original agreement.

Commercial Staff

DD/S/[redacted]

Distribution:
Orig. & 1-- [redacted] Subject File
1 -- SR Division [redacted]
1 -- [redacted]
1 -- [redacted] Chrono.

SECRET

29 July 1958

MEMORANDUM FOR: The Record

SUBJECT: Project AEDINOSAUR - Conversation with Attorney, 29 July 1958

1. No further information having been received from [redacted] it was decided to call our attorney in New York immediately and have him get in touch with [redacted] at [redacted] Accordingly, I talked with [redacted] who will call [redacted] and inquire as to his relation with [redacted] will then call his attention to the fact that under our agreement the manuscript, proofs, etc., are the sole property of the Agency, and that [redacted] was specifically told we would not accept publication by [redacted] or any other concern in the U. S.

2. [redacted] said he has recently been in touch with a [redacted] [redacted], and also has talked by telephone with [redacted] in San Francisco. [redacted] insisted that Phase 1 does not cover negatives or plates. I informed [redacted] that we are content to settle the account for Phase 1 with [redacted] without having him make negatives or plates, providing we pay only the actual cost of typesetting, proofs, and layout. [redacted] has received the following billings from [redacted]

[redacted] (Typesetting in Russian, 635 pages @ [redacted])	- [redacted]
[redacted] (Reproduction proofs @ [redacted] a page)	- [redacted]
[redacted] (Design and layout)	- [redacted]
[redacted] fee	- [redacted]
[redacted] bonus (15 days @ [redacted])	- [redacted]
Locating European publisher	- [redacted]
Miscellaneous Expenses (Communication, tolls, etc.)	- [redacted]
Total	[redacted]

Payments totaling [redacted] have been made to [redacted]. The item of [redacted] re locating a European publisher may be questionable. [redacted] will inform me of the results of his conversation with [redacted]

/S/

Chief, Commercial Staff

Distribution:
Orig. & 1 - [redacted] Subj. File
1 - SR - Attn: Mr. [redacted]
1 - [redacted] Chrono
1 - [redacted] Chrono

8 August 1958

MEMORANDUM FOR: The Record

SUBJECT: AEDINOSAUR--Current Developments

1. On 7 August 1958 I met with [redacted] in New York. [redacted] had asked him for further payments on account, but [redacted] will make no more payments until authorized by us. He will be away from his office on vacation from 8 August until 25 August.

2. [redacted] told [redacted] he had made no arrangements with [redacted] [redacted] r publication of the book in question. He also expressed surprise that we had been billed for three sets of reproduction proofs and said he did not know the third set had been made. He said he had not provided any reproduction proofs to [redacted] [redacted]

3. In accordance with our telephone conversation of today, [redacted] will arrange through the Contacts Office to get the full story from [redacted] on their dealings with [redacted] After talking to [redacted] called the [redacted] who said they had the third set of proofs in their vault, in accordance with standard paractice. They said this set had not been out of their possession.

4. [redacted] has asked [redacted] if they can destroy the type because of the difficulty of storage. [redacted] requests that the type not be destroyed until the book appears in Europe, which will be in two or three weeks. We will have [redacted] office direct [redacted] [redacted] to hold the type for several weeks.

Chief, Commercial Staff

Distribution:

Orig. & 1--[redacted] Subj. File
1--SR Div. (Mr. [redacted]
1--[redacted] Chrono
1--[redacted] Chrono

SECRET

Body-91

DISPATCH

CLASSIFICATION: ~~SECRET~~

DISPATCH SYMBOL AND NO.

TO

INFO

HEADQUARTERS FILE NO.

FROM Chief, SR via Chief, WE

DATE 9 AUG 1958

SUBJECT REDWOOD AEDINOSAUR

Arrangements for Publication of Dr. Zhivago

RE: "43-3" — (CHECK "X" ONE)

MARKED FOR INDEXING

NO INDEXING REQUIRED

INDEXING CAN BE JUDGED BY QUALIFIED HQ. DESK ONLY

ACTION REQUIRED Comments and actions re: (1) Arrangements for forwarding books, (2) return one set of reproduction proofs, (3) reaction to publishing miniature edition Dr. Zhivago.

REFERENCE(S)

1. First of all Headquarters would like to state that it has been extremely pleased with fine cooperation and expeditious handling of the publication of Pasternak's Dr. Zhivago.

2. As knows, our primary objective in this operation is to make this philosophical novel available to the large number of Soviet tourists and officials now visiting Western Europe and the Brussels Fair. We are, therefore, looking forward to obtaining and distributing the first thousand copies of the book. Toward this end, it is requested that the first 200 of the books be forwarded by where they will be picked up and distributed by If it is convenient for we would like to have 200 of the books sent to Headquarters, 200 to 100 to and 100 to

3. To cover the cost of the books and any other expenses incurred in getting the book published please ~~send T/A~~ Rebate to Headquarters to be charged against AEDINOSAUR.

4. If feels that it is appropriate, we would like to ask to return one set of the reproduction proofs when the latter has completed proofreading or printing the book. The reproduction proofs should be forwarded to Headquarters.

5. Headquarters would also appreciate thinking on the following proposition: After has published the regular Russian edition of the book which will be distributed at the Brussels Fair and throughout Western Europe, we would like to consider publishing a miniature light weight edition of the book which could be mailed or carried into the Soviet Union more easily than the regular size book. For security reasons it would be best if put out such an edition. Printing consultants at Headquarters advise us that such an edition could be printed on bible stock (or similar light weight paper) and would look something like a small "pocketbook". Since the miniature edition would not be intended for the Brussels Fair but for long range dissemination within the Soviet Union, there would not be such a time factor as there has been with the regular edition. Depending upon the cost and the dimensions of the finished product, Headquarters would be willing to purchase 1,000 to 2,000 copies of the miniature books.

a. If felt that it would be appropriate, might be used to sound out on this matter. To explain his interest in this undertaking, could say that he has heard that there is a demand in the emigre world for a miniature edition of Dr. Zhivago and that he has a specific order for 1,000 to 2,000 books. If should raise the question of the miniature books cutting into the sale of the regular books, could assure that the new books will not be sold on the Western European market.

8 August 1958

Distribution:
2 -
2 - WE/2
2 - SR/2
1 - RI
SR/2:

FORM 10-57 53 USE PREVIOUS EDITION. REPLACES FORMS 51-28, 51-28A AND 51-29 WHICH ARE OBSOLETE.

CLASSIFICATION: ~~SECRET~~

CONTINUED

PAGE NO.

the capability of giving the book to travelers going into the USSR for internal distribution. Some American travelers will similarly carry the book into the Soviet Union. Plans are also being made to mail a certain number of the books to students and members of the Soviet intelligensia.

5. An attempt is being made [redacted] to inform Pasternak that an Escrow account from the sale of the book has been set up in his name. Pasternak will be told that funds from this account will be available if he is ever in a position to use them.

[redacted]

SECRET

8 September 1958

MEMORANDUM FOR PP NOTES

SUBJECT: Publication of Pasternak's Dr. Zhivago

1. The Russian edition of Boris PASTERNAK's novel Dr. Zhivago will be published this week by [redacted] in Holland. Arrangements have been made for [redacted] to receive the first thousand copies of the book off the press. These will be distributed to Soviet visitors at the Brussels Fair and in Western Europe [redacted] The [redacted] has been instrumental in having the original Russian edition of the book published. Observing that this great anti-communist philosophical novel was being published in Italian, French, English and German, and realizing that there was little chance of Soviet authorities publishing it in the Soviet Union, we felt that the book should be published in Russian for Soviet readers. A copy of the original Russian manuscript was obtained from [redacted] who agreed that it should be published but asked that it not be done in the U.S. Pasternak had himself requested that for his personal safety and other reasons the Russian edition of the book not be published in the U.S. Every effort was made to honor the author's petition.

2. Inorder to expedite the publication of the book, arrangements were made to have the manuscript typeset in New York. When this work was completed, negatives were made from the reproduction proofs [redacted] had been in correspondence with FELTRINELLI, the Italian publisher who claimed to hold all foreign rights to the publication of the book, and it was mutually agreed that the Russian edition would be published joinly under both their names.

[redacted] will distribute and sell the book whereever he can in Europe, the U.S., the Far East, etc. through his normal publishing channels.

4. Approximately 800 of the first thousand books have been sent to Brussels, Frankfurt, Munich, Berlin and Paris. These books will be distributed to Soviet tourists at the Brussels Fair and in Western Europe by [redacted] assets. Arrangements are also being made to make the book available to [redacted] that have

jointly with Feltrinelli, the Italian publisher who claims to hold all foreign rights.

As additional copies become available, they will be furnished to [redacted] for use in contact and mailing operations and for travellers to take into the USSR. An effort is being made [redacted] [redacted] to establish an escrow account in Pasternak's name for the author's share in the royalities from the sale of the book.

8 September 1958

MEMORANDUM FOR:

SUBJECT: Notes - SR Division

Availability of "Dr. Zhivago" in Russian. Approximately 800 of the first 1000 Russian language copies of Boris Pasternak's novel, "Dr. Zhivago," have been transmitted to for distribution to Soviet personnel and tourists in Western Europe and attending the Brussels Fair. The Russian edition of the book is expected to be published this week by Mouton, a well-known publishing firm in Holland.

Pasternak is recognized by non-Soviet critics to be the greatest living Russian writer. "Dr. Zhivago" is considered to be the best Russian novel to appear since the Revolution and to be an important stimulant to independent thinking. The Soviet Union rejected "Dr. Zhivago" for publication in the USSR.

SR Division has been instrumental in having the original Russian edition published so that this significant literary work can be made available to Soviet travellers during the summer tourist season. A copy of the original manuscript was obtained In deference to the author's request that the book not be published in Russian in the U.S., a European publisher was used. To expedite the publication, typesetting of the Russian manuscript was performed in N.Y. and negatives of the reproduction proofs prepared

this attachment is being forwarded to [redacted] for his guidance.

Commercial Staff

Distribution:
Orig. & 1--[redacted]/Subject File (w/att.)
1--[redacted] w/att.)
1--[redacted] (w/att.)
1--OGC (w/att.)
1-[redacted] Chrono. (w/att.)

Attachment to
Memorandum of
10 September 1958

The following is the agreed plan of action which we desire [redacted] acting on our behalf, to follow in his dealings with [redacted]

1. Point out to [redacted] that nothing can be accomplished toward settlement of our relationship until all copies of the reproduction proofs now outstanding are recovered and brought to [redacted] office. We know one copy is now at [redacted] and it has been our understanding that a fourth copy has been secured in a safe deposit vault in New York City.

2. Certain points require rather stern negotiation with [redacted] Firstly, we would like him to justify to us his eligibility for the [redacted] payment provided for in paragraph 10 of the basic agreement with him. We have never received a report on his activities in this respect and have no basis for justifying this substantial payment. (For your guidance, it is our informal opinion that [redacted] did little or nothing in pursuit of this requirement.) Secondly, the invoice from the [redacted], dated 10 July 1958, billed for [redacted] Our contract with [redacted] called for [redacted]

3. It is our desire that it be made completely clear to [redacted] that we are aware of his untrustworthy behavior during our relationship, and that we feel that we are being most lenient in our final dealings with him.

4. It is requested that, after completion of the above steps, [redacted] draft a settlement agreement to cover the final settlement with [redacted] This agreement should contain the standard provisions pertinent to such an agreement and a special provision stating that [redacted] has not and will not enter into any relationship with any persons at any time involving [redacted] It is requested that a draft of this agreement be provided the clients for review prior to execution.

5. The approved agreement and necessary funds will be provided to [redacted] so that he may arrange the final settlement with [redacted]

10 September 1958

MEMORANDUM FOR: The Record

SUBJECT: Status of AEDINOSAUR as of 9 September 1958

1. [redacted] met on 9 September 1958 to discuss the current status of the project and to formulate a plan of action for the handling of [redacted] from this point forward.

2. [redacted] reported the status of the various phases of the project is as follows:

(a) European Edition - Delivery by the printer of the initial 1000 completed books has been made [redacted] The printer's normal, [redacted] distribution channels will soon be handling the book. As regards any interest of Commercial Staff, this phase can be considered completed successfully.

(b) [redacted] The [redacted] representative presented our position (as outlined in teletype message drafted [redacted] on 8 September. [redacted] This phase, therefore, also requires no further action on our part.

3. As regards the last phase of the project, i.e., [redacted] it was agreed that we would follow the plan of action outlined in the unclassified attachment to this memorandum. A copy of

FILE NO.

CLASSIFIED MESSAGE

~~SECRET~~

ROUTING

1 SR/2
2
3
4
5
6

ORIG :
UNIT :
EXT : 538
DATE : 10 October 1958

TO :

FROM: DIRECTOR

CONF:

INFO :

RE Filing (check one):
No CS Record Value. Destroy.
RI file this copy as indicated
Branch copy filed as indicated
RE Indexing (check one):
Marked
Signature:

PRECEDENCE

DEFERRED OCT 11 16 05Z58

X ROUTINE REC'D CABLE SECT.

PRIORITY INITIALS

OPERATIONAL IMMEDIATE INITIALS

TO INFO CITE DIR

REDWOOD AEDINOSAUR

C/S COMMENT: *RECOMMENDED BE URGED, THRU CONTACT, PROCEED MILAN AND TAKE UP PROBLEM WITH FELTRINELLI.

1. BELIEVE FELTRINELLI TAKING LEGAL ACTION AGAINST PRIMARILY FOR FINANCIAL REASONS. HOWEVER MUST ALSO CONSIDER LIKELIHOOD AND EFFECT SOVIET AND CP PRESSURE AGAINST FELTRINELLI.

2. REF PARA 3, CONCUR PROCEED SOONEST MILAN TO SETTLE MATTER DIRECTLY WITH FELTRINELLI AS SUGGESTED. ADVISE RESULTS NEGOTIATIONS.

3. TO PROTECT HIMSELF SHOULD HAVE COVER STORY RE SOURCE REPRODUCTION PROOFS. SUGGEST SOURCE BE "PROMINENT RUSSIAN EMIGRE."

4. FYI AGAIN ATTEMPTING PUBLISH RUSSIAN EDITION BOOK. WE INFORMED FELTRINELLI HAS REQUESTED FIND NEW YORK LAWYER TO BRING SUIT AGAINST

END OF MESSAGE

RI COPY

C/WE
RELEASING OFFICER

COORDINATING OFFICERS

~~SECRET~~

AUTHENTICATING OFFICER

FORM 4-58 1389 a

Copy No.

FILE NO.

CLASSIFIED MESSAGE

S-E-C-R-E-T

ORIG :
UNIT :
EXT :
DATE : 13 OCTOBER 1958

TO :
FROM : DIRECTOR
CONF :
INFO :

ROUTING 1 2 3 4 5 6

RE Filing (check one):
No CS Record Value. Destroy.
RI file this copy as indicated
Branch copy filed as indicated
RE Indexing (check one):
Marked
Signature

PRECEDENCE
DEFERRED — OCT 13 22 32 z58
X ROUTINE — REC'D CABLE SECT.
PRIORITY — INITIALS
OPERATIONAL IMMEDIATE — INITIALS

TO INFO CITE DIR

REDWOOD/AEDINOSAUR/PSYCH

REF

WAS SUPPOSED TO PUBLISH BOOK JOINTLY WITH FELTRINELLI BUT FOULED UP AND PRINTED ONLY NAME FELTRINELLI AS PUBLISHER IN BOOK.

2. FELTRINELLI MAY NOW BE UNDER INCREASING SOV OR CP PRESSURE TO SQUELCH PUBLICATION.

3. REQUEST FURTHER DETAILS ON ADDRESSEE, DESTINATION AND SHIPMENT DATE PLATES. UPON RECEIPT INFO HQS WILL ADVISE RE POSSIBLE ACTION.

END OF MESSAGE

RI COPY

ROUTING	INITIAL
RI/AN	
RI/TY	
~~DESTROY~~	
RI/FI	

COORDINATING OFFICERS

RELEASING OFFICER

S-E-C-R-E-T

FORM 4-58 1389a REPRODUCTION BY OTHER THAN THE ISSUING OFFICE IS PROHIBITED. Copy No.

[redacted] for any single activity will remain unchanged.

SECRET

NOTIFICATION OF PROJECT APPROVAL

PROJECT: **AEDINOSAUR**

ACTION		AREA
	NEW PROJECT	DIVISION SR
	AMENDMENT NO.	
X	RENEWAL (FY 1959)	BRANCH PP
	TERMINATION	DESK
	MEMO REQUEST	

AUTHORIZATION

APPROVING AUTHORITY	AMOUNT	FISCAL YEAR
13 October 1958		1959

CONDITIONS OF APPROVAL

Renewal in the amount of for FY 1959 approved.

PP/OPS/PP REF. NO.	SIGNATURE	DATE
	(Signed)	14 October 1958

DISTRIBUTION

1	DD/P	1	SSA-DD/S	1	COVERT BUDGET BRANCH	1	AREA DIVISION CHIEF OF ADMIN.	1	PP/OPS/PR	2	PP/OPS/PP

Body-103

FORM NO. 849
1 DEC 55

SECRET

(5)

Estimate of
Funds Required

5. The following project proposals were developed in FY 1958 as the result of activities financed out of D&TO funds and have been submitted as standard projects:

6. As most of the AEDINOSAUR FY 1958 obligations were incurred in the last quarter of the fiscal year, it is impossible now to evaluate the result of these operations. Activities financed were:

a.

b. Publications
Typesetting and photo-offset proofs of Pasternak's novel, "Dr. Zhivago," have been purchased and final publishing arrangements are in process of being completed.

c.

d. Editing and publishing arrangements for the French-language version of autobiography have been initiated.

7. Estimate of funds required for other developmental activities and unforeseen targets of opportunity in FY 1959 (Russian language publication of special books, articles, special operations, etc.).

8. The authorization for C/SR to commit D&TO funds up to

REQUEST FOR PROJECT RENEWAL

1. It is requested that Project AEDINOSAUR, the D&TO project for the SR Division, be renewed for FY 1959 in the amount of The project was included in the FY 1959 Operational Program for the SR Division in the amount of The SR Division plans to expand its PP operations and anticipates that there will be special operations which will require an increase in D&TO funds over the amounts obligated in FY 1957 and FY 1958. The activities which can be foreseen are enumerated in paragraphs 3 and 4.

2. Funds approved and obligated by fiscal year since project initiation:

	Funds Approved	Funds Obligated
FY 1957		
FY 1958		

3. Assets and operations to be continued or activated out of D&TO funds for FY 1959:

b. SR Division has agreed to contribute toward the publication of a book entitled "Europe in the Jet Age", which will contain a chapter on the Soviet Union. The book will be published by the Commercial Staff's project

4. The following events likely to occur during FY 1959 may require expenditures not provided for in existing projects:

REQUEST FOR [redacted] PROJECT RENEWAL

DIVISION PROJECT CLEARANCE SHEET

1. ACTION: Request for Renewal, FY 1959

a. Project Cryptonym AEDINOSAUR

b. Division SR

c. Branch [redacted]

d. [redacted] and Extension [redacted]

2. DIVISION CONCURRENCES:

9 Sept. 1958 Date

9 Sept 1958 Date

3 September 1958 Date

15 Sept 58 Date

16 Sep 58 Date

~~SECRET~~
(When Filled In)

STAFF COORDINATION

PROJECT: AEDINOSAUR

		DIVISION SR
	AMENDMENT NO.	DIVISION: SR
X	RENEWAL (FY 1959)	BRANCH
	TERMINATION	DESK

ORGANIZATIONAL ELEMENT	SIGNATURE	COPY NO.	DATE	MEMORANDUM ATTACHED: YES	NO	DATE
ASSA-DD/S	/s/	2	10/7/58			
		1 & 3	7 Aug 1958			
~~PP/C/PRD~~		1				

~~RECOMMEND~~ APPROVAL

	SIGNATURE	DATE
for CPP		13 Oct. 1958
	SIGNATURE	DATE

(This space reserved for comments of SSA-DD/S; CPP)
Funds programmed in operating budget

Body-107

FORM 5-58 848 USE PREVIOUS EDITIONS. (5)

FILE NO.

CLASSIFIED MESSAGE

~~S-E-C-R-E-T~~

ORIG :
UNIT :
EXT :
DATE : 14 OCTOBER 1958 588

ROUTING 1 2 3 4 5 6

TO :

FROM : DIRECTOR

CONF :

INFO :

RE Filing (check one):
No CS Record Value. Destroy.
RI file this copy as indicated
Branch copy filed as indicated
RE Indexing (check one):

PRECEDENCE
DEFERRED OCT 14 19 56 z58
ROUTINE REC'D CABLE SECT.
X PRIORITY INITIALS
OPERATIONAL IMMEDIATE INITIALS

TO INFO CITE DIR

REDWOOD/AEDINOSAUR/PSYCH

REF

FYI FELTRINELLI CLAIMS HOLD COPYRIGHT ALL FOREIGN PUBLICATION DR. ZHIVAGO. IN ORDER TO CLARIFY LEGAL SITUATION RE DEVELOPING SUITS BY FELTRINELLI AGAINST ETC. DESIRE KNOW SOONEST:

1. WHAT ARE PERTINENT/ITALIAN COPYRIGHT REGULATIONS RE FOREIGN AUTHOR?

2. DOES FELTRINELLI HOLD COPYRIGHT IN ACCORDANCE WITH ITALIAN COPYRIGHT LAW.

END OF MESSAGE

C/S COMMENT: * CONCERNING PUBLISHER SENDING PLATES RUSSIAN EDITION OF DR. ZIVAGO BEING SENT TO U.S.

SR
C/WE/2
C/WE/4

RELEASING OFFICER COORDINATING OFFICERS CSR/2 AUTHENTICATING

~~S-E-C-R-E-T~~

Body-108

CLASSIFIED MESSAGE

~~S-E-C-R-E-T~~

1	SR/2	4
2		5
3		6

DATE : 15 OCT 58

TO : DIRECTOR

FROM :

ACTION: SR 6

INFO :

RE Filing (check one):
No CS Record Value. Destroy.
RI file this copy as indicated
Branch copy filed as indicated
RE Indexing (check one):
Marked

OCT 15 2006Z 58

ROUTINE

TO INFO DIR CITE

REDWOOD AEDINOSAUR

RE:

1. WITH RECEIPT REF ON STRICT ORDERS NOT SELL BOOK COMMERCIALLY BUT USE PRESENT COPIES FOR DISTRIBUTION SOVIET VISITORS. SINCE MANY PEOPLE KNOW OF THIS DISTRIBUTION BESIEGED BY OWN MEMBERS AND OTHERS WITH REQUESTS TO BUY. REFUSALS AND LAME EXCUSES CAUSING STRAINED FEELINGS ALL SIDES. NO ANSWER FROM TO LETTER REQUESTING PURCHASE.

2. PLEASE ADVISE SOONEST CURRENT STATUS REF PARA 1 PROBLEM. REQUEST ANSWER LETTER, STATE SELLING PRICE AND DELIVERY DATE.

END OF MESSAGE

CS COMMENT: *ADVISED THAT UNTIL FELTRINELLI AND DISAGREEMENT SETTLED SHOULD WITHHOLD ADVERTISING.

ROUTING	INITIAL
RI/AN	
RI/TY	
~~DESTROY~~	
RI/FI	

~~S-E-C-R-E-T~~

FORM 4-58 1389 USE PREVIOUS EDITIONS REPRODUCTION BY OTHER THAN THE ISSUING OFFICE IS PROHIBITED Copy No. (35)

FILE NO.

CLASSIFIED MESSAGE

~~S-E-C-R-E-T~~

ROUTING

1	SR/2	4	
2		5	
3		6	

DATE : 16 OCT 58

TO : DIRECTOR

FROM

ACTION: SR 6

INFO

RE Filing (check one):
No CS Record Value. Destroy.
RI file this copy as indicated
Branch copy filed as indicated
RE Indexing (check one):
Marked
Signature

OCT 17 0538Z 58

ROUTINE

TO DIR INFO CITE

REDWOOD AEDINOSAUR

12835

1. FOR CONTACT WITH HOWEVER BELIEVES ACCOUNT PER REF INACCURATE SINCE PLATES ACTUALLY PROVIDED TO NEITHER SHIPPED PLATES TO USA.

2. FOR ATTEMPT ARRANGE TO SETTLE WITH FELTRINELLI FAILED SINCE OVERRULED BY DIRECTOR OF WHO IRRITATED BY ADVERSE PUBLICITY AND HEATEDLY TERMINATED DISCUSSION WITH

3. DISCUSSED SITUATION WITH AGREED USF TRUSTED LAWYER APPROACH HOWEVER FEELS THIS ONLY LIKELY RESULT IN EXTRICATION SETTLE COST OF [illegible]1,000 [illegible] BOOKS DELIVERED, AND KEEP INVOLVEMENT FROM PUBLICITY. OFFERS NO PROSPECT BRING AND FELTRINELLI TO AGREEMENT WHICH IS NECESSARY TO SETTLE WHOLE AFFAIR.

4. NOT ASKING TAKE ACTION BUT DOES HAVE ANY CHANNEL TO FELTRINELLI WHICH MIGHT HELP CALM DOWN THIS TEMPEST WHICH HAS ARISEN OVER BLUNDER?

~~S-E-C-R-E-T~~

CLASSIFIED MESSAGE

S-E-C-R-E-T

FILE NO.

ROUTING

1		4	
2		5	
3		6	

DATE :

TO :

FROM :

ACTION:

INFO :

RE Filing (check one):
No CS Record Value. Destroy. ☐
RI file this copy as indicated ☐
Branch copy filed as indicated ☐
RE Indexing (check one):
Marked ☐ None required ☐
Signature:

TO INFO CITE

PLEASE KEEP [redacted] ADVISED BY CABLE OF ANY INFO RE FELTRINELLI'S INTENTIONS WHICH [redacted] CAN DEVELOP.

5. [redacted]

[redacted] APPROACH [redacted] DIRECTLY TO DISCUSS PLACING LARGE ORDER OF SEVERAL THOUSANDS FOR BOOKS AND USE THIS CONVERSATION AS GAMBIT TO INQUIRE HOW [redacted] PROPOSES GET DISPUTE SETTLED. THIS TO GIVE [redacted] STIMULUS TO SETTLE QUICKLY. NO LARGE ORDER NEED ACTUALLY BE PLACED UNLESS NEEDED.

6. DOES HQ HAVE ANY FURTHER SUGGESTIONS?

7. RE [redacted] SITUATION STILL NOT CLARIFIED. WILL ADVISE.

END OF MESSAGE

S-E-C-R-E-T

FORM 4-58 1389 USE PREVIOUS EDITIONS

 Copy No. (35)

10-24-58

9

U R G E N T   U R G E N T

AS FAR AS WE HAVE ASCERTAINED, THE ITALIAN PUBLISHER HAS SECURED WORLD RIGHTS FOR THE ORIGINAL LANGUAGE AND THE TRANSLATIONS, INCLUDING BROADCASTING RIGHTS. THE WORK WAS FIRST PUBLISHED IN ITALY, WHICH FACT BRINGS ARTICLE 6 OF THE REVISED BERN CONVENTION INTO PLAY BETWEEN ITALY AND THE GERMAN FEDERAL REPUBLIC. THE ITALIAN PUBLISHER HAS ASSIGNED TO A GERMAN PUBLISHER ALL GERMAN RIGHTS. AS FAR AS WE KNOW, HE HAS RETAINED THE ORIGINAL LANGUAGE BROADCASTING RIGHTS HIMSELF. CONSEQUENTLY, ONLY THE ITALIAN PUBLISHER OR HIS ASSIGNEE MAY LEGALLY AUTHORIZE BROADCASTS WHICH ORIGINATE IN GERMANY OF THE WORK IN THE ORIGINAL LANGUAGE. THE ITALIAN PUBLISHER, ACTING AS THE AUTHOR S AGENT, HAS REFUSED TO AUTHORIZE RFE TO USE THE WORKS TEXT FOR THEIR TRANSMISSIONS. IN OUR OPINION IT IS DOUBTFUL IF WE CAN SUCCESSFULLY DEFEND ACTION BASED UPON ARTICLE SIX REFERS TO ABOVE. CONSEQUENTLY WE SHOULD NOT PUT OURSELVES IN JEOPARDY BY BROADCASTING CONTENT OF NOVEL BEYOND PERMISSIBLE LIMITS OF REVIEW.

END OF MSG

CLASSIFIED MESSAGE

~~SECRET~~

FILE NO.

ROUTING

1		4	
2		5	
3		6	

ORIG :
UNIT :
EXT :
DATE : 24 October 1958

TO : SEE ADDRESSEES BELOW

FROM: DIRECTOR

CONF: SR 6

INFO :

RE Filing (check one):
No CS Record Value. Destroy.
RI file this copy as indicated ☑
Branch copy filed as indicated
RE Indexing (check one):
Marked ☑

PRECEDENCE

DEFERRED — OCT 24 16 20 58 — REC'D CABLE SECT.

ROUTINE

X PRIORITY — INITIALS

OPERATIONAL IMMEDIATE — INITIALS

TO

INFO

CITE DIR

RI copy – AEDINOSAUR
Branch copy – Dr. Zhivago

BOOK MESSAGE

PSYCH

1. PENDING OFFICIAL SOV REACTION TO PASTERNAK'S RECEIPT NOBEL PRIZE FOR NOVEL "DR. ZHIVAGO" DESIRE ASSETS GIVE MAXIMUM FACTUAL PLAY WITHOUT ANY PROPAGANDISTIC COMMENTARY THIS EVENT IN ORDER AVOID OVERPLAY EXCELLENT INHERENT PROPAGANDA VALUE. SUGGEST INCLUDE FOLLOWING POINTS:

A. DR. ZHIVAGO IS GREAT HUMANISTIC MASTERPIECE.

B. THIS FIRST TIME RUSSIAN LIVING USSR HAS RECEIVED NOBEL PRIZE FOR LITERATURE (IVAN BUNIN RECEIVED ~~XXXX~~ PRIZE AS EMIGRE). STRESS FACT PASTERNAK RUSSIAN. AVOID REFERENCE TO HIM AS SOVIET.

C. NOVEL IS CRITICAL SEVERAL ASPECTS SOV REGIME.

RI COPY

COORDINATING OFFICERS

RELEASING OFFICER

~~SECRET~~

AUTHENTICATING OFFICER

Copy No.

FORM 4-58 1389 a

(35)

CLASSIFIED MESSAGE

~~SECRET~~

ORIG :
UNIT :
EXT :
DATE : 24 October 1958

FILE NO.

ROUTING 1 2 3 4 5 6

TO :

FROM : DIRECTOR

CONF :

INFO :

PAGE 2

RE Filing (check one):
No CS Record Value. Destroy.
RI file this copy as indicated
Branch copy filed as indicated
RE Indexing (check one):
Marked None required
Signature:

PRECEDENCE: DEFERRED / ROUTINE / X PRIORITY / OPERATIONAL IMMEDIATE

INITIALS

TO INFO CITE DIR

D. NOVEL STILL NOT PUBLISHED IN USSR.

2. AS MAJOR OBJECTIVE, DESIRE USE EVERY OPPORTUNITY HAVE SOV CITIZENS READ NOVEL AND LEARN ABOVE FACTS.

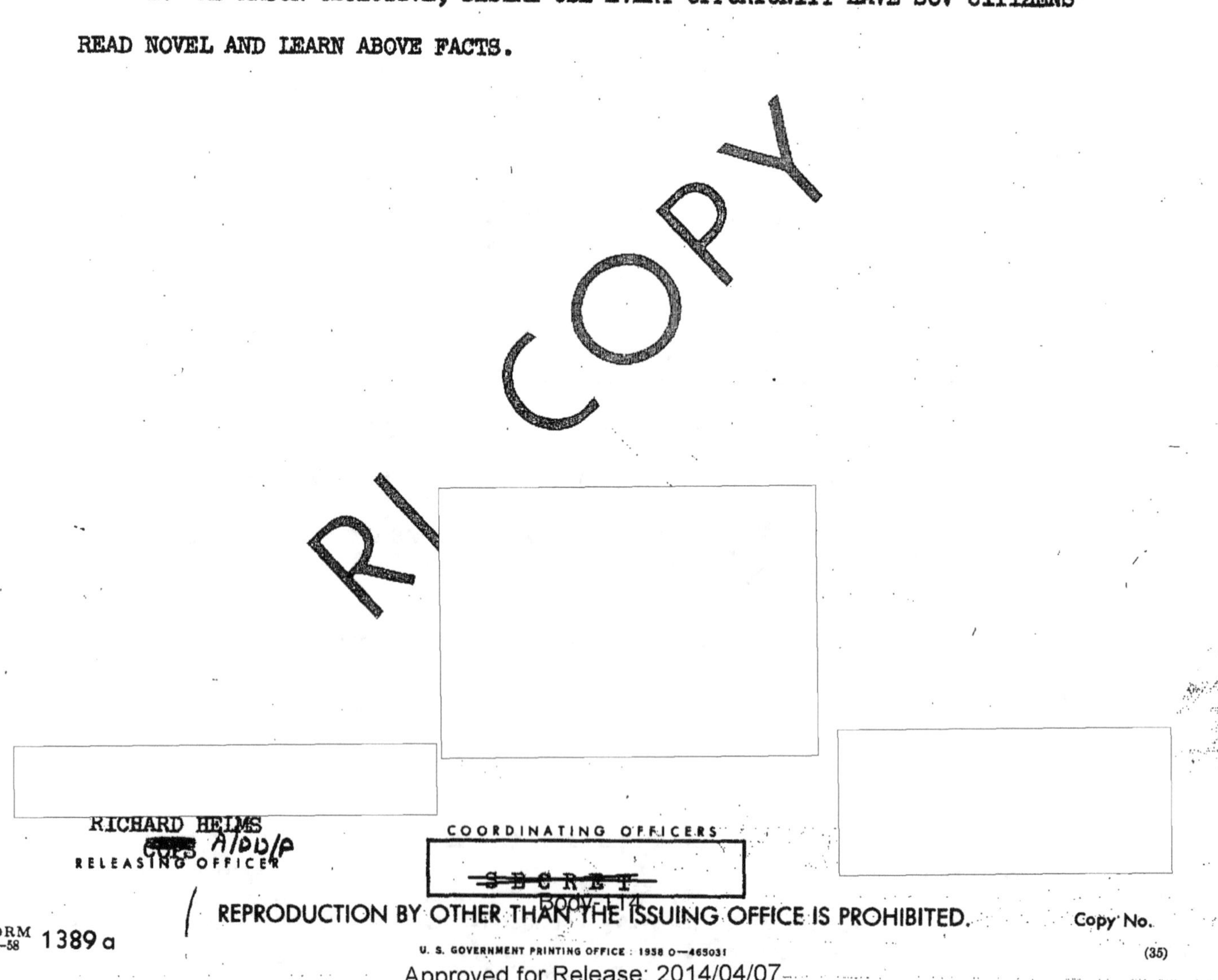

RICHARD HELMS
A/DD/P
RELEASING OFFICER

COORDINATING OFFICERS

~~SECRET~~

Copy No.

FORM 4-58 1389 a

U. S. GOVERNMENT PRINTING OFFICE : 1958 O—465031

(35)

FILE NO

CLASSIFIED MESSAGE

~~SECRET~~

ROUTING	
1 SR/2	4
2	5
3	6

DATE : 25 OCT 58

TO : DIRECTOR

RE Filing (check one):
No CS Record Value. Destroy. ☐

FROM :

ACTION:

INFO :

OCT 25 1833Z 58

ROUTINE

TO DIR INFO CITE

REDWOOD AEDINOSAUR PSYCH

RE

36 COPIES SHIPPED 24 OCTOBER. FORWARDING TOTAL 175 COPIES.

END OF MESSAGE

RI COPY

ROUTING	INITIAL
RI/AN	
RI/TY	
~~DESTROY~~	
RI/FI	

~~SECRET~~

FORM 4-58 1389 USE PREVIOUS EDITIONS

REPRODUCTION BY OTHER THAN THE ISSUING OFFICE IS PROHIBITED. Copy No.

(35)

FILE NO.

CLASSIFIED MESSAGE

~~SECRET~~

667

ORIG :
UNIT :
EXT :
DATE : 27 OCTOBER 1958

TO :

FROM : DIRECTOR

CONF :

INFO :

RE Filing (check one):
No CS Record Value. Destroy.
RI file this copy as indicated ✓
Branch copy filed as indicated

ROUTING

1	SR/2	4	
2		5	
3		6	

OCT 28 23 02 z58
REC'D CABLE SECT.

PRECEDENCE				INITIALS
	DEFERRED		PRIORITY	
R	ROUTINE		OPERATIONAL IMMEDIATE	INITIALS

TO | INFO | CITE DIR

REDWOOD/AEDINOSAUR/PSYCH

TO FULFILL IMMEDIATE DEMAND BOOKS, REQUEST 60 BOOKS IN LOTS OF AS LARGE SIZE AS PERMITS. REMAINING BOOKS.

END OF MESSAGE

CS COMMENT: * 36 COPIES SHIPPED SEA POUCH 24 OCTOBER. FORWARDED TOTAL 175 COPIES.

RI COPY

ROUTING	INITIAL
RI/AN	
RI/TY	
~~DESTROY~~	
RI/FI	

RELEASING OFFICER

COORDINATING OFFICERS

~~SECRET~~

Body-116

AUTHENTICATING OFFICER

FORM 4-58 1389 a

REPRODUCTION BY OTHER THAN THE ISSUING OFFICE IS PROHIBITED. Copy No.

U. S. GOVERNMENT PRINTING OFFICE : 1958 O—465031

(35)

CLASSIFIED MESSAGE

~~S-E-C-R-E-T~~

FILE NO.

ROUTING

1	4
2	5
3	6

DATE :

TO :

FROM :

ACTION:

INFO :

RE Filing (check one):
No CS Record Value. Destroy. ☐
RI file this copy as indicated ☐
Branch copy filed as indicated ☐
RE Indexing (check one):
Marked ☐ None required ☐
Signature:

PAGE 2

TO INFO CITE

COMPLEXES. LEFTIST PRESS AND WRITERS IN FREE WORLD SHOULD BE PARTICULARLY EFFECTIVE. [redacted] ALSO INTERNATIONAL PEN GROUP SHOULD BE ENLISTED MAKE DIRECT APPEAL TO KHRUSCHEV ALLOW PASTERNAK APPEARANCE.

[redacted]

6. CAN USE [redacted] GROUP TO PLAY LINE PARA 2 ABOVE TO EAST ZONE AND EXPLOIT FACT IF SOVIETS KEEP PASTERNAK FROM GOING STOCKHOLM. GERMAN PRESS ALREADY BEGINNING ON OWN INITIATIVE MAKE PROPER EDITORIAL COMMENT BUT CAN SPARKPLUG FURTHER THROUGH [redacted] ASSETS.

1. PLS ADVISE.

END OF MESSAGE

RI COPY

Body 117
~~S-E-C-R-E-T~~

FILE NO

CLASSIFIED MESSAGE

~~S-E-C-R-E-T~~

ROUTING

1		4	
2		5	
3		6	

DATE : 28 OCT 58

OCT 28 1840Z58

TO : DIRECTOR

FROM :

ACTION

INFO

RE Filing (check one):
No CS Record Value. Destroy. ☐
RI file this copy as indicated ☑
Branch copy filed as indicated ☐
RE Indexing (check one):

PRIORITY

TO DIR INFO CITE

REDWOOD PSYCH

1. SINCE SO FAR UNAWARE YOUR THINKING URGENTLY RECOMMEND PSYCH EXPLOITATION SOV DILEMMA RE PASTERNAK APPEARANCE TO ACCEPT NOBEL PRIZE. PRAVDA EXECRATION PASTERNAK PROBABLY AUGURS PREVENTION HIS TRIP STOCKHOLM AND POSSIBLY SERIOUS OFFICIAL REPRISALS AGAINST HIM PERSONALLY.

2. FEEL PROP THEMES SHOULD BE DEVISED TO SHOW SOV SUPPRESSION DR ZHIVAGO AS PROOF OF AIM SUPPRESS ALL INDEPENDENT THOUGHT AND TOTALLY ENSLAVE ALL PERSONS UNDER SOV HEGEMONY. SUCH LINE SHOULD TEND DETER UNCOMMITTED AREAS FROM FALLING FOR SOV BLANDISHMENTS. SHOULD ALSO FURTHER DECIMATE EXTRA BLOC CP MEMBERSHIP.

3. PROP SHOULD CHALLENGE USSR TO MAKE EVEN SO NIGGARDLY CONCESSION TO HUMAN DECENCY IN CULTURAL FIELD AS TO LET PASTERNAK APPEAR WITH WIFE TO ACCEPT AWARD JUST AS ALL OTHER WINNERS FROM FREE COUNTRIES HAVE DONE AS OF RIGHT NOT PRIVILEGE BUT QUESTION WHETHER SOVIETS DESIRE STOOP TO SAME LEVEL IN THIS MANNER AS NAZIS WHO PREVENTED CARL VON OSSIETSKY ACCEPT PEACE PRIZE 1938.

4. SUGGEST IMPLEMENTATION THIS RECOMMENDATION MAY HELP PASTERNAK, CAN HAVE ONLY GOOD PSYCH EFFECT AND CANNOT LOSE. MAXIMUM IMPACT ANTICIPATED BY COPIOUS EDITORIAL COVERAGE IN PRESS AND RADIO URGING PEOPLE IN FREE WORLD WRITE KHRUSCHEV LETTERS OF PROTEST AND PUBLICIZING SUCH LETTERY BY LARGE GROUPS OF ALL POLITICAL

~~S-E-C-R-E-T~~

of the Communist system, the other an aberration, a turning against the system, which will be held up as a solemn and effective warning against all literary deviators.

5. One lesson for the Free World is perhaps that it has been over-sanguine in its appraisal of the potential cultural liberalization or "thaw" in the Soviet Union and, a fortiori, in its satellites. The unwavering determination of the Communist Party of the Soviet Union to push through to its ultimate goals is only intensified by incidents such as this, undeterred by considerations of "fair play" to its own citizens or of impact on Free World opinion. The falsity of the liberalization promises of the Chinese Communist rectification program had already indicated this basic truth.

6. Another and even more chilling lesson which we have only begun to face is that inner tensions, whether political, social, economic or cultural, must not be optimistically regarded as a source of weakness in the Communist system. In Communist eyes, indeed, they are the inner principle of its dynamic strength, the dialectical basis for the creative interaction of historical necessity and human will. The fact that Communists believe this to be true, does not, of course, automatically make it so. But it would be well for us to adopt as a background to policy the propositions that stresses and strains are not necessarily vulnerabilities and that actions predicated on the assumption that they are will probably be self-defeating.

30 October 1958

MEMORANDUM FOR: Director of Central Intelligence

THROUGH: Deputy Director/Intelligence

SUBJECT: Pasternak and the Nobel Prize - The "Literary Hungary"

1. Pasternak's "rejection" of the Nobel Prize dramatizes again the hard lesson of Hungary, that the Soviet regime will brutally crush any direct challenge to its basic principles. In its eyes Pasternak had become a symbol and an instrument of counter-revolution and as such he could only be dealt with in drastic fashion comparable to the treatment of the Budapest insurgents.

2. Reactions of revulsion and shock cannot conceal from Free World consciousness the sense of its own impotence to further the cause of liberalization within the Bloc. Hopes that a "Renaissance of humanism" will in the near future undermine the monolith of Communism have been dashed. Any further attempt on our part to portray the personal ordeal of Pasternak as a triumph of freedom will only, as in the case of Hungary, heighten the tragic irony which informs it.

3. An objective judgment of Pasternak as a literary figure would probably acknowledge that he represents an extension of the pre-Bolshevik tradition of Russian literature in what may be called its current of "European decadence." The "cosmopolitanism" which enabled him to translate Shakespeare, Schiller, Goethe and other European classics with such finesse was in its essence an "alien" inheritance, which even his political detachment could not make acceptable to the Communist regime. So long as his impact was contained within the Soviet Union, it could be tolerated; when it came to appear as a chosen vessel of Free World cold war, it had to be crushed. The earlier western emphasis on Dudintsev's Not by Bread Alone may also have exacerbated the Soviet reaction to what they inevitably regarded as a deliberate provocation.

4. It is quite possible that the Kremlin is pleased that this crisis arose in the way it did, pari passu with the award of the Nobel prize to the three Soviet physicists. It is thus provided with an almost ideal opportunity to demonstrate the difference between the two creations: one a triumph of Soviet science and a manifestation of the power

Dr. Zhivago Local Document

30 Oct 58

SUPPORT FROM BALOK

SUBJECT : [redacted], U.S. PUBLISHER OF PASTERNAK'S DR. ZHIVAJO X PASTERNAK'S DR. ZHIVAJO.

1. [redacted] [redacted] BACKGROUND AND LATEST DEVELOPMENTS OF PASTERNAK'S BOOK DR. ZHIVAJO.

2. PASTERNAK GAVE THE MANUSCRIPT TO GOCOMO FELTINELLI X GIACOMO FELTINELLI, A PUBLISHER IN MILAN X MILAN, ITALY. THIS EVENT OCCURRED DURING THE "BIG THAW" X "BIG THAW", THAT IS, AFTER STALIN'S X STALIN'S DEATH. ILYA EHRENBURG X ILYA EHRENBURG READ THE MANUSCRIPT AND ACCORDING TO THE INTERVIEW HE GAVE TO GERHARD RUGE X GERHARD RUGE, A WEST GERMAN NEWSMAN IN MOSCOW X MOSCOW, EHRENBURG "LIKED IT TO A CERTAINPOINT".

3. IN MAY 1958 X MAY 1958, [redacted] SUGGESTED TO [redacted] X [redacted] (SPELLING ?) OF [redacted] TO LET FELTINELLI COME TO THE U.S. IN CONNECTION WITH A BOOK CONVENTION. FELTINELLI HOLDS THE COPY RIGHT TO DR. ZHIVAJO. [redacted] FELT THAT FELTINELLI'S PRESENCE COULD HAVE BEEN EXPLOITED FOR THE BENEFIT OF THE U.S. GOVERNMENT. [redacted], HOWEVER, ADVISED [redacted] THAT THERE WAS "TOO MUCH RED-TAPE INVOLVED" AND THUS THE PROJECT FAILED.

4. [redacted] ~~IS OF THE OPINION THAT EVEN NOW IT WOULD BE MOST ... FOR THE U.S. TO LET FELTINELLI COME HERE. HE BELIEVES~~

CLASSIFIED MESSAGE

~~S-E-C-R-E-T~~

DATE : 30 OCT 58

1
2
3 6

TO : DIRECTOR

FROM :

ACTION:

INFO :

RE Filing (check one):
No CS Record Value. Destroy. ☐
RI file this copy as indicated ☑
Branch copy filed as indicated ☐

OCT 31 0016Z 58

OUTIN E

TO DIR INFO CITE

PSYCH

RE:

WITHOUT KNOWING YOUR ABILITY TO ACCOMPLISH; SUBMIT THIS IS PRECISELY CORRECT TIME ATTEMPT ACHIEVE BOYCOTT OF LITERARY OR OTHER CULTURAL FESTIVALS IN WHICH SOVIET UNION IS PARTICIPANT, SUCH AS VENICE FILM FESTIVAL OR OTHER SIMILAR CULTURAL JAMBOREES, OR AT LEAST ATTEMPT INSPIRE WIDE SUPPORT OF PREMISE THAT SOVIET UNION SHOULD NOT IN FUTURE BE INVITED PARTICIPATE. WOULD OF COURSE BE MORE EFFECTIVE IF MIDDLE EASTERN AND OTHER NEUTRALIST ELEMENTS SUPPORT SUCH POSITION.

END OF MESSAGE

CS COMMENT: *ACTION UNIT DETERMINED AS THOUGH INDICATOR REDWOOD USED.

ROUTING	INITIAL
RI/AN	
RI/TY	
~~DESTROY~~	
RI/FI	

~~S-E-C-R-E-T~~

Body-122

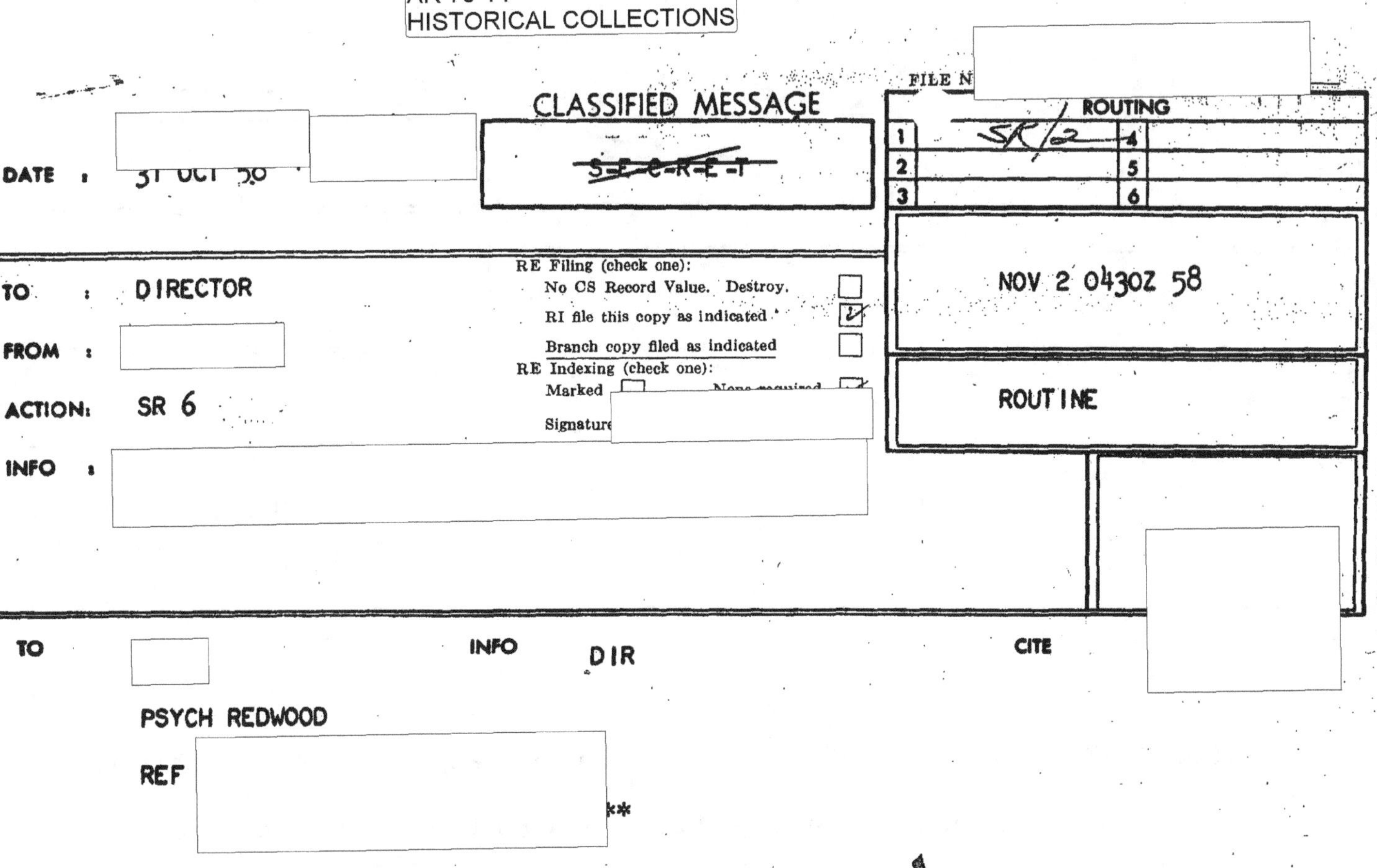

CLASSIFIED MESSAGE

S-E-C-R-E-T

FILE N…

ROUTING

1 SR/2

DATE : 31 OCT 58

TO : DIRECTOR

FROM :

ACTION: SR 6

INFO :

RE Filing (check one):
No CS Record Value. Destroy.
RI file this copy as indicated ☑
Branch copy filed as indicated
RE Indexing (check one):
Marked None required ☑
Signature

NOV 2 0430Z 58

ROUTINE

TO INFO DIR CITE

PSYCH REDWOOD

REF **

1. SUPPRESSION PASTERNAK POSSIBLE BLOW TO THOSE WHO HAVE INSISTED THAT SOVIETS ENJOY INTERNAL FREEDOM FOR EXPRESSION AND ENJOYMENT OF ARTS.

2. PERHAPS OPPORTUNITY EXISTS TO OBTAIN PUBLIC OBJECTIONS BY PICASSO ROBERSON CHAPLIN BEAUVOIR ET AL.

3. APPEALS FROM THESE PERSONS TO KHRUSHCHEV MIGHT CARRY GLOBAL IMPACT IN ARTISTIC AND INTELLECTUAL WORLD.

4. SHOULD THESE PERSONS AND OTHERS LIKE THEM FAIL TO RESPOND TO WELL PUBLICIZED APPEAL FOR THEIR VOICES, THEIR REFUSALS MIGHT ALSO TEND REPUDIATE THEIR PAST AND FUTURE PRONOUNCEMENTS THIS SUBJECT.

6. YOUR COMMENTS APPRECIATED.

END OF MESSAGE

Body-123

S-E-C-R-E-T

FORM 4-58 1389 USE PREVIOUS EDITIONS

 Copy No. (35)

FILE NO.

CLASSIFIED MESSAGE

~~SECRET~~

ROUTING

1		4	
2		5	
3		6	

DATE :

TO :

FROM :

ACTION:

INFO :

RE Filing (check one):
No CS Record Value. Destroy. ☐
RI file this copy as indicated ☑
Branch copy filed as indicated ☐
RE Indexing (check one):
Marked ☐
Signature:

PAGE-2-

TO INFO CITE

C/S COMMENT: * Requested all [redacted] assets to exploit the Pasternak rejection of the Nobel prize.

** Forwarded suggested actions regarding the Pasternak case.

~~SECRET~~

CLASSIFIED MESSAGE

~~SECRET~~

FILE NO.

ORIG :
UNIT :
EXT : 49
DATE : 4 November 1958

ROUTING

1	SR/2	4	
2		5	
3		6	

TO :

FROM: DIRECTOR

CONF:

INFO :

RE Filing (check one):
No CS Record Value. Destroy.
RI file this copy as indicated ☑
Branch copy filed as indicated
RE Indexing (check one):

PRECEDENCE

DEFERRED Nov 5 23 05 : 58

X ROUTINE REC'D CABLE SECT.

PRIORITY INITIALS

OPERATIONAL IMMEDIATE INITIALS

TO INFO CITE DIR

REDWOOD PSYCH

REF *

1. APPRECIATE ACTION.

2. DUTCH PUBLISHER, MOUTON, ANNOUNCED ON 2 NOVEMBER WILL PUBLISH UNABRIDGED RUSSIAN EDITION BOOK IN ABOUT 8 WEEKS. TO AVOID DUPLICATION PLEASE NOTIFY HQS FELTRINELLI REPLY PRIOR MAKING ANY COMMITMENTS TO

END OF MESSAGE

RI COPY

ROUTING
RI/AN
RI/TY
~~[illegible]~~
/FI

RELEASING OFFICER COORDINATING OFFICERS AUT

~~SECRET~~

4-58 1389 a REPRODUCTION BY OTHER THAN THE ISSUING OFFICE IS PROHIBITED. Copy No.

U. S. GOVERNMENT PRINTING OFFICE : 1958 O—465031 (35)

FILE NO.

CLASSIFIED MESSAGE

S-E-C-R-E-T

ROUTING
1 SR/
2
3
4
5
6

DATE : 58

TO : DIRECTOR

FROM :

ACTION: SR 6

INFO :

RE Filing (check one):
No CS Record Value. Destroy.
RI file this copy as indicated
Branch copy filed as indicated
RE Indexing (check one):
Marked None required

NOV 4 2123Z 58

PRIORITY

TO DIR INFO CITE

REDWOOD AEDINOSAUR

2. MOUTON CALLED PRESS CONFERENCE 2 NOV IN HOTEL DES INDES HAGU. FOLLOWING IS RESUME OF ARTICLES ON "ILLEGAL" PRINTING WHICH APPEARED DUTCH EVENING PAPERS EXCEPT TELEGRAAF WHICH MORNING EDITION. SOME PAPERS REFUSED PRINT STORY WHILE OTHERS MERELY ALLUDED TO PRESS CONFERENCE AND FACT AGREEMENT REACHED.

3. TELEGRAAF: WITH ALL FUSS ABOUT ZHIVAGO, MYSTERY HAS ARISEN AND MOST OF ANSWERS REMAIN BE FOUND IN NETH AND HAGU IN PARTICULAR. ACCORDING EEKHOUT, SOVIET VISITORS TO EXPO GIVEN FREE COPIES IN VATICAN PAVILION IN WHICH FELTRINELLI, WHO HAS BOOK RIGHTS, APPEARED AS PUBLISHER ALTHOUGH HE HAD NOT PLACED ORDER FOR PRINTING OF RUSSIAN EDITION. THESE COPIES ORIGINATED FROM ILLEGAL SOURCE WHICH PROVED BE MOUTON ACTING IN COMPLETE IGNORANCE. F AND M NOW MADE CONTRACT FOR NEW RUSSIAN EDITION OF BOOK. EEKHOUT CLAIMS FELTRINELLI WROTE HIM 1 JULY SAYING ABOUT SEND HIM PHOTOCOPY OF BOOK. SEVERAL DAYS LATER DE RIDDER RECEIVED TELEPHONE CALL FROM CONTACT IN PARIS WHO TOLD HIM HE BRINGING MANUSCRIPT. DE RIDDER ACCEPTED DELIVERY OF BOOK ON ASSUMPTION PERSON FROM PARIS WAS SENT BY FELTRINELLI. WEEKS LATER DE RIDDER RECEIVED VISIT VAN DER BEEK WHO ORDERED 1,000 COPIES

RI COPY

S-E-C-R-E-T

Body 128

FORM 4-58 1389 USE PREVIOUS EDITIONS

 Copy No.

CLASSIFIED MESSAGE

~~S-E-C-R-E-T~~

FILE NO.

ROUTING

1		4	
2		5	
3		6	

DATE :

TO :

FROM :

ACTION:

INFO :

RE Filing (check one):
No CS Record Value. Destroy. ☐
RI file this copy as indicated ☐
Branch copy filed as indicated ☐
RE Indexing (check one):
Marked ☐ None required ☐
Signature:

TO INFO CITE

LEGAL EDITION. ON 1 NOV CONTRACT WAS SIGNED FOR PRINTING LEGAL EDITION. EEKHOUT EXPLAINED STORY BECAUSE OF MISLEADING ACCOUNTS IN WHICH HE MORE OR LESS IMPUTED PARTICIPATING POLITICAL AFFAIR. EEKHOUT SAID THEY INVOLVED IN POLITICS WITHOUT KNOWING IT. (COMMENT: PORTION SIMILAR TO TELEGRAAF ON ORIGINAL ARRANGEMENTS) SOMEONE CAME FROM PARI TO BRING MANUSCRIPT WHICH MOUTON THOUGHT WAS FROM FELTRINELLI BUT LATER LEARNED THIS NOT CASE. MOTIVES OF FRENCHMAN NOT CLEAR TO THIS DAY. (COMMENT: PORTION FOLLOWS SIMILAR TO TELEGRAAF ON BEEK.) IN DEALING WITH BEEK, MOUTON DID NOT KNOW HIS RELATIONSHIP WITH VREDE EN VRIJHEID, AN ANTI-COMMUNIST ORGANIZATION, WHICH SEEMS HAVE DISTRIBUTED BOOK TO RUSSIAN VISITORS AT VATICAN PAVILION. FELTRINELLI WAS IN HAGU 1 NOV AND MOUTON ASSURED HIM THAT PRINTING EXPENSES WILL BE BORN BY BEEK ONLY AND THEY ATTEMPTING TURN ILLEGAL PRINTING INTO LEGAL ONE. EVERYTHING TURNED OUT ALRIGHT AND CONTRACT SIGNED FOR 5,000 COPIES IN RUSSIAN. FELTRINELLI WANTS FIRST EDITION CONTINUED BE CONSIDERED AS ILLEGAL. PARIS MANUSCRIPT DIFFERS FROM FELTRINELLI ONLY SLIGHTLY. BEEK'S COPIES SIMILAR TO FELTRINELLI'S WITH EXCEPTION TYPO ERRORS AND SOME RULES LEFT OUT. BUT WHO HAD MANUSCRIPT PRINTED AND NOT PUBLISHED? FELTRINELLI SENT MANUSCRIPT UNREGISTERED BUT MOUTON DID NOT GET IT. WHERE IS IT? HOW DID FRENCHMAN AND BEEK GET TEXT SINCE FELTRINELLI SAYS HE DID NOT PROVIDE THEM WITH IT?

~~S-E-C-R-E-T~~

CLASSIFIED MESSAGE

~~S-E-C-R-E-T~~

FILE NO.

ROUTING

1		4	
2		5	
3		6	

DATE :

TO :

FROM :

ACTION:

INFO :

RE Filing (check one):
No CS Record Value. Destroy. ☐
RI file this copy as indicated ☐
Branch copy filed as indicated ☐
RE Indexing (check one):
Marked ☐ None required ☐
Signature:

PAGE -5-

TO INFO CITE

7. PARIS MATCH: ARTICLE CLAIMS CLANDESTINE EDITION MADE IT POSSIBLE FOR PASTERNAK RECEIVE NOBEL PRIZE.

8. ALTHOUGH PRESSURE AND FLOW ORDERS FROM ABROAD HAD INDUCED FELTRINELLI AND MOUTON COME AGREEMENT, SITUATION NOT YET CLEAR BETWEEN FELTRINELLI AND BEEK WHO MAY STILL BE ON HOOK. IT CONCEIVABLE FELTRINELLI, NOW SATISFIED THAT HE HAS SETTLED WITH MOUTON AND PUBLICLY "DISGRACED" BEEK, WILL LET MATTER DROP. ON OTHER HAND, BEEK UNDER INCREASING PRESSURE FROM PRESS AND FACES POSSIBLE CHARGES FROM FELTRINELLI THAT HE STOLE MANUSCRIPT.

END OF MESSAGE

~~S-E-C-R-E-T~~

Body-128

FORM 4-58 1389 USE PREVIOUS EDITIONS

(35)

CLASSIFIED MESSAGE

~~S-E-C-R-E-T~~

FILE NO

ROUTING

1		4	
2		5	
3		6	

DATE :

TO :

FROM :

ACTION:

INFO :

RE Filing (check one):
No CS Record Value. Destroy. ☐
RI file this copy as indicated ☐
Branch copy filed as indicated ☐
RE Indexing (check one):
Marked ☐ None required ☐
Signature: ____________

TO INFO CITE

OBVIOUSLY AWARE THAT MOUTON WAS PRINTING RUSSIAN EDITION FOR FELTRINELLI. IT WAS IMPOSSIBLE FILL HIS ORDER WITHIN MONTH AS REQUESTED. TO DE RIDDER'S STUPEFACTION, BEEK TOOK PRINTING PLATES OUT OF HIS BRIEFCASE. BEST OUR KNOWLEDGE NO RUSSIAN EDITION EVER PUBLISHED AND WE TRIED CONTACT FELTRINELLI TO INFORM HIM THIS STARTLING VISIT BUT HE NOT AVAILABLE. IN ORDER PRESERVE FELTRINELLI'S RIGHTS, WE NOW REPRODUCING BOOK PHOTO-MECHANICALLY IN ORDER PREVENT BOOK GOING TO ANOTHER PUBLISHER. 1,160 COPIES GIVEN TO BEEK WHO DID NOT TELL FOR WHOM BOOKS INTENDED. EEKHOUT HEARD THEN BOOKS DISTRIBUTED IN VATICAN PAVILION. BUT UNTIL THEN HAD BEEN UNAWARE INVOLVED IN POLITICAL AFFAIR. AFTERWARDS LEARNED PARIS MANUSCRIPT NOT IDENTICAL WITH FELTRINELLI MANUSCRIPT, BUT BEEK'S PHOTOCOPY QUITE SIMILAR TO FELTRINELLI'S. FELTRINELLI SEEMED FIND NO OBJECTION TO HAGU ILLEGAL EDITION. AGREEMENT REACHED BETWEEN FELTRINELLI AND EEKHOUT, ITALIAN SHOWED UNDERSTANDING FOR MOUTON ACTION BUT MYSTERY REMAINS: WHERE IS FELTRINELLI'S PHOTOCOPY WHICH SENT BY POST TO HAGU?

4. HAAGSCH DAGBLAD: WE HAD INTERVIEW WITH FELTRINELLI WHO ITALIAN PUBLISHER AND MAIN CHARACTER IN PIRATE EDITION DR ZHIVAGO. (PORTION GARBLED-BEING SERVICED) IS WAY TO LOND. FELTRINELLI SAID: "I CONSIDERING BRINGING ACTION AGAINST VAN DER BEEK WHO IS RESPONSIBLE FOR PIRATE PUBLICATION. MY INTENTION NOW PUBLISH

~~S-E-C-R-E-T~~

CLASSIFIED MESSAGE

~~S-E-C-R-E-T~~

FILE NO.

ROUTING

1		4	
2		5	
3		6	

DATE :

TO :

FROM :

ACTION:

INFO :

RE Filing (check one):
No CS Record Value. Destroy. ☐
RI file this copy as indicated ☐
Branch copy filed as indicated ☐
RE Indexing (check one):
Marked ☐ None required ☐
Signature:

PAGE -3-

TO INFO CITE

BOOK THROUGH MOUTON, THAT IS I PUBLISH AND DISTRIBUTE, MOUTON WILL DO SETTING AND PRINTING, NOTHING MORE. EACH ORDER MUST HAVE MY CONSENT. PRINTING WILL AMOUNT TO 5,000 COPIES. I THINK BOOK WILL BE ON MARKET 1 DECEMBER." IT KNOWN FELTRINELLI DID NOT WISH PUBLISH BOOK IN RUSSIAN THIS SPRING AND HE SABOTAGED NEGOTIATIONS WITH MOUTON. FELTRINELLI IS KNOWN BE COMMUNIST. HE DENIED ANY SABOTAGE OF PUBLICATION, STATING: "YOUR COMPATRIOTS DID NOT COME UP FAST ENOUGH WITH DETAILED ESTIMATES OF EXPENSES." WE ASKED FELTRINELLI IF HE COMMUNIST. "I AM NOT MEMBER OF COMMUNIST PARTY" HE SAID. "I AM NOT ASKING YOU THAT". "THEN I CANNOT ANSWER YOUR QUESTION" HE SAID DRYLY. HE DESCRIBED MOUTON HANDLING OF ILLEGAL PUBLICATION STUPID AND WILDWEST LIKE.

5. SECOND ARTICLE IN HAAGSCH DAGBLAD: DURING FIRST WEEK SEPTEMBER SEVERAL HUNDRED COPIES ZHIVAGO OFFERED FREE TO RUSSIAN TOURISTS IN VATICAN PAVILION AT EXPO. THEY PART 1,160 COPIES PRINTED HAGU. THEY ONLY COPIES PRINTED IN RUSSIAN IN WORLD. ACCORDING SOME REPORTS, COPIES THESE BOOKS BEING PASSED FROM HAND TO HAND IN MOSCOW AND LENINGRAD. (COMMENT: REMAINDER OF ARTICLE VERY SIMILAR TO TELEGRAAF).

6. <u>HET BINNENHOF</u>: SERIES OF WILDWEST DEVELOPMENTS SURROUND RUSSIAN PRINTING OF DR ZHIVAGO FROM WHICH IT RESULTS MOUTON HAS PUBLISHED ILLEGAL AND WILL PUBLISH

~~S-E-C-R-E-T~~

FORM 4-58 1389 USE PREVIOUS EDITIONS

 Copy No. (35)

CLASSIFIED MESSAGE

FILE NO.

~~S-E-C-R-E-T~~

ROUTING

1	SR/2	4
2		5
3		6

DATE : 3 NOV 58

TO : DIRECTOR

FROM :

ACTION: SR 6 *

INFO :

RE Filing (check one):
No CS Record Value. Destroy. ☐
RI file this copy as indicated ☑
Branch copy filed as indicated ☐

NOV 4 0706Z 58

ROUTINE

TO DIR INFO CITE

REF

1. THAT SOME WEEKS AGO HE HAD WRITTEN GIANGIACOMO FELTRINELLI THAT BIG AUTHORITATIVE "CLEAN" RUSSIAN EDITION OF DOCTOR ZHIVAGO AN URGENT REQUIREMENT. URGED FELTRINELLI COOPERATE WITH HIM STATING HE ENTIRELY AT HIS DISPOSAL FOR SUCH PUBLICATION AND WILLING, ABLE ORGANIZE SUPPORT, ROUND UP GERMAN OR INTERNATIONAL PUBLISHERS. NO ANSWER YET RECEIVED.

2. ON MONTHS LECTURE TOUR. NEXT MEETING 1 DECEMBER. CAN THEN PASS ANY GUIDANCE HEADQUARTERS MAY WISH.

END OF MESSAGE

RI COPY

ROUTING	INITIAL
RI/AN	
RI/TY	
[illegible]	
RI/FI	

Body-131
~~S-E-C-R-E-T~~

FORM 4-58 1389 USE PREVIOUS EDITIONS

 Copy No.

4. There has been some question as to the copyright actually held by Feltrinelli.

5. In conclusion, the story as we have it is that asked Feltrinelli for the Russian and English rights. Feltrinelli sold Collins only the English rights. never gave us any details on their transactions with Feltrinelli.

Pasternak himself did not want the Russian edition to be brought out in the U.S. He was reported as favoring a neutral country.

Distribution:
Orig - Addressee
1 -
1 -
P -
1 -

~~SECRET~~

5 November 1958

MEMORANDUM FOR: Chief, [redacted]

SUBJECT: Manuscript of Dr. Zhivago

1. After checking with [redacted] who handled the publication of the Russian edition and the files on this matter, the following story emerges:

a. CIA first heard in October 1957 about Pasternak's novel in a cable sent by [redacted] who at that time was in [redacted] [redacted]

b. On 29 November 1957, WE asked [redacted] whether Collins had acquired the publication rights of the novel, how he acquired them, and what arrangements could be made for publications in other languages. [redacted]

c. The answer to these questions was that Collins was translating the Pasternak manuscript into English and could not spare a copy. On the other hand, [redacted] had another copy of the manuscript which they were willing to lend us. [redacted]

d. This manuscript was received at Headquarters where two copies were made. [redacted] [redacted]

2. From the above, it appears that [redacted] got at least one copy of the Russian original from Feltrinelli in a legal way. This was used by Collins for translation into English. [redacted] did not tell us how the other copy was procured. [redacted] [redacted] the basis of the Russian edition eventually put out by Mouton in Holland.

3. It seems obvious that Feltrinelli made copies of the original Russian available whenever he gave the authorization for a foreign edition. On 19 December 1957, for example, we received information that a Russian manuscript had been located in Germany. [redacted]

~~SECRET~~

CLASSIFIED MESSAGE

SECRET

DATE : 5 NOV 1958

TO : DIRECTOR

FROM :

ACTION :

INFO :

RE Filing (check
No CS Record Value. Destroy.
RI file this copy as indicated
Branch copy filed as indicated

ROUTING
1 4
2 5
3 6

NOV 5 2053Z 58

ROUTINE

TO DIR INFO CITE

REDWOOD

RE A.

B.

C.

1. PROPOSE DR ZHIVAGO BOOK PUBLICATION IN RUSSIAN USING REDUCED FORMAT BUT UNABRIDGED CONTENT, THIN PARCHMENT PAPER, BOOK DIVIDED IN THREE PARTS, EACH PAPER BOUND. TOTAL NOT EXCEED THOUSAND COPIES. PURPOSE COVERT DISTRIBUTION TO SOV SAILORS, TOURIST, ALSO BALLOON EAST GERMANY.

2. PROPOSAL BASED VICIOUS SOV ANTI PASTERNAK CAMPAIGN DOMESTIC PRESS UNDOUBTEDLY STIRRING DEEP INTEREST HOME AUDIENCES IN CONTENTS BOOK NOT AVAILABLE LOCALLY. PRESENT VERSION BOOK TOO BULKY FOR MAXIMUM COVERT IMPORTATION USSR VIA SAILORS, TOURISTS.

3. UNABLE MANUFACTURE LOCALLY PARA 1 VERSION BOOK. COULD HQS ARRANGE PRINTING SOONEST, DELIVERY TO AS COPIES BECOME AVAILABLE. BELIEVE TIME ELEMENT ESSENTIAL IF FULL PSYCH EXPLOITATION THEME BE ACHIEVED VIA

4. FYI: VIEW SUBSTANCE REF A, BELIEVE COPYRIGHT VIOLATION NOT MAJOR PROBLEM. FURTHERMORE RE REF B, ACCORDING OBTAINED EARLY MANUSCRIPT DR ZHIVAGO BOOK SUPPOSEDLY FROM USSR THRU CHANNEL DIFFERENT FROM FELTRINELLY'S. ATTEMPTED OBTAIN MANUSCRIPT FOLLOWING REF C PROPOSAL, ~~BUT HE REFUSED RELEASE,~~ STATING OBLIGATED PROTECT PASTERNAK,

SECRET

FORM 4-58 1389 USE PREVIOUS EDITIONS

 Copy No. (35)

CLASSIFIED MESSAGE

~~S-E-C-R-E-T~~

FILE NO.

DATE :

TO :

FROM :

ACTION :

INFO :

RE Filing (check one):
No CS Record Value. Destroy. ☐
RI file this copy as indicated ☐
Branch copy filed as indicated ☐
RE Indexing (check one):
Marked ☐ None required ☐
Signature:

ROUTING

1		4	
2		5	
3		6	

PAGE -2-

TO INFO CITE

WOULD RELEASE MANUSCRIPT ONLY IF FELTRINELLI FAILED PUBLISH.

END OF MESSAGE

C/S COMMENT: *CABLE PRE-DATES CS FILES.

**Confirmed that BBC Russian broadcasts of Dr. Zhivago began on 4 October.

***Requested confirmation that BBC had begun broadcasting extensive portion of Russian language version of Dr. Zhivago.

~~S-E-C-R-E-T~~

Body-135

FORM 4-58 1389 USE PREVIOUS EDITIONS

REPRODUCTION BY OTHER THAN THE ISSUING OFFICE IS PROHIBITED. Copy No. (35)

☐ UNCLASSIFIED ☐ INTERNAL USE ONLY ☐ CONFIDENTIAL ☐ SECRET

ROUTING AND RECORD SHEET

SUBJECT: (Optional)

FROM: RID/RPG

NO.

DATE

TO: (Officer designation, room number, and building)	DATE RECEIVED	DATE FORWARDED	OFFICER'S INITIALS	COMMENTS (Number each comment to show from whom to whom. Draw a line across column after each comment.)
1. RID/AN				The attached document was in:
2. RI/MIS				
3. RI/Files				
4.				
5.				
6.				
7.				
8.				
9.				
10.				
11.				
12.				ABSTRACT ~~X~~ INDEX
13.				DATE 5 NOV 58
14.				
15.				

Body-136

FORM 1 DEC 56 610 USE PREVIOUS EDITIONS ☐ SECRET ☐ CONFIDENTIAL ☐ INTERNAL USE ONLY ☐ UNCLASSIFIED

GPO 1961 : O—593644

CLASSIFIED MESSAGE

~~SECRET~~

FILE NO.

ROUTING

1		4	
2	WE/2	5	
3		6	

Nov 5 22 32 58
REC'D CABLE SECT.

ORIG :
UNIT :
EXT :
DATE : 5 NOVEMBER 1958 620

TO :
FROM : DIRECTOR
CONF : WE 6
INFO :

RE Filing (check one):
No CS Record Value. Destroy.
RI file this copy as indicated ✓
Branch copy filed as indicated
RE Indexing (check one):
Marked None required ✓
Signature:

PRECEDENCE	DEFERRED	X	PRIORITY	INITIALS
	ROUTINE		OPERATIONAL IMMEDIATE	INITIALS

TO INFO CITE DIR

REDWOOD AEDINOSAUR

REF

2

A. HIS CLIENT PREPARED PAY ANY ROYALTIES OR COSTS LEGALLY DUE

B. NEVER HAD BUT ONE COPY REPRODUCTION PLATES AND HAS NO KNOWLEDGE EXISTENCE ANY OTHER COPIES, BUT

C. CANNOT REVEAL HIS CONTACTS.

1 2

2. REQUEST

A. HQS FEELS HAVE DONE FINE JOB IN COVERING THIS AFFAIR WHICH FULLY WORTH TROUBLE IN VIEW OBVIOUS EFFECT ON SOVIETS.

B. HQS WILLING PAY LAWYER AND SETTLEMENT COSTS.

NOV 6 1958

COORDINATING OFFICERS

RELEASING OFFICER ~~SECRET~~ AUTHENTICATING OFFICER

CLASSIFIED MESSAGE

~~SECRET~~

FILE NO.

ROUTING

1		4	
2		5	
3		6	

ORIG :
UNIT :
EXT :
DATE : 5 NOVEMBER 1958

NOV 5 22 32 Z 58
REC'D CABLE SECT.

TO

FROM : DIRECTOR

CONF :

INFO :

RE Filing (check one):
No CS Record Value. Destroy.
RI file this copy as indicated
Branch copy filed as indicated
RE Indexing (check one):
Marked   None required
Signature:

PRECEDENCE		DEFERRED		PRIORITY	INITIALS
		ROUTINE		OPERATIONAL IMMEDIATE	INITIALS

PAGE TWO

TO INFO CITE DIR

3. FYI: NO NEED TAKE ACTION GET FURTHER COPIES PRINTED AS [redacted] ORDERS APPEAR ADEQUATE.

END OF MESSAGE

C/S COMMENT:

*Concerned Feltrinelli publication of the Pasternak book.

RI COPY

DC/SR -- in draft

COORDINATING OFFICERS

RELEASING OFFICER

~~SECRET~~

AUTHENTICATING OFFICER

FORM 4-58 1389 a REPRODUCTION BY OTHER THAN THE ISSUING OFFICE IS PROHIBITED. Copy No.

U. S. GOVERNMENT PRINTING OFFICE : 1958 O—465031 (35)

CLASSIFIED MESSAGE

~~S-E-C-R-E-T~~

FILE NO.

ROUTING

1		4	
2		5	
3		6	

DATE :

TO :

FROM :

ACTION :

INFO :

RE Filing (check one):
No CS Record Value. Destroy. ☐
RI file this copy as indicated ☐
Branch copy filed as indicated ☐
RE Indexing (check one):
Marked ☐ None required ☐
Signature:

TO INFO CITE

SAME DATE AL BINA HAD ARTICLE

3. AL NAHAR WILL RUN UP RELEASE RE HOWARD FAST AND FEATURE PASTERNAK STORY IN LITERARY SECTION.

END OF MESSAGE

C/S COMMENT: *ACTION UNIT DETERMINED AS THOUGH INDICATOR REDWOOD USED.

** APPARENTLY WRONG REFERENCE. POSSIBLY INTENDED.

~~S-E-C-R-E-T~~ Bodx-139

FORM 4-58 1389 USE PREVIOUS EDITIONS

 Copy No. (35)

CLASSIFIED MESSAGE

~~S-E-C-R-E-T~~

FILE NO.

DATE : 6 NOV 58

TO : DIRECTOR

FROM :

ACTION: SR 6 *

INFO :

RE Filing (check one):
No CS Record Value. Destroy. [ ]
RI file this copy as indicated [✓]
Branch copy filed as indicated [ ]

ROUTING

1	SR/2	4	
2		5	
3		6	

NOV 6 0954Z 58

ROUTINE

TO DIR INFO CITE

PSYCH

RE

1. PRESS COVERAGE PASTERNAK CASE:

A. HIS WINNING NOBEL PRIZE COVERED PAGE 1 BY AL HAYAT, AL NAHAR AND AL BINA OCT 24.

B. HIS EXPULSION FROM SOVIET WRITERS UNION COVERED PAGE 1 BY AL HAYAT, AL NAHAR AND AL BINA OCT 27.

C. HIS TURNING DOWN NOBEL PRIZE COVERED PAGE 1 BY AL HAYAT, AL NAHAR AND PAGE 3 BY AL BINA OCT 30.

D. SOVIET WRITERS ATTACK HIM COVERED BY AL HAYAT AND AL NAHAR ON 1 NOV.

E. HIS LETTER TO KHRUSCHEV COVERED BY AL HAYAT, AL NAHAR AND AL BINA NOV 2.

SUBSTANTIAL COVERAGE IN AL JARIDA , AL AMAL, AL BAYRAQ AND TO LIMITED EXTENT IN PRO NASIR PAPERS SIYASAH (ALSO RECEIVED AL SIYASAH), AL KIFAH, AND BEIRUT AL MASSA.

2. AL BINA 31 OCT HAD FRONT PAGE EDITORIAL "NOBEL PRIZE SEEN THOUGH PASTERNAK CASE." THEME: FREE THOUGHT AND DIALECTICAL MATERIALISM DO NOT GO TOGETHER.

~~S-E-C-R-E-T~~

SECRET
(WHEN FILLED IN)

ROUTING AND RECORD SHEET

INSTRUCTIONS: Use officer designations in the "TO" column. Number each comment to correspond with the number in the "TO" column. Draw a line across the sheet under each comment. Each officer should date and initial (check mark insufficient) before further routing. This Routing and Record sheet should NOT be removed from the attached RECORD document.

FROM: RI/ RI/AN

DOCUMENT NUMBER

DOCUMENT DATE

TO	ROOM NO.	DATE RECEIVED	DATE FORWARDED	OFFICER'S INITIALS
1. SR/2		17 NOV 1958		
2.				
3. SR				
4.				
5.				
6.				
7.				
8.				
9.				
10.				
11.				
12.				
13.				
14. RI/FI				

COMMENTS

NOTE: If a copy or attachments are removed from the attached document, note the location of the copy and/or attachment hereon. If this RECORD COPY is to be retained in the files at the Desk, call the Central File Section for permanent loan.

Sov Counselor in B. Past.

file Di "3"

FILE TITLE: AEDINOSAUR

FILE NUMBER

ENCLOSURE

ABSTRACT X

DATE PROCESSED 7 Nov 1958

INDEX

FORM NO. 1 OCT. 55 610a

SECRET

DISPATCH

CLASSIFICATION: ~~SECRET~~

DISPATCH SYMBOL AND NO.

TO: Chief, SR

INFO: Chief, WE

HEADQUARTERS FILE NO.

FROM:

DATE: NOV 7 1958

SUBJECT: REDWOOD
Soviet Writers' Union Stand Against Pasternak

RE: "43-3" — (CHECK "X" ONE)
MARKED FOR INDEXING
NO INDEXING REQUIRED
X INDEXING CAN BE JUDGED BY QUALIFIED HQ. DESK ONLY

ACTION REQUIRED: For your information

REFERENCE(S)

2. the case had been extremely badly handled by the Soviet Writers' Union which had issued emotional statements without taking any political advise. He insisted on the fact that the Soviet Government had not taken part in this incident whereas Secretary of State Dulles immediately seized the opportunity to take a stand against the Soviet Union, thereby forcing the Soviet Government to make a reply.

3. for ten years the Soviet Writers' Union has provided Pasternak with a large salary and a house. This is done for many Soviet writers to give them the necessary leisure to produce works of art. However none of Pasternak's books or poetry had ever had success with the Russian public. Many of his poems were published in Pravda in 1946 and 47 but did not catch the public's attention. under the rules of the Writers' Union, each member has to ask permission to have a work published in a foreign country, but that Pasternak had his book published in Italy three years ago without informing the Writers' Union and without offering to share some of his earnings with them as repayment for what he had been accepting from them. All in all, from the point of view of the Writers' Union, Pasternak's behavior was fraudulent. Their stand against him was for these reasons rather than because he had criticized the Soviet system, and many popular Soviet writers have been much more critical of some aspects of Soviet life without suffering the slightest persecution.

6 Nov 58
Distribution:
2-SR
2-WE

FORM 10-57 53 (40) USE PREVIOUS EDITION. REPLACES FORMS 51-28, 51-28A AND 51-29 WHICH ARE OBSOLETE.

CLASSIFICATION: ~~SECRET~~

CONTINUED

PAGE NO.

SECRET
(WHEN FILLED IN)

ROUTING AND RECORD SHEET

INSTRUCTIONS: Use officer designations in the "TO" column. Number each comment to correspond with the number in the "TO" column. Draw a line across the sheet under each comment. Each officer should date and initial (check mark insufficient) before further routing. This Routing and Record sheet should NOT be removed from the attached RECORD document.

FROM: RI/ RI/AN

DOCUMENT NUMBER

DOCUMENT DATE

1

TO	ROOM NO.	DATE RECEIVED	DATE FORWARDED	OFFICER'S INITIALS
1.				
2.				
3.				
4.				
5. SR/2/PP	1 DEC 1958			
6.				
7.				
8.				
9.				
10.				
11.				
12.				
13.				
14. RI/FI				

COMMENTS

NOTE: If a copy or attachments are removed from the attached document, note the location of the copy and/or attachment hereon. If this RECORD COPY is to be retained in the files at the Desk, call the Central File Section for permanent loan.

1cc retained by SR/2/PP

RECORD COPY

FILE TITLE

FILE NUMBER

ENCLOSURE

ABSTRACT X

DATE PROCESSED 18 Nov 1958

INDEX

Body-143

FORM NO. 1 OCT. 55 610a

SECRET

VIA: Air (SPECIFY AIR OR SEA POUCH)

DISPATCH NO.

~~Secret~~
CLASSIFICATION

TO : Chief, WE
Attn: Chief, WE/2

DATE: 18 November 1958

FROM : Acting

SUBJECT: GENERAL— REDWOOD/AEDINOSAUR/Psych

SPECIFIC— Forwarding of Copies of Dr. Zhivago

Reference:

1. To date, the following shipments of Dr. Zhivago have been made to Headquarters:

24 October	-	36 copies by sea pouch
28 October	-	12 copies by sea pouch
31 October	-	60 copies by air pouch
4 November	-	30 copies by sea pouch
14 November	-	35 copies by sea pouch

2. Of the overall total received one copy was passed to during his recent visit and seven copies have been retained for operational reference use. Thirty-two copies have been retained by .

3. Including the copies forwarded to is in receipt of a total of 1,065 copies. The remaining 63 copies will be turned over by as soon as their legal differences have been settled.

Attachments: books as described above (usc)

Distribution:
3 Hqs w/atts.
2

18 November 1958

CS COPY

Body-144

~~Secret~~
CLASSIFICATION

FORM NO. MAR. 1949 51-28 A

IO/1

18 November 1958

MEMORANDUM FOR THE RECORD

SUBJECT: Telephone Conversation with

2. While trip was originally set up in the broad context of publications in general, the Dr. Zhivago book has become an important feature. saw Feltrinelli in Milan some time in late October. The purpose of seeing him was to inquire about obtaining rights for the book Feltrinelli took the position that he would not give rights to a publisher's agent, but he informed that if he should receive requests from specific publishers, he would probably go along.

3. Feltrinelli, , may decide to give rights in one of two ways, and it is at this point that there arises a possibility of duplication. He may, for example, decide to grant exclusive rights to the first publisher in a given language who may write to him, or he may on the other hand grant rights wholesale to all comers. He remarked to that as of the date of visit he had already received five requests for rights We have no other information as to how Feltrinelli may or may not have responded to these requests.

4. So far as is concerned, we have a control over which should prevent any publication of Dr. Zhivago which would duplicate an edition possibly being sponsored by some other CIA asset in the field. was carefully briefed before his departure, by , to the effect that he could talk to publishers or anyone else whom he chose to see, but that his authority was restricted to submitting recommendations to is not authorized to sign contracts with publishers, commit funds, etc.

FILE NO.

CLASSIFIED MESSAGE

S-E-C-R-E-T

549

ORIG :
UNIT : SR/2/PP
EXT :
DATE : 18 November 1958

TO :

FROM: DIRECTOR

CONF: SR 6

INFO

RE Filing (check one):
No CS Record Value. Destroy.
RI file this copy as indicated
Branch copy filed as indicated
RE Indexing (check one):
Marked
Signature

ROUTING

PRECEDENCE: DEFERRED / X ROUTINE / PRIORITY / OPERATIONAL IMMEDIATE

TO   INFO   CITE DIR 01078

01078

REDWOOD AEDINOSAUR PSYCH

REF

1. RE PARA ONE REF:

A. REPORTEDLY PUBLISHING COMPLETELY NEW RUSSIAN EDITION.

B. HAS BEEN INTERESTED IN OBTAINING COPIES MINIATURE EDITION AND HAS REQUESTED HQS PUBLISH IT. IN VIEW GREAT DEMAND SOV INTELLECTUALS OBTAIN COPIES BOOK AND PROBLEMS CIRCULATING NORMAL EDITION, HQS CONSIDERING PUBLICATION BLACK MINIATURE EDITION. COMMENTS RE PUBLICATION WILL BE APPRECIATED.

C. DER SPIEGEL ARTICLE HALF TRUTH HALF ERROR. EDITION INTENDED BE LEGAL. UNDERSTOOD HE HAD RIGHTS, EMPLOYEE FAILED TO GET SPECIFIC APPROVAL FELTRINELLI. PUBLISHING ONLY IN LATTER'S NAME MADE EDITION ILLEGAL. FELTRINELLI DISPUTE FOLLOWED. BY RECENT AGREEMENT WILL PRINT NEW RUSSIAN EDITION FOR FELTRINELLI. PUBLICATION DATE ABOUT 1 JAN 1959.

AEDINOSAUR

RI COPY

RELEASING OFFICER   COORDINATING OFFICERS   AUTHENTICATING OFFICER

SECRET

Body 147

FORM 4-58 1389 a   (35)

Copy No.

Approved for Release: 2014/04/07

FILE NO.

CLASSIFIED MESSAGE

~~S-E-C-R-E-T~~

ORIG :
UNIT :
EXT :
DATE :

ROUTING			
1		4	
2		5	
3		6	

TO :

FROM: DIRECTOR

CONF:

INFO :

RE Filing (check one):
No CS Record Value. Destroy. ☐
RI file this copy as indicated ☐
Branch copy filed as indicated ☐
RE Indexing (check one):
Marked ☐ None required ☐
Signature:

PAGE TWO

PRECEDENCE: DEFERRED / ROUTINE / PRIORITY (INITIALS) / OPERATIONAL IMMEDIATE (INITIALS)

TO INFO CITE

2. RE PARA TWO REF:

A. TEXT USED FOR FIRST [redacted] FELTRINELLI EDITION CAME FROM [redacted].

B. DUE [redacted] RAPID PRINTING [redacted] GAVE APPROX SIX HUNDRED COPIES TO SOV VISITORS AT FAIR.

3. IF [redacted] INTERESTED CAN PROVIDE FURTHER DETAIL ABOVE.

END OF MESSAGE

CS COMMENT: * CONCERNING RUSSIAN EDITION DR ZHIVAGO.

RI COPY

COORDINATING OFFICERS

Chief, WE
RELEASING OFFICER

~~S-E-C-R-E-T~~

Body 148

FORM 4-58 1389 a

Copy No. (35)

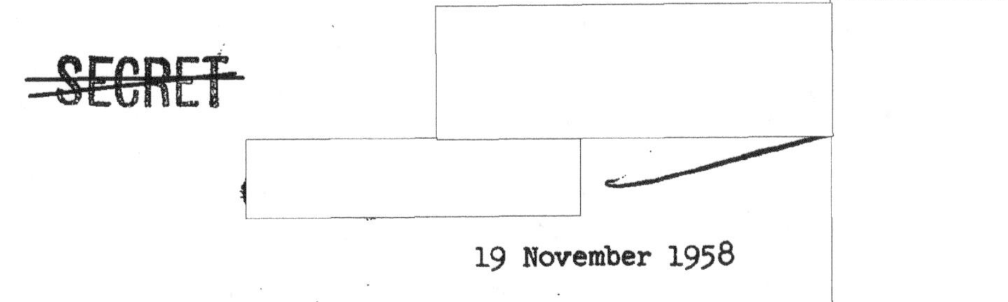

~~SECRET~~

19 November 1958

MEMORANDUM FOR: Chief of Operations, DDP

SUBJECT : History of the Dr. Zhivago Manuscript

1. According to ~~reports based~~ upon ~~various~~ interviews with PASTERNAK, the author completed the manuscript for Dr. Zhivago in 1954. Dr. Zhivago was first mentioned in the Soviet press in 1954 when the organization of the Soviet Union of Writers, Znamya, published ten poems intended as an appendix to the novel. In an introductory note, PASTERNAK said that the novel would be completed that summer.

2. The author submitted the manuscript to the State Publishing House shortly after the 20th Party Congress in 1956. The manuscript was accepted and allegedly scheduled for publication at the end of 1956.

3. During the summer of 1956 the author received a letter from the Union of Writers of the USSR, signed by the First Secretary, Alexsej SURKOV, and a number of prominent writers, refusing publication and accusing him of using his "great gift" to "resuscitate in the soul of our people ideals which have been dead for a long time."

4. In June 1956 PASTERNAK gave a copy of the manuscript to a representative of the Italian Communist publisher Giangiacomo FELTRINELLI and to two other visitors from abroad. Later, PASTERNAK wrote to FELTRINELLI and accepted the latter's proposal to act as agent for the publication of all translations of the novel. PASTERNAK ~~also~~

~~SECRET~~

informed his foreign publishers that they should ignore any letter he might write under duress requesting that the manuscript not be published.

Regarding attribution, the book could be a direct copy of either the Feltrinelli edition or the Michigan edition, or it could be fictitious. A miniature edition attributed to an innocuous, fictitious publisher appears to be preferable as it would avoid incurring additional legal problems that might result from using the name of one of the bona fide publishers.

5. Conclusion and recommendation:

In view of the security, legal, and technical problems involved, it is recommended that a black miniature edition of "Dr. Zhivago" be published at headquarters using the first Feltrinelli text and attributing it to a fictitious publisher. This recommendation is submitted for your approval.

Acting Chief, SR Division

Concur:

C/PP	Date
C/IO	Date
C/WE	Date

Approved:

ADD/P	Date

Distribution:
Orig & 1 - Addressee
1 - C/PP
1 - C/IO
1 - C/WE
1 - SR/COP/PP

SECRET

name without the latter's consent - thereby becoming an illegal edition.

b. According to a recent statement by Feltrinelli, Mouton will print a new Russian-language edition for Feltrinelli. The publication date is tentatively set for about 1 January 1959.

c. The University of Michigan Press has announced it will put out a Russian-language edition of "Dr. Zhivago" on 21 November 1958. Reportedly, the Michigan publication will be a new edition.

d. Over 500 copies of the illegal Russian-language edition of the novel were distributed to Soviet visitors at the Brussels Fair and in Western Europe last summer. Many of these copies are presumed to be circulating in the USSR.

e. Publication of a miniature edition at headquarters would require approximately three months.

4. <u>Discussion:</u>

The following possibilities for publishing a miniature edition have been considered: (a) To print a miniature edition of the book in a country which is not a member of the Geneva Universal Copyright Convention. This idea is rejected because of the security and control problems involved. (b) To print a black miniature edition using either of the two Feltrinelli-Mouton texts or that of the University of Michigan. The Michigan edition is rejected

The second Feltrinelli-Mouton edition is rejected because of the uncertainty of its availability.

19 November 1958

MEMORANDUM FOR: Acting Deputy Director (Plans)

SUBJECT: Miniature edition of "Dr. Zhivago"

1. **Problem:**

To publish a miniature edition of "Dr. Zhivago" which can be circulated in the Soviet Union more easily than the normal edition.

2. **Assumptions:**

a. There appears to be no prospect that the novel will be published in the USSR.

b. It is believed there is a tremendous demand on the part of Soviet students and intellectuals to obtain copies of this book.

c. Soviet customs officers may become increasingly alert to efforts to introduce copies of "Dr. Zhivago" into the USSR.

d. A miniature edition, more easily concealed and infiltrated into the USSR, would receive wide internal circulation.

3. **Facts Bearing on the Problem:**

a. The original Russian edition of "Dr. Zhivago" was intended to be legal but turned out to be illegal. As Dutch publisher Mouton was corresponding with Feltrinelli for publication rights, [redacted] A Mouton employee, however, failed to obtain specific approval from Feltrinelli prior to publication. Consequently the book came out only in Feltrinelli's

CLASSIFIED MESSAGE

~~S-E-C-R-E-T-~~

ROUTING			
1	2	4	
2		5	
3		6	

DATE : 21 NOV 58

TO : DIRECTOR

FROM :

ACTION: SR 6 *

INFO :

RE Filing (check one):
No CS Record Value. Destroy. ☐
RI file this copy as indicated ☑
Branch copy filed as indicated ☐
RE Indexing (check one):
Marked ☐
Signature:

NOV 22 0140Z 58

ROUTINE

TO DIR INFO CITE

RE:

PLEASE SEND 15 COPIES RUSS EDITION DR ZHIVAGO FOR FORWARDING USSR THRU

END OF MESSAGE

C/S COMMENT: * ACTION UNIT DETERMINED AS THOUGH INDICATOR REDWOOD USED.

RI COPY

ROUTING	INITIAL
RI/AN	
RI/TY	
~~[illegible]~~	
RI/FI	

~~S-E-C-R-E-T-~~

FORM 4-58 1389 USE PREVIOUS EDITIONS REPRODUCTION BY OTHER THAN THE ISSUING OFFICE IS PROHIBITED. Copy No. (35)

Dr Zhivago

~~SECRET~~

21 November 1958

MEMORANDUM FOR THE RECORD

SUBJECT: Publication of Dr. Zhivago

	Country	Publisher	Form of Publication	When Published	Language	Rights
WE	Great Britain	Collins & Harvill Press, London	Hardback book	4 Set. 58	English	Yes
	France	Gallimard & Co. Paris	book	Aug. 58	French	Yes
	Italy	Giangiacomo Feltrinelli Via Andegari 6, Milan, Italy	book	Nov 1957	Italian	Yes
	Sweden	Albert Bonnier	book	31 Oct 58	Swedish	Yes
	Norway					
	Denmark	Gyldendal Press	book	28 Oct 58	Danish	Yes
	Finland	Tammi OY (Social-Democratic Co-operatives' publisher)	book	Dec. 58	Finnish	Yes
	Iceland	Almenna Bokavelagid, Reykjavik	book		Icelandic	Yes
	Netherlands	Mouton & Co. Publishers and Printers Herderstraat 5, The Hague, Netherlands		2nd edition ready 1 Jan 59	Russian	Yes*

*Special controls by Feltrinelli, who has indicated he will not permit Mouton to fill orders that smell like intelligence exploitation of the book.

~~SECRET~~

~~SECRET~~

	Country		Publisher	Form of Publication	When Published	Language	Rights
	Portugal		(none, see Brazil)				
	Spain		(none, see Venezuela)				
EE	W.Germany		S.Fischer Verlag Frankfurt am Main	book	Nov. 58	German	Yes
	Poland	1.	Orbis, London	book	after 1/1/59	Polish	May get
		2.	Polish Literary Journal Opinia Warsaw	excerpts in Magazine	late 1957	Polish	?
	Czechoslovakia		none				
	Hungary		none				
SE	Greece		John Yerolimbos [redacted] Athens	book possibly condensed	Nov. 58	Greek	No
			[redacted]	serializ.	Talking stage	Greek	hopes to get
	Yugoslavia		Peter Zivanovic, v-p of Yugoslav semi-official publishing house	book	indefinite because of apparent Soviet pressure	Serbian	
	Bulgaria						
	Rumania						
	Turkey						
SR	Soviet Union		(see Netherlands)				Yes
			Black				No

~~SECRET~~

	Country	Publisher	Form of Publication	When Published	Language	Rights
NEA	Africa South					
	Saudi Arabia, Iraqi, Jordan, Sudan, Kuwait					
	Africa North					
	Iran	Etelaat, journal	serialization	Nov. 58	Persian	No
		Tehran Journal	serialization	Nov. 58	English	No
		Roshanfekr	excerpts	after Nov. 58	Persian	No
	Pakistan	[redacted]	book	still in talking stage	Urdu	No
	India					
	Ceylon	Leading English-language daily	serialized condensation	Nov. 58	English	No
	Egypt-Syria					
	Lebanon	Dar Al Alim Lil Milayiin Beirut	book	talking stage	Arabic	Not yet
		Al Ahliyyah, Beirut	"	"	"	"
		Al Khal Publishing House Beirut	"	"	"	"
CI/ICD [redacted]	Israel	Jerusalem Post report on 24/10/58 that a Hebrew edition is to be published, date and place unknown.				
WH	Brazil	Editora Itatiata or Italiana or Itaidia Belo Horizonte	book	Nov. or Dec. 1958	Portuguese	Yes

	Country	Publisher	Form of Publication	When Published	Language	Rights
WH	Venezuela	La Estera (daily) Caracas	serialization	Nov. 58	Spanish	No
	Mexico					
FE	Japan	Sekai Shuho Tokyo magazine	serialization	5 Nov. 58	Japanese	No
	China	Chen Pao (Truth daily) Hong Kong	serial	Nov. 58	Chinese	No
	Malaya	Singapore Straits Times, Singapore	serial	Nov. 58	English	No
	Indonesia		condensation	Talking stage	Indonesian	No
	Vietnam	a newspaper	serialized	Nov. 58	Vietnamese	No
		a newspaper	serialized	Nov. 58	Chinese	No
	Thailand					
	Burma					

Dr Zhivago

21 November 1958

MEMORANDUM FOR: Chief, Psychological and Paramilitary Staff

SUBJECT: Operational Funds for Purchase and Distribution of 40 Copies of the British Edition of Dr. Zhivago by Boris Pasternak

REFERENCE: Project [redacted] FY 1959

1. This memorandum proposes approval of the recommendation contained in paragraph 5.

2. As you are aware, [redacted] is attempting to facilitate the exploitation of Dr. Zhivago by making copies of the English language edition available [redacted] It has been considered advisable to use the British edition for this purpose, rather than the American one.

3. A number [redacted] [redacted] have requested copies of the British edition in quantities small enough to make it feasible for [redacted] [redacted] to ship them directly. In addition, the [redacted] Division desires to have some 40 copies available at Headquarters for pro rata distribution to the requesting area divisions.

4. The cost of copies of the book [redacted] [redacted] will be charged to the [redacted] concerned.

5. It is recommended that out of the [redacted] [redacted] the sum of [redacted] for FY 1959 be made available to cover the cost of 40 copies of Dr. Zhivago for Headquarters distribution on a pro rata basis to the requesting area divisions.

6. Please direct inquiries concerning this proposal to [redacted]

Approved:

25 Nov 1958

Date

Distribution:
Original and 1-Addressee [redacted]

SECRET

Dr. Zhivago

SECRET

21 November 1958

MEMORANDUM FOR: Chief, [redacted]

SUBJECT: Operational Funds for Purchase and Distribution of 640 Copies of the British Edition of Dr. Zhivago by Boris Pasternak

REFERENCES: (a) [redacted] FY 1959

(b) Memo for CPP, 21 Nov 58, concerning 40 copies of the British edition

1. This memorandum proposes approval of the recommendation contained in paragraph 4.

2. The [redacted] Division desires to acquire 640 copies of the British edition by the most expeditious means in order to distribute them to [redacted] which do not have [redacted] It has been determined that the acquisition of 640 copies would place an undue burden on [redacted], and that the fastest means of getting these copies to Headquarters is with the aid of the Commercial Staff.

3. We propose therefore, to ask that Commercial Staff, through a secure channel, acquire these 640 copies at a cost of approximately [redacted] a copy, or [redacted] accounting to be made in the customary manner.

4. It is recommended that out of the [redacted] the sum of [redacted] for FY 1959 be made available to cover the cost of procurement of 640 copies of Dr. Zhivago for Headquarters distribution to the area divisions. After distribution to the area divisions at Headquarters, [redacted] will determine the apportionment of costs and charge each division accordingly. Area divisions involved (FE, NEA, EE, SR and WH) have agreed to pay their proportionate shares of this shipment and [redacted] will be credited accordingly with no actual final cost to this project.

SECRET

~~SECRET~~

Approved:

(Signed)

Date

25 NOV 1958

(21 Nov 58)
Distribution:
Original and 1-Addressee
1-
1-Chief Finance
1-Commercial Staff
1-Each Area Division
2-

~~SECRET~~

At the beginning of July of this year, there appeared at the Dutchman MOUTON's print shop, a very secretive visitor who appeared to be well informed about the preparation of the Russian edition of Dr. Zhivago. MOUTON's sales director, Peter de RIDDER, asked the visitor to be patient until he could get together with FELTRINELLI and could begin the preparation. The unknown individual reached in his briefcase and wordlessly exhibited the negatives of the complete photostatic copy of Dr. Zhivago which obviously originated from an illegal Russian edition from behind the Iron Curtain. The Dutchman wasn't too sure if it would be in the interests of the MOUTON Firm and that of FELTRINELLI to accept this edition, but one had to think of the possibility of another printer being found who didn't have to worry about this. RIDDER accepted the edition without the directors of the international syndicate knowing about it. RIDDER tried to reach FELTRINELLI by telephone in order to legalise the printing at the last minute.

The individual in the Brussels Vatican pavilion who talked with the Soviet tourists was not unknown to PASTERNAK. He was called Vladimir Graf TOLSTOY, a grand nephew of Count Leo Nikolayevich TOLSTOY and had visited PASTERNAK at the end of July in his village near Moscow. Leo N. TOLSTOY was very friendly with PASTERNAK's father, the painter Leonid PASTERNAK, while Boris PASTERNAK was serving in a literary capacity in the Soviet system. TOLSTOY immigrated to America. He became a professor at the Jesuit University at Georgetown in Washington, D.C., and entered the service of the Militant American Cultural and Propaganda Organization which goes under the name of Committee for a Free Europe. From the Coffers of this Committee, TOLSTOY's nephew Vladimir, financed the printing of the Russian edition of Dr. Zhivago.

Paris Match

Article claims clandestine edition made it possible for PASTERNAK to receive Nobel Prize.

Telegraaf

With all the fuss about ZHIVAGO, mystery has arisen and most of the answers remain to be found in the Netherlands and the Hague in particular. According to KEEHOUT, Soviet visitors to the exposition were given free copies in Vatican pavilion in which FELTRINELLI, who has book rights, appeared as publisher although he had not placed an order for printing of Russian edition. These copies originated from

SECRET

D 4, Nov.

Memorandum For: Director of Central Intelligence

Subject : Article in the National Review Bulletin of 15 November 1958 Concerning the Book "Dr. Zhivago"

1. This memorandum is for information only.

2. on 15 November 1958 the National Review Bulletin carried an article on the publication of the book "Dr. Zhivago" asserting that CIA was responsible for the Dutch publication of the book. An extract of this article as it appeared in the National Review Bulletin is set forth as Attachment "A".

3. A source of this office has advised that Ralph De Toledano wrote the article which appeared in the National Review Bulletin. De Toledano, author of "Spies, Dupes and Diplomats," is a member of the extreme right wing element and was a close associate of Senator McCarthy. De Toledano entered on duty with OSS in December 1944, but was terminated in February 1945

4. Considerable material has appeared in the European press concerning the publication of "Dr. Zhivago." Attachment "C" contains a summary of material which has appeared in Der Speigel, issue of 29 October 1958, in the Paris Match, and in the Dutch publications Haagsch Dagblat and Het Binnenhoff. The Der Speigel article asserted that Vladimir Graf Tolstoy, the grandnephew of Count Leo Nikolyevich Tolstoy, financed the printing of the Russian edition of "Dr. Zhivago" from funds of the Committee for Free Europe. The article went on to assert that Vladimir Tolstoy had visited Boris Pasternak, the author of "Dr. Zhivago," in July in Russia.

5. The editors of the National Review and the National Review Bulletin have had numerous articles in the past charging that the Committee for Free Europe and Radio Free Europe are CIA sponsored and financed. It is possible that Ralph De Toledano, as part of the basis for his assertion in the 15 November 1958 article that "Dr. Zhivago" was published through the work of CIA, used some of the

material described above. It is a well-known fact that the various editors and contributors to the National Review and National Review Bulletin follow closely material appearing in the Western European press.

6. Further work is being done on this matter, and you will be advised of the results of this further investigation.

Director of Security

Attachments: A, B and C

Distribution:

Orig & 1 - D/CI
1 - DD/CI
1 - IG
1 - OGC
1 - ID
1 - Acting DD/P
1 - Asst. to D/CI
1 - ER

OS/ Cord: (24 November 1958)

illegal source which proved to be MOUTON acting in complete ignorance. FELTRINELLI and MOUTON have now made contract for the new Russian edition of the book. EEKHOUT claims FELTRINELLI wrote him on 1 July asking about sending him photocopy of book. Several days later DE RIDDER received telephone call from contact in Paris who told him he was bringing manuscript. DE RIDDER accepted delivery of book on assumption that the person from Paris was sent by FELTRINELLI. Weeks later DE RIDDER received visit from VAN DER BEEK who ordered 1,000 copies, obviously aware that MOUTON was printing Russian edition for FELTRINELLI. It was impossible to fill his order within month as requested. To DE RIDDER's stupefaction, BEEK took printing plates out of his briefcase. To the best of our knowledge no Russian edition was ever published and we tried to contact FELTRINELLI to inform him of this startling visit but he was not available. In order to preserve FELTRINELLI's rights, we are now reproducing the book photo-mechanically in order to prevent book from going to another publisher. 1,160 copies were given to BEEK who did not tell for whom the books were intended. EEKHOUT heard then that the books were distributed in the Vatican Pavilion. But until then he had been unaware involved in political affair. Afterwards learned that Paris manuscript was not identical with FELTRINELLI manuscript, but BEEK's photocopy was quite similar to FELTRINELLI's. FELTRINELLI seemed to find no objection to Hague illegal edition. Agreement reached between FELTRINELLI and EEKHOUT, Italian showed understanding for MOUTON action but mystery remains: Where is FELTRINELLI's photocopy which was sent by post to Hague?

Haagsch Dagblad

We had an interview with FELTRINELLI who is the Italian publisher and main character in the pirate edition of Dr. Zhivago. FELTRINELLI said: "I am considering bringing action against VAN DER BEEK who is responsible for the pirate publication. My intention now is to publish the book through MOUTON, that is I will publish and distribute, MOUTON will do the setting and printing, nothing more. Each order must have my consent. The printing will amount to 5,000 copies. I think the book will be on the market on 1 December." It is known that FELTRINELLI did not wish to publish the book in Russian this spring and that he sabotaged negotiations with MOUTON. FELTRINELLI is known to be Communist. He denied any sabotage of publication stating: "Your compatriots did not come up fast enough with detailed estimates of expenses." We asked FELTRINELLI if he was a Communist. "I am not a member of the Communist Party" he said. "I am not asking you that." "Then I cannot answer your question", he said dryly. He described MOUTON's handling of illegal publication as stupid and wildwest like.

Second Article in Haagsch Dagblad

During the first week of September several hundred copies of Dr.

Zhivago were offered free to Russian tourists in Vatican Pavilion at the exposition. They were part of 1,160 copies printed at the Hague. They were the only copies printed in Russian in the world. According to some reports, copies of these books are being passed from hand to hand in Moscow and Leningrad.

Het Binnenhof

A series of wildest developments surround the Russian printing of Dr. Zhivago from which it results that MOUTON has published illegal and will publish legal edition. On 1 November a contract was signed for the printing of a legal edition. REMHOUT explained the story because of misleading accounts in which he more or less imputed participating in political affairs. REMHOUT said they were involved in politics without knowing it. Someone came from Paris to bring the manuscript which MOUTON thought was from FELTRINELLI, but later learned this was not the case. Motives of the Frenchman is not clear to this day. In dealing with BEEK, MOUTON did not know his relationship with Vrede en Vrijheid, an anti-Communist organization, which seems to have distributed the book to Russian visitors at the Vatican Pavilion. FELTRINELLI was in the Hague on 1 November and MOUTON assured him that printing expenses will be born by BEEK only and they are attempting to turn the illegal printing into a legal one. Everything turned out all right and contract was signed for 3,000 copies in Russian. FELTRINELLI wants the first edition continued to be considered as illegal. Paris manuscript differs from FELTRINELLI's only slightly. BEEK's copies are similar to FELTRINELLI's with exception of typographical errors and some rules left out. But who had the manuscript printed and not published? FELTRINELLI sent the manuscript unregistered but MOUTON did not get it. Where is it? How did the Frenchman and BEEK get the text since FELTRINELLI says he did not provide them with it?

ATTACHMENT "Q"

Article Appearing in _Der Spiegel_ Issue of 29 October 1958 about _Dr. Zhivago_

The article started off by mentioning Soviet tourists who have for several months been visiting the Brussels World Fair and have been in the last few weeks visiting an exhibit of the Vatican which is of particular interest. The Soviet visitors had been interested not so much in the Vatican Church or in the Vatican pavilion, which is called the "Church of the Still" which the Catholic clerics have designated as the clergy in the countries behind the Iron Curtain. The Soviet citizens have gone much more to the pavilion-helpers which they have made plain through words and gestures, but they had come with some mutual reservations. They are in such cases directed after a few discreet steps to the Vatican's Information Office for the Church of the eastern areas and they were greeted by a Slovenian priest who spoke with them awhile in the Russian language. The Soviet guests left with a book under their arm which was given to them as a gift, and this book was not the Bible, but a novel, a Russian edition of the _Dr. Zhivago_ by Boris PASTERNAK which is forbidden in the Soviet Union.

The author was given the Nobel Prize for Literature last Thursday by the Swedish Academy. The sixty-eight year old writer, PASTERNAK, who lives in a villa somewhat near Moscow, wrote _Dr. Zhivago_ over a period of ten years.

The Neue Zuercher Zeitung stated that the book was a very good Russian novel of freedom. It is the only fully free and completely non-censored edition of a Russian's concept of this epic and it is the only worthwhile writing of all the Soviet literature of this year. The book tells the story of a middle-class intellectual, Dr. Yuryi Andreyevich ZHIVAGO, who has maintained an independent critical outlook on the events in Russia from the October Revolution of 1917 to the Stalinist Terror and has changed it happily.

PASTERNAK gave a copy of his manuscript to the Director of the Mailaender Firm, Dr. Giangiacomo FELTRINELLI, and gave him the right for publishing the book in Western countries. After a period of several months, there appeared in the Mailaender Company the Italian; from Gallimard in Paris, the French; and from COLLINS and HARVILLE Press in London, the English edition of _Dr. Zhivago._ At the same time, the German edition appeared in August of this year. Also, the Russian version of Slavic text, the printer and publisher MOUTON in the Hague.

ATTACHMENT "A"

Excerpt from *National Review*, Volume I, No. [illegible], November 15, 1958

"At Home"

Washington

"That quaint workship of amateur subversion, the Central Intelligence Agency, may be exorbitantly expensive -- but from time to time it produces some noteworthy goodies. This summer, for instance, CIA forgot its feud with some of our allies and turned on our enemies -- and *mirabile dictu*, succeeded most nobly.

The Russian text of Boris Pasternak's novel, DOCTOR ZHIVAGO, was recently turned over to a Dutch publisher. [illegible] thousand copies of the book were then quietly shipped to the Vatican pavilion at the Brussels Fair, and there handed out free to visiting Soviet citizens. In Moscow, these books were passed from hand to hand as [illegible] a copy of [illegible] in a college dormitory. The Kremlin, through its ambassador in Italy, protested bitterly to Feltrinelli, who "owns" [illegible] rights to DOCTOR ZHIVAGO -- and last week a suit was filed against the Dutch publisher to force him to cease and desist. But the damage has been done, and the award of a Nobel Prize to Mr. Pasternak was the icing on a cake which Comrade Khrushchev has had some difficulty in digesting.

Soviet discomfiture over Pasternak was [illegible] on a small scale here when the WASHINGTON POST frowned editorially on its erstwhile good friend, Mr. Cyrus Eaton. To the dismay of the let's-[illegible]-to-the-Russians [illegible] in the nation's capital, the POST took [illegible] certain words spoken by Mr. Eaton before a large audience [illegible] National Press Club. The [illegible] industrialist went far beyond [illegible] demands for unilateral [illegible] disarmament, recognition of Red China, and other forms of appeasement. The WASHINGTON POST considers tender solicitude [illegible] American interest a form of pricking "propaganda misconceptions."

Mr. Eaton, however, found it in his over-[illegible] heart to justify the Soviet massacre of Hungary, to depict [illegible] Khrushchev as a man with abounding love for the United States, and to [illegible] the treatment of Mr. Pasternak by the Communists as a demonstration of overzealous patriotism among the Soviet younger generation. The WASHINGTON POST, hardly blushing, remarked: "Some of Mr. Eaton's uncritical observations sound embarrassingly like those of Henry Wallace during his period of [illegible] gullibility about Russia." How true, said the pot to the kettle."

SECRET

25 November 1958

MEMORANDUM FOR: Acting Deputy Director (Plans)

SUBJECT: Publication of the Russian Edition of Dr. Zhivago

1. This memorandum is for information only.

2. SR first became interested in the possibilities of a Russian edition of Pasternak's Dr. Zhivago in the Fall of 1957. In November of that year, Giangiacomo Feltrinelli, an Italian communist publisher, announced that he had obtained the original Russian manuscript from Pasternak and that he would publish it in Italian. Reports [redacted] indicated that the manuscript had been smuggled out of the Soviet Union and that the book probably would not be published in the USSR.

3. In January 1958, [redacted] the original Russian manuscript of Dr. Zhivago. A first reading of the manuscript indicated that this was a great literary work which would produce a psychological impact upon Soviet readers. In the early months of 1958, discussions were held between representatives of SR and IO Divisions and with members of the [redacted] to determine how a Russian edition of the book might be published. It was decided that, if at all possible, the book should be brought out by a legitimate publisher.

4. A considerable effort was made to find such a publisher.

SECRET

e: Seays

16. There have been a number of articles in the European press regarding the mysterious Frenchman, distribution of the book to Soviet visitors at the Vatican Pavilion, and the copies that have been smuggled back into the Soviet Union.

17. The University of Michigan has announced that it will publish a Russian edition of Dr. Zhivago. the Michigan edition will be on the market the first week in December. Michigan University Press will publish the book without having a copyright from Feltrinelli. Kyrill Schabert, President of Pantheon Books, Inc., has engaged a New York lawyer to sue the University for Feltrinelli. Mr. Fred D. Wieck, Director of the University of Michigan Press states, however, that he has been informed by legal counsel (Weil, Gotshal & Manges) that all rights to the book are vested only in Pasternak and that Feltrinelli has no greater copyright than anyone else. Michigan is, therefore, prepared to engage in a legal dispute with Feltrinelli and feels that it will win any suit which Feltrinelli might bring against them.

Acting Chief, SR Division

Page Denied

5. While efforts were being made to find a publisher who could obtain the rights from Feltrinelli, it was decided to explore the possibility of having the manuscript typeset in the United States in order to expedite the publication and make it available for the Brussels Fair. It was felt that the manuscript could be typeset in the U.S. and that photo offset negatives and reproduction proofs could then be sent to a European publisher who had obtained the copyright from Feltrinelli.

7. In June 1958, discussions were held with and the latter stated that he could arrange to have the typesetting completed by 1 August 1958. Representatives of the Commercial Division and the Legal Counselors Office assisted SR in drawing up a contract and in providing us with a New York lawyer, who was to represent the Agency in this project. According to the final contract which was signed by and , the latter was to arrange for the typesetting and manufacture of reproduction proofs and to find and designate a European publisher.

8. completed his first two tasks, but he did not find a European publisher. Contrary to instructions given him, he contacted copy of our reproduction proofs to Upon learning of this, was told that we were deeply concerned about his breach of contract and unethical conduct. He was asked to get the set of reproduction proofs back as soon as possible.

9. Efforts were made to prevent from using our reproduction proofs, and if possible, to prevent or delay any publication of Dr. Zhivago in the Russian language. In August 1958, a representative of SR went out and held discussions with In these discussions, the following reasons were given for not wanting to publish the book:

~~SECRET~~

☐ UNCLASSIFIED ☐ INTERNAL ONLY ☐ CONFIDENTIAL ☐ SECRET

ROUTING AND RECORD SHEET

SUBJECT: (Optional) Dr Zhivago Memo

FROM:

NO.

DATE 25 November 1958

TO: (Officer designation, room number, and building)	DATE RECEIVED	DATE FORWARDED	OFFICER'S INITIALS	COMMENTS (Number each comment to show from whom to whom. Draw a line across column after each comment.)
1. ADD/P	NOV 26 '58			
2.				
3.				ATTACHED
4.				
5. The Director	11/26			1 to 5 These details on the Russian edition of Dr. Zhivago deserve your reading on an FYI basis.
6.				
7. Dr				
8.				
9.				
10.				
11.				
12.				
13.				
14.				
15.				

FORM 1 DEC 56 610 USE PREVIOUS EDITIONS ☐ SECRET ☐ CONFIDENTIAL ☐ INTERNAL USE ONLY ☐ UNCLASSIFIED

a. Publication of the Russian edition of Dr. Zhivago in the U.S. would lessen the effectiveness of the book and would seriously harm relations of the U.S. with other governments involved in this operation.

b. The author, Pasternak, specifically requested that the book not be published in the United States for his personal safety and other reasons.

c. If the book were published by [redacted] the Italian publisher, Feltrinelli, who holds all publishing rights, could bring suit. Lawyers in the publishing business had advised us that Feltrinelli would have good grounds to bring suit against [redacted]

d. We had reason to believe that [redacted] was given reproduction proofs in an unorthodox manner and that these proofs are in fact the property of the U. S. Government.

10. [redacted] agreed not to use our reproduction proofs and to delay publication of the book until after the European edition appeared.

11. In the meantime In July 1958, before completion of the typesetting in New York, we received a report that a Dutch publisher, Mouton, was corresponding with Feltrinelli regarding publication of the Russian edition. [redacted] t Mouton was, in fact, planning to publish the book and that Mouton had a copy of the original Russian manuscript. Reportedly, Mouton also had obtained the Russian copyright from Feltrinelli. Since there was no rights problem, [redacted] Mouton would be willing to publish the book by 15 September if [redacted] It was also requested that [redacted] we obtain the first 1000 copies off the press. Mouton agreed to these conditions. The typesetting was completed in July, [redacted] the negatives and reproduction proofs were forwarded [redacted] on 1 August.

12. The printing of the book was accomplished in early September and we obtained the first thousand copies which were distributed to [redacted] About 500 copies of the book were given to Soviet visitors at the Brussels Fair and the remaining number were distributed to SR assets for covert distribution. It was assumed that Mouton would distribute the remaining number of books through his own normal publishing channels.

13. [redacted] there had been a disagreement between Feltrinelli and Mouton on the handling of the publication. An investigation revealed that an employee of Mouton was supposed to see Feltrinelli at the Frankfurt Book Fair in August to make final arrangements for the publication. The employee failed to see Feltrinelli but, assuming that Feltrinelli would have no objections to the publication, gave his approval for the printing. When Feltrinelli heard that the book was being distributed at the Vatican Pavilion, he immediately labeled it as an illegal edition brought out without his approval.

14. At a press conference in The Hague on 2 November 1958, Feltrinelli elaborated upon how the illegal edition of the book was published. Supposedly, an "unknown Frenchman" gave an employee of Mouton a set of reproduction plates and ordered a thousand copies of the book. These books were than illegally distributed at the Brussels Fair. Feltrinelli announced that Mouton will print for him a new legal edition of the book. This will be a limited edition of 5,000 copies and is scheduled to be on the market on or about 1 January 1959.

Dr. Zhivago

26 November 1958

MEMORANDUM FOR: Acting Chief, SR Division

SUBJECT : Latest Information Regarding [redacted] Russian Edition of Dr. Zhivago

Regarding the [redacted] Russian edition of Dr. Zhivago, the following information was obtained on 26 November 1958 from [redacted]

1. After discussion with a representative of [redacted] edition, [redacted] found out that the binding of the book will not be completed before Monday, 1 December 1958 (or possibly a few days later).

2. Since the binding has not been completed, none of the books have been sent to any distribution points as of this date.

3. [redacted] is attempting to obtain a preliminary hand-bound copy of the book so that we can compare it with the Feltrinelli-Mouton edition.

Chief, SR/2

SR/RP

CLASSIFIED MESSAGE

FILE NO.

S-E-C-R-E-T

ROUTING

1	SR/2	4
2		5
3		6

DATE 29 NOV 58

TO : DIRECTOR

FROM :

ACTION: SR 6

INFO :

RE Filing (check one):
No CS Record Value. Destroy. ☐
RI file this copy as indicated ☑
Branch copy filed as indicated ☐
RE Indexing (check one):

NOV 29 1622Z 58

ROUTINE

TO DIR INFO CITE

REDWOOD AEDINOSAUR PSYCH

1. DE RIDDER MADE COMPARISON RUSSIAN PRINT OF DR ZHIVAGO PLATES FURNISHED BY VAN DER BEEK WITH PRINT OTHER PRESSES IN WEST. DE RIDDER CONVINCED PRINT SIMILAR TO RUSSIAN EDITION CHURCHILL MEMOIRS PUBLISHED AFTER WAR BY NY PRINTER. DE RIDDER THINKS PRINTER WAS SPONSORED BY TOLSTOI FOUNDATION, IS PRESENTLY BANKRUPT AND NO LONGER IN PRINTING BUSINESS.

2. NOT KNOWN WHETHER DE RIDDER HAS INFORMED FELTRINELLI OF ABOVE AND

END OF MESSAGE

RI COPY

ROUTING	INITIAL
RI/AN	
RI/TY	
DESTROY	
RI/FI	

Body-179

S-E-C-R-E-T

FORM 4-58 1389 USE PREVIOUS EDITIONS

Copy No.

FILE NO.

CLASSIFIED MESSAGE

~~S-E-C-R-E-T~~

ORIG :
UNIT :
EXT :
DATE : 10 December 1958

ROUTING
1 SR/2

TO :
FROM : DIRECTOR
CONF: SR 6
INFO :

RE Filing (check one): No CS Record Value. Destroy. RI file this copy as indicated. Branch copy filed as indicated
RE Indexing (check one): Marked / None required
Signature:

DEFERRED — DEC 10 23 06 z58
ROUTINE — REC'D CABLE SECT.
X PRIORITY — INITIALS
OPERATIONAL IMMEDIATE — INITIALS

O INFO CITE DIR

REDWOOD PSYCH

REF A.

B.

1. APPROVE NEGOTIATE

2. HQS WILLING PURCHASE TWO THOUSAND COPIES.

3. FYI DEPENDING UPON PRICE, MAY PURCHASE ADDITIONAL ONE OR TWO THOUSAND COPIES AFTER RUSSIAN EDITION PUBLISHED.

END OF MESSAGE

C/S COMMENT: *CONCERNED HQS PLANS TO PUBLISHING RUSSIAN EDITION OF PASTERNAK AUTOBIOGRAPHY.

ROUTING	INITIAL
RI/AN	
RI/TY	
~~DESTROY~~	
RI/FI	

~~S-E-C-R-E-T~~

FORM 4-58 1389a REPRODUCTION BY OTHER THAN THE ISSUING OFFICE IS PROHIBITED. Copy No.

U. S. GOVERNMENT PRINTING OFFICE : 1958 O—465031 (35)

NEA

DISPATCH

CLASSIFICATION: ~~CONFIDENTIAL~~

DISPATCH SYMBOL AND NO.

TO: Chief, NEA

INFO: Chief, SR

HEADQUARTERS FILE NO.

FROM:

DATE: 12 December 1958

SUBJECT: REDWOOD/PSYCH
Comments on Russian Publication of "Dr. Zhivago"

RE: "43-3" — (CHECK "X" ONE)
MARKED FOR INDEXING
NO INDEXING REQUIRED
INDEXING CAN BE JUDGED BY QUALIFIED HQ. DESK ONLY

ACTION REQUIRED

REFERENCE(S)

1. 26 November 1958

2. In Para. 3 of the attached memo mentions that he has promised a Russian language copy of "Dr. Zhivago" to and also to . Inasmuch as Para. 4 of ref states that the book being transmitted per ref should not be given by Americans directly to Soviets we are asking that Headquarters forward by air parcel post two copies of the Russian language edition published by Prompt compliance with this request will be appreciated.

Enclosure:
Memo as above

11 December 1958

Distribution:
2-NEA w/encl in dupl
3-SR w/encl in sc
2- w/encl

CS COPY

(b)(1)
(b)(3)

Body-181

FORM 10-57 53 (40) USE PREVIOUS EDITION. REPLACES FORMS 51-28, 51-28A AND 51-29 WHICH ARE OBSOLETE.

CLASSIFICATION: ~~CONFIDENTIAL~~

CONTINUED

~~CONFIDENTIAL~~

MEMO: Re Russian Language Copies of Dr. Zhivago 10 Dec 1958

1. Ref dispatch assumes that the only copies available in the USSR are those from the Brussels Fair, or those of the illegal edition otherwise distributed in Western Europe. I doubt if this is correct, I assume it has been read in a Moscow Russian edition by a large number of Soviet officials.

the normal procedure for a Russian book of serious interest is:

A. Pre-screening while it is still in galley. Dr. Zhivago survived this stage, where most objectionable books are caught.

B. Printing of what he calls a "pilot" edition, direct from corrected galleys, soft cover binding, fair paper. Normally this pilot edition is in about 100 copies, but in the case of a book like this, at least 500 and perhaps 1000 would be run off and distributed quite widely and passed on from one person to another.

C. After this pilot copy review, the book is revised, if necessary, and run off in the regular way.

2. Soviets are aware that University of Michigan Press announced publication Russian language edition, for sale early December. This was in all book trade magazines and also mentioned in Edmund Wilson's review in the New Yorker, Nov 15, 1958.

3. I have already given an English language copy, and have promised him and a Russian language copy when received.

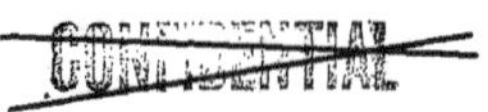

~~SECRET~~
(WHEN FILLED IN)

ROUTING AND RECORD SHEET

INSTRUCTIONS: Use officer designations in the "TO" column. Number each comment to correspond with the number in the "TO" column. Draw a line across the sheet under each comment. Each officer should date and initial (check mark insufficient) before further routing. This Routing and Record sheet should NOT be removed from the attached RECORD document.

FROM: RI/ RI/AN

DOCUMENT NUMBER

DOCUMENT DATE

1

TO	ROOM NO.	DATE RECEIVED	DATE FORWARDED	OFFICER'S INITIALS
1.		24 DEC 1958		
2.				
3.				
4.				
5.				
6.				
7.				
8.				
9.				
10.				
11.				
12.				
13.				
14. RI/FI				

COMMENTS

NOTE: If a copy or attachments are removed from the attached document, note the location of the copy and/or attachment hereon. If this RECORD COPY is to be retained in the files at the Desk, call the Central File Section for permanent loan.

1 CC retained in SR/2/PP

FILE TITLE

FILE NUMBER

ENCLOSURE

ABSTRACT X

INDEX

DATE PROCESSED Bucy-183
12 Dec 68

FORM NO. 1 OCT. 55 610a

~~SECRET~~

d. Special care should be taken in concealing the book at border points and inside the USSR.

e. It is better to give the book to travelers going by air since the likelihood of getting the book through is much greater than if it is taken in by train.

5. We would appreciate knowing how many of the books have been given to Soviet citizens and any of their reactions. Additional books can be ordered directly from Mouton & Co. Herderstraat 5, The Hague Netherlands. A new legal edition will be ready around 1 January 1959. If it is difficult for the [redacted] to order additional copies, Headquarters can assist in obtaining them.

18 November 1958

Attachments: s/c
Books

Distribution:

CS COPY

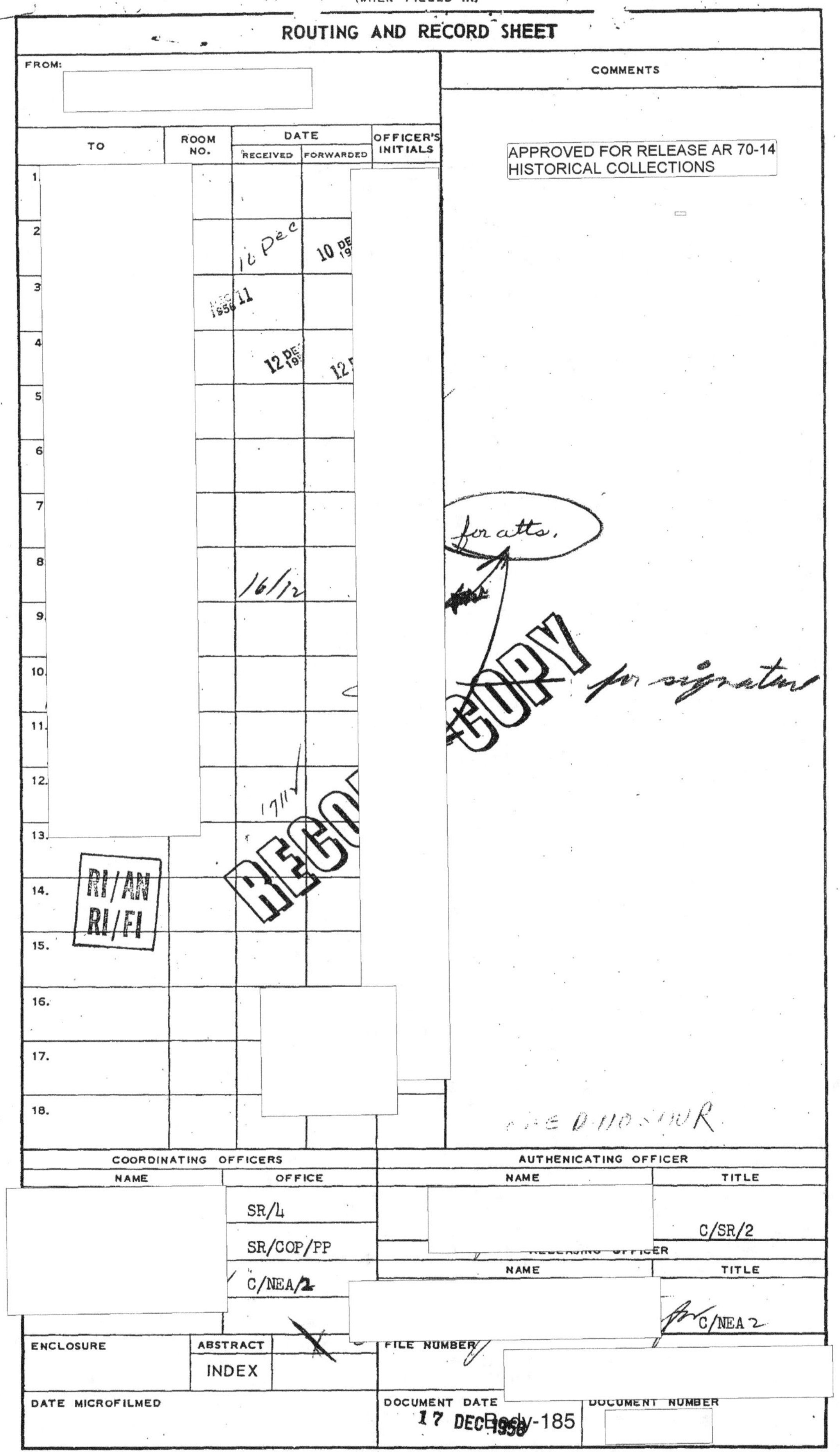

ROUTING AND RECORD SHEET

FROM:

TO	ROOM NO.	DATE RECEIVED	DATE FORWARDED	OFFICER'S INITIALS
1.				
2.		12 Dec	10 DEC	
3.		11 1956		
4.		12 DEC	12	
5.				
6.				
7.				
8.		16/12		
9.				
10.				
11.				
12.		17/12		
13.				
14. RI/AN				
15. RI/FI				
16.				
17.				
18.				

COMMENTS

for atts.

RECORD COPY

for signature

COORDINATING OFFICERS NAME	OFFICE
	SR/4
	SR/COP/PP
	C/NEA/2

AUTHENTICATING OFFICER NAME	TITLE
	C/SR/2

RELEASING OFFICER NAME	TITLE
	for C/NEA 2

ENCLOSURE | ABSTRACT | INDEX | FILE NUMBER

DATE MICROFILMED | DOCUMENT DATE 17 DEC 1956 | DOCUMENT NUMBER

Body-185

FORM 3-58 610b

DISPATCH — SECRET

TO: [redacted]

FROM: Chief, SR

DATE: 17 DEC 1958

SUBJECT: REDWOOD/PSYCH
Distribution of Russian copies of Dr. Zhivago.

RE: "43-3" — (CHECK "X" ONE)
MARKED FOR INDEXING
NO INDEXING REQUIRED
INDEXING CAN BE JUDGED BY QUALIFIED HQ. DESK ONLY

1. We are forwarding under separate cover 9 copies of the Russian edition of Dr. Zhivago. We regret that we cannot send you the number of copies requested but this is all the number that are available at Headquarters.

2. As you know, the whole Soviet treatment of the Pasternak affair has already made the author a symbol of the Soviet intellectuals' aspirations for creative freedom. [redacted] there has been a student demonstration in Moscow University regarding the regime's censorship of the book. Other reports indicate that a number of Soviet intellectuals and students have been desperately attempting to get copies of the book.

3. Because of the inherent value of the book to a Soviet reader and because of the broader problem that it presents to the regime, we would like to make the book available to as many Soviet readers as possible. For various reasons, however, the book must be handled with great care. As a result of the dispute between Feltrinelli and Mouton, the Dutch publisher, the book was published as an illegal edition. About 500 copies of the book were then distributed to Soviet visitors at the Brussels Fair. Articles in the West European press made it known that Soviet visitors were obtaining these copies; we may, therefore, assume that Soviet authorities are aware of the fact that a certain number of the books have already been taken into the USSR and that efforts may be made to smuggle in other books. Soviet customs officials may have been instructed to search travelers' baggage for this particularly hot item.

4. To avoid having the book confiscated and to prevent Soviet authorities linking the book to [redacted] the following precautions should be taken in distributing it:

a. The [redacted] should provide travelers or agents with a good cover story regarding the source of the book. Under no circumstances should the traveler say that the book came from an American official. The following are a few stories which might be used:

(1) The book was bought from a Russian emigre in a city where the traveler had been before he went to the Soviet Union.

(2) The book was obtained from someone who got it at the Brussels Fair.

(3) It was bought at a Russian book store in [redacted] [redacted] etc.

b. The book should only be given to reliable travelers or agents.

c. For the time being, it should not be given to American travelers going to the USSR; nor should Americans give it directly to Soviet officials or visitors.

CS COPY

FORM 10-57 53b (40) USE PREVIOUS EDITION. REPLACES FORMS 51-28, 51-28A AND 51-29 WHICH ARE OBSOLETE. CLASSIFICATION SECRET Body 186 CONTINUED PAGE NO.

CLASSIFIED MESSAGE

~~S-E-C-R-E-T~~

FILE NO

ROUTING

1	SR/3	4	
2		5	
3		6	

DATE : 17 DEC 58

DEC 17 2013Z 58

TO : DIRECTOR

FROM :

ACTION: SR 6

INFO

RE Filing (check one):
No CS Record Value. Destroy. ☐
RI file this copy as indicated ☑
Branch copy filed as indicated ☐
RE Indexing (check one):
Marked ☐
Signature:

PRIORITY

TO DIR INFO CITE

REDWOOD PSYCH

RE

file Dr Z

1. FIRM HAS COPY OF RUSSIAN TEXT BUT ONLY RIGHTS FOR FRENCH EDITION. RUSSIAN RIGHTS REST WITH FELTRINELLI WHO PLANS PUBLISH BUT DATE UNKNOWN .

2. NEXT STEP MAY BE APPROACH FELTRINELLI VERIFY STATEMENT AND IF NECESSARY OFFER INDUCEMENTS ASSURE PUBLICATION. REALIZE HE MAY REFUSE OR USE DELAYING TACTICS. THIS FOR HQS. DECISION AND ACTION.

3. IF ABOVE IMPRACTICAL AND YOU DESIRE PUBLISH UNAUTHORIZED EDITION WILL ATTEMPT TAKE STEPS PROVIDE PUBLISHER HERE WHO WILLING LEND HIS NAME AND REASONABLY "JUDGMENT PROOF". SAME COMPANY COULD PUBLISH POCKET EDITION DR. ZHIVACO.

END OF MESSAGE

C/S COMMENT: *APPROVED NEGOTIATE .

RI COPY

ROUTING	INITIAL
RI/AN	
RI/TY	
~~DESTROY~~	
RI/FI	

~~S-E-C-R-E-T~~

FY 1959 be made available to cover an advance for the cost of procurement of 515 copies of the Russian-language edition of Dr. Zhivago for Headquarters distribution to the area divisions. Accounting will be in accordance with Agency Regulation. At the time of distribution to the area divisions at Headquarters, [redacted] will apportion costs and charge each division for its share. Area divisions involved have agreed to pay their proportionate shares of this shipment and [redacted] accordingly will be credited with little (if any) final cost.

5. [redacted] Division requires 1,600 additional copies of this edition for its own purposes, but is using other means of financing the purchase.

6. The edition is not to be confused with a Russian-language edition published by [redacted] at an announced retail price of [redacted]

/S/

APPROVED:

(Signed) [redacted]

Chief, [redacted]

7 JAN 1959

Date

Dr. Zhivago

Memo

5 January 1959

MEMORANDUM FOR: [redacted]

SUBJECT: Operational Funds for Purchase and Distribution of 515 copies of Russian-Language Dutch-Manufactured Edition of Dr. Zhivago

REFERENCES: a. Project [redacted] FY 1959

b. Memorandum for [redacted] dated 21 November 1958, concerning 40 copies of the British Edition

c. Memorandum for [redacted] dated 21 November 1958, concerning 640 copies of the British Edition.

1. This memorandum proposes approval of the recommendation contained in paragraph 4.

2. The [redacted] desires to acquire 515 copies of the Russian-language Dutch-manufactured edition of Dr. Zhivago by the most expeditious means in order to distribute them to [redacted] It has been determined that attempting to acquire this number of books through [redacted] would impose an undue burden, apart from the security considerations involved. (The Italian publisher, Giangiacomo Feltrinelli, is believed to have told the Dutch printer and publisher that he will veto any large order that smacks of intelligence exploitation of this edition.)

3. Pantheon Books, Inc., of New York, publishers of the American edition, has recently advertised that it will accept orders for the Dutch-made edition. This Division has discussed the matter with IO Division [redacted] The stated retail price is [redacted] and some discount for an order of this size may bring the single-copy price down to [redacted] We propose, therefore, to ask that IO Division acquire, through a secure channel, these 515 copies at an approximate cost of [redacted] per copy, or [redacted] will need an advance of funds to do this.

4. It is recommended that out of the [redacted] the sum of [redacted] for

26 January 1959

MEMORANDUM FOR: [redacted]

SUBJECT: Mouton edition of Dr. Zhivago

1. In accordance with your request, I asked [redacted] to order, through Pantheon in New York, 515 copies of the forthcoming Mouton local edition of Dr. Zhivago.

2. I am informed by [redacted] that Pantheon knows nothing whatever about any such edition. [redacted] has also heard through some other channel that the Mouton edition will not be available until late Spring.

3. Assuming the edition does come out as expected, we may anticipate a certain amount of trouble in bringing to the United States such a large number of copies in view of a conflict with rights apparently granted to the University of Michigan for sale in this country. The fact is, of course, that the 515 copies in question would be obtained for us [redacted] as a logistical service, and that they would not be resold. However, [redacted] might have a certain amount of difficulty in explaining to the U.S. customs authorities what they were going to do with them.

4. Under the circumstances, I have asked [redacted] to do nothing further about ordering from Mouton until further word from us. If we consider it advisable, [redacted] will proceed and will take their chances with the U.S. customs.

5. Please let me know what the next move is.

[redacted] (26 Jan. 1959)
Distribution:
2 - Addressee
1 - RI
3 - [redacted]

~~SECRET~~

c. Likelihood of suit by Feltrinelli.

d. [redacted] was in possession of stolen U.S. property.

9. [redacted] and latter [redacted] agreed not to use our reproduction proofs and to delay publication of the book until after the European edition appeared.

10. In the meantime we got word [redacted] about Dutch publisher, Mouton, corresponding with Feltrinelli, etc. Agreement is made for first thousand copies of the book.

11. We obtain first ###### thousand copies of the book off the press and of these send 500 copies to the Brussels Fair.

12. On October 9 [redacted] reported disagreement between Feltrinelli and Mouton. Feltrinelli labels book being distributed at Vatican Pavalion illegal edition.

13. 2 November 1958 Feltrinelli holds press conference in the Hague and elaborates upon the illegal edition of the book. "An unknown French man came to Mouton and ordered 1,000 copies of the book."

14. To bring about quick settlement of dispute between Feltrinelli and Mouton we ask [redacted] to order several thousand copies from Mouton. Also settlement out of court.

Feb 3 59

SUBJECT: The Story of Dr. Zhivago

1. We first became interested in the possibilities of a Russian edition of Pasternak's Dr. Zhivago in the fall of 1957. Feltrinelli Report, smuggled out

2. In January 1958 [redacted] provided us with a photostateof the manuscript. Discussions held between representatives of [redacted] and the [redacted] to determine how a Russian edition of the book might be published--if at all possible through a legitimate publisher.

3. Efforts to find publisher. [redacted]

4. While efforts were being made to find a publisher we decided to explore the possibility of having manuscript typeset in the U.S. in order to exploit the publication.

5. The Office of Security offers us a knight in sterling armor. [redacted] [redacted]

6. Negotiations with [redacted] New York lawyer and signing of contract for typesetting and manufacture of reproduction proofs and to find European publisher.

7. [redacted] completes first two tasks in time alloted but does not find European publisheer. On the contrary takes page proofs to [redacted] [redacted].

8, Efforts to prevent [redacted] from using our peproduction proofs. Trip [redacted] in August. Discussions with [redacted] Reasons given for not wanting [redacted] to publish the book.

a. Seriously harm relations ~~of the~~ U.S. with other governments involved.

b. The author specifically requested that it not be published in U.S.

DISPATCH

CLASSIFICATION: SECRET

DISPATCH SYMBOL AND NO.

HEADQUARTERS FILE NO.

TO: Chief, SR

INFO: Chief, NEA
Chief, FE

FROM:

DATE: 27 February 1959

SUBJECT: REDWOOD/PSYCH
Passing of Russian Copy of Dr. ZHIVAGO to

RE: "43-3" — (CHECK "X" ONE)
MARKED FOR INDEXING
NO INDEXING REQUIRED
INDEXING CAN BE JUDGED BY QUALIFIED HQ. DESK ONLY

ACTION REQUIRED: For your information

REFERENCE(S): , 28 November 1958

2. had previously lent an English translation of the book to and she asked if she might pass it on to some of her friends. said she was certainly free to do so and suggested in a joking manner that she give the book to one of her Russian friends in the Soviet Embassy to read and discuss. She took the book and nothing more was said until, having had the book for several weeks, stopped at house one day to tell him that she still had the book and intended to return it very soon. told her not to worry because he had written to a friend of his in the States requesting an additional copy.

3. On the 18th when came to , conversation was entirely in a light vein until just before they were to depart. then told that he had received his additional copy of Dr. Zhivago and asked her if she would trade copies with him since the new copy was discovered to have been printed in the Russian language. friend had sent the book on with a note stating that English language copies were unavailable and so he sent on a copy which he had obtained at the Brussels Fair in the hope could use it. said he was about to return the book when he remembered and the previous discussion concerning passing the book to the Russians. suggested that she pass the book on to one of her acquaintances and then discuss it with him or her later on. She was cautioned not to mention that she had obtained the book from an American as it might appear to the Russians to be an act of provocation which might cause her embarrassment. It was explained to her that she could tell them that went to the Brussels Fair and purchased the copy which she then forwarded to her accepted the idea with enthusiasm and said she would give the book to both a Soviet and White Russian and then compare their reactions, after which she would discuss it with . We have no idea to whom will give the book but we will keep you advised when she discusses the matter with us.

27 February 1959

Distribution:

2 SR 2 FE
2 NEA 2

FORM 10-57 53 (40) USE PREVIOUS EDITION. REPLACES FORMS 51-28, 51-28A AND 51-29 WHICH ARE OBSOLETE.

CLASSIFICATION: SECRET

CONTINUED

SECRET
(WHEN FILLED IN)

ROUTING AND RECORD SHEET

INSTRUCTIONS: Use officer designations in the "TO" column. Number each comment to correspond with the number in the "TO" column. Draw a line across the sheet under each comment. Each officer should date and initial (check mark insufficient) before further routing. This Routing and Record sheet should NOT be removed from the attached RECORD document.

FROM:  RI/AN

DOCUMENT NUMBER

DOCUMENT DATE

TO	ROOM NO.	DATE RECEIVED	DATE FORWARDED	OFFICER'S INITIALS
1.		12 MAR 1959	16 MAR 1959	
		17 MAR 1959		
		25 MAR 1959		
10.				
11.				
12.				
13.				
14. RI/FI				

COMMENTS

NOTE: If a copy or attachments are removed from the attached document, note the location of the copy and/or attachment hereon. If this RECORD COPY is to be retained in the files at the Desk, call the Central File Section for permanent loan.

FILE TITLE

FILE NUMBER

ENCLOSURE

ABSTRACT

INDEX

DATE PROCESSED 27 Feb 1959

FORM NO. 610a
1 OCT. 55

SECRET

ROUTING AND RECORD SHEET

FROM:

TO	ROOM NO.	DATE RECEIVED	DATE FORWARDED	OFFICER'S INITIALS
1. C/WE/3			4 MAR 1959	
2.				
3. ~~C/WE~~				
4.				
5.				
6. RI/DP		5/3		
7.				
8.				
9.				
10.				
11.				
12. RI/AN RI/FI				
13.				
14.				
15. ~~RI/D&P~~				
16.				
17.				
18.				

COMMENTS

Sep Cover Attachment
Back Sea Pouch.

AEDINOSAUR

COORDINATING OFFICERS NAME	OFFICE

AUTHENTICATING OFFICER NAME	TITLE
	C/WE/3

RELEASING OFFICER NAME	TITLE

ENCLOSURE: copies of Dr. Zhivago

ABSTRACT | INDEX

DATE MICROFILMED

DOCUMENT DATE: 4 March 1959 / 5 MAR 1959

DOCUMENT NUMBER:

FORM 3-58 610b

DISPATCH	CLASSIFICATION ~~SECRET~~	DISPATCH SYMBOL AND NO.
TO INFO		HEADQUARTERS FILE NO.
FROM Chief, WE		DATE MAR 1959
SUBJECT Operational Transmittal of Dr. Zhivago		RE: "43-3" — (CHECK "X" ONE) MARKED FOR INDEXING X NO INDEXING REQUIRED INDEXING CAN BE JUDGED BY QUALIFIED HQ. DESK ONLY
ACTION REQUIRED Possible action.		
REFERENCE(S)		

Attached are ~~eight~~ ten copies of Dr. Zhivago in the Russian language. These are sent for possible use in connection with any Soviet contacts the station either now has or will in the future establish.

4 March 1959

Attachments: Under Separate Cover, sea pouch,
copies of Dr. Zhivago

Distribution:
3 - w/atts. U.S.C.
2 - WE/3 w/o/atts.
1 - RI w/o/atts.

CS COPY

5 Mar 59

FORM 10-57 53 (40) USE PREVIOUS EDITION. REPLACES FORMS 51-28, 51-28A AND 51-29 WHICH ARE OBSOLETE. CLASSIFICATION ~~SECRET~~ Body-196 CONTINUED

Country	Publisher	Language	Form of Publication	Date of Publication	Rights
Iran	Etelaat, Tehran Journal	Persian	serial	Nov.'58	No
Iran	Tehran Journal, Tehran	English	serial	Nov.'58	No
Iran	Roshanfekr, Tehran Magazine	Persian	excerpts	Dec.'58	No
	6. Western Hemisphere				
United States	Pantheon Books, Inc., New York	English	book	7 Sept.'58	Yes
United States	University of Michigan Press, Ann Arbor, Mich.	Russian	book	Feb.'59	Yes
Mexico	Editorial Noguer, Mexico City and Barcelona, Spain	Spanish	book	Oct.'58	Yes
Argentina	Editorial Forjador, Buenos Aires	Spanish	book	Dec.'58	No
Argentina	Editorial Quetzal, no city of publication given	Spanish	condensation	Dec.'58	No
Argentina	El Nacional, Buenos Aires Newspaper	Spanish	serial	Nov.'58	Yes
Cuba	El Excelsior, Havana Newspaper	Spanish	serial	Nov.'58	Not known
El Salvador	La Prensa Grafica, San Salvador	Spanish	condensation	Dec.'58	Yes
Venezuela	La Esfera, Caracas Newspaper	Spanish	serial	Nov.'58	No
Brazil	Editora Itatiaia Belo Horizonte	Portuguese	book	Dec.58	Yes
Brazil	Ultima Hora, Rio de Janeiro and Sao Paulo, Newspaper.	Portuguese	serial	Feb.'59	Yes

23 March 1959

MEMORANDUM FOR THE RECORD

SUBJECT: Editions of Dr. Zhivago

REFERENCE: Memorandum for the Record, dated 21 November 1958, subject: "Publication of Dr. Zhivago

1. Since October 1958, Dr. Zhivago by Boris Pasternak has been published in book form in Spanish, Russian, Hebrew, Arabic and Urdu, and serially in a number of other languages, including Turkish and Thai. What follows is a revised list of publications, actual or planned, in all countries known to this Division to date.

2. The first edition anywhere was published in Milan, Italy, by Giangiacomo Feltrinelli, Via Andegari 6, Milan, who claimed world copyright for the book. Feltrinelli has sold publication rights for various languages in a score of countries, either directly or through publishers who got on his bandwagon early, such as William Collins of London.

3. Europe

Country	Publisher	Language	Form of Publication	Date of Publication	Right
Great Britain	Collins & Harvill Press, London	English	book	4 Sept.'58	Yes
France	Gallimard & Co., Paris	French	book	Aug.'58	Yes
France	Kultura, Paris	Polish	book	Spring '59	Yes
Italy	Feltrinelli (see para 2 above)	Italian	book	Nov.'57	Yes
West Germany	S.Fischer Verlag Frankfurt/Main	German	book	Nov.'58	Yes
Denmark	Gyldendal Press, Copenhagen	Danish	book	Oct.'58	Yes
Finland	Tammi O/Y (Social-Democratic Co-Op Publisher), Helsinki	Finnish	book	Dec.'58	Yes

~~SECRET~~

Country	Publisher	Language	Form of Publication	Date of Publication	Rights
Iceland	Almenna Bokavelagid, Reykjavik	Icelandic	book	Spring '59	Yes
Norway	Gyldendal Norsk Forlag, Oslo	Norwegian	book	Nov.'58	Yes
Sweden	Albert Bonnier, Stockholm	Swedish	book	Oct.'58	Yes
Netherlands	Mouton & Co., Herderstraat 5, The Hague	Russian	book	Sept.'58	No
Netherlands	Mouton & Co., Herderstraat 5, The Hague	Russian	book	Spring '59	Yes
Greece	John Yerolimbos, Athens	Greek	condensation	Nov.'58	No
Greece	Kathimeri, Athens Newspaper	Greek	serial	April '58	No
Turkey	Cumhuriyet, Istanbul	Turkish	serial	March '59	No
Poland	Opinie, Warsaw Literary Journal	Polish	excerpts	late '57	Not known
Yugoslavia	Petar Zivanovic, v-p of semi-official publishing house	Serbian	book	Indefinite because of apparent Soviet pressure	Not known

3. **Near East**

Country	Publisher	Language	Form of Publication	Date of Publication	Rights
Lebanon	Dar Al Thaqafa, Beirut	Arabic	book	Feb.'59	Yes
Lebanon	Baalbaki, Beirut	Arabic	condensation	1958	No
Egypt	Al Bulis, Cairo Police Magazine	Arabic	serial	Nov.'58	Not known
Egypt	Al-Jumhuriyah, Cairo Gov't Newspaper	Arabic	serial	Mar.'59	Not known
Israel	Am Oved, Tel Aviv	Hebrew	book	Nov.'58	Not known

Announcement of the Egyptian government daily's intention to publish the novel was made 16 March, shortly after President Nasser and Premier Khrushchev began airing their differences in public.

5. Asia

Country	Publisher	Language	Form of Publication	Date of Publication	Rights
Japan	Jiji Tsushin-sha, Tokyo	Japanese	2-vol.book	Mar.'59	Yes
Japan	Sekai Shuho, Tokyo Magazine	Japanese	serial	Nov.'58	No
Hong Kong	Hong Kong Times	Chinese	serial	Nov.'58	Not known
Hong Kong	Chen Pao (Truth Daily)	Chinese	serial	Nov.'58	No
Hong Kong	China Daily Mail	English	condensed serial	Nov.'58	Not known
Singapore	Straits Times, Newspaper	English	serial	Nov.'58	No
Indonesia	Pembangunan, Djakarta	Indonesian	still in talking stage		Not known
Thailand	Siam Nikorn, Bangkok Daily Newspaper	Thai	serial	Nov.'58	No
Viet Nam	Front for Defense of Cultural Freedom in Viet Nam, Saigon	Vietnamese	book	Summer '59	Yes
Viet Nam	Cach Mang Quoc Gia, Saigon Newspaper	Vietnamese	serial	Nov.'58	No
Viet Nam	Tu Do, Saigon Newspaper	Vietnamese	excerpts	Nov.'58	No
Viet Nam	Committee for Supporting Anti-Communist Movement in North Viet nam, Saigon	Vietnamese	picture book		No.
Ceylon	Colombo Newspaper	English	condensed serial	Nov.'58	No
Pakistan	Translux, Karachi	Urdu	book	Jan.'59	Yes

~~SECRET~~

27 March 1959

MEMORANDUM FOR THE RECORD

SUBJECT: Exploitation of Dr. Zhivago

1. At the time of the OCB agreement that [redacted] would not exploit the publication of Dr. Zhivago, the position of Boris Pasternak, its author, was such that any obvious cold-war association of Pasternak with the West brought with it a risk of personal reprisal against him or his family.

2. It was decided that exploitation of Dr. Zhivago would be undertaken solely by this Agency, because of the sensitivity of the operation, and that the hand of the United States Government should not be shown in any manner. [redacted]

3. This Agency has proceeded, in line with this directive to exploit Dr. Zhivago where it has proved feasible to do so, bearing in mind the security considerations.

4. In one form or another, including full-length and condensed books and serials in indigenous languages, this book has been spread throughout the world, with assistance from this Agency in a number of areas where interest might not normally be great. [redacted]

reviews and critical articles on the book and its author, including a long article, with pictures of Pasternak and the British edition, in Blitz, a pro-Soviet English-language magazine. This article, while anti-Pasternak, revealed by its appearance that interest in Dr. Zhivago was widespread [redacted].

~~SECRET~~

10. Meanwhile a new attempt to get a cheap [redacted] export edition [redacted] is being made. Although cheap, it would be a full-length edition. The full-length edition is preferable because the promotion of this book is as literature, not as cold-war propaganda, in line with the original verbal policy guide lines.

11. SR Division believes that the original premise on which the clandestine exploitation of Dr. Zhivago was launched is no longer valid, namely, the possibility of personal reprisal against Pasternak or his family. SR Division's view is that the world-wide discussion of the book and Pasternak's own subsequent statements have shown that his personal position has not become worse. In other words, an all-out overt exploitation of Dr. Zhivago would not harm Pasternak, more than he has already harmed himself. If there is no longer any personal danger to the author, it may be well to review the OCB policy decision to determine whether [redacted] should not now begin to exploit the book as literature.

12. I would therefore recommend that

a. The original policy on which exploitation of Dr. Zhivago was based be reviewed at the appropriate level;

SECRET

b. Overt U.S. exploitation of this book be made on the basis of a full-length edition in English

c. No attempt be made to put out a U.S.-sponsored abridged edition, which would become a cold-war article no matter how painstakingly it was edited.

Distribution:

Orig -
1 -
1 -
1 -
1 -
1 - clipboard
1 - chrono

4

SECRET

7. In other areas of the world, in which [redacted] was anxious to have Dr. Zhivago published, the area divisions were canvassed for their reactions. The areas have since been partially or wholly covered by indigenous publication, although not in the range of languages desired [redacted] Nevertheless, in the judgment of those in this Agency who know the field best, there has been adequate if not thorough coverage. Moreover, those indigenous publishers who could make a commercial go of this book in their own languages have, by and large, done so. [redacted]

by American travelers or officials. It would be quite natural for an American who speaks or reads Russian to be carrying and reading the book which has been number one on the best seller list for the past three months. He can always say that he purchased it before he left for his trip, or in the case of an official in Western Europe, that he received it from a friend in the U.S. For travelers who do not know a few words of Russian to justify their possession of the book, the Pantheon or Collins English edition can be used.

5. Besides the Michigan edition, we are producing at Headquarters a miniature edition intended exclusively for clandestine distribution. It will appear as one or two volumes and should be completed around 15 April. We believe that because of its small size and ease of concealment this will be the best edition to give travelers going to the Soviet Union. We also intend to use this edition in contacts with Soviets abroad, particularly at the Vienna Festival. In passing the miniature edition, travelers can say that they purchased it [redacted] or obtained it from someone who in turn bought it [redacted]. Copies of this edition will be forwarded to you when they are completed.

6. We feel that Dr. Zhivago is an excellent springboard for conversations with Soviets on the general theme of "Communism versus Freedom of Expression". Travelers should be prepared to discuss with their Soviet contacts not only the basic theme of the book itself--a cry for the freedom and dignity of the individual--but also the plight of the intellectual in the communist society. The whole Pasternak affair is indeed a tragic but classic example of the system of thought control which the party has always used to maintain its position of power over the intellectual. Like jamming, censorship, and the party ideological decrees for writers and artists, the banning of this book is another example of the means which the regime must use to control the Soviet mind. It is a reflection of the "Nekul'turnost'" the intellectual barbarity, and the cultural sterility which are features of the closed society.

7. In discussing the Pasternak affair with Soviets we would like to stimulate their thinking and raise doubts about the tenets of "socialist realism" and the need for ideological controls over the artist. Perhaps a good opening to such conversations is to ask the Soviet interlocutor about the latest developments in Soviet drama, poetry, art, etc. A sympathetic but curious attitude toward the innovations and trends in the Soviet artistic world will usually set a friendly tone for the conversation. After discussing the latest artistic developments, a Westerner can inquire about what makes the works of Soviet writers such as Sholokhov, Pasternak, Magarita Aliger, Fedin, Leonid, and Katayev as great as they are. After discussing the works of these writers, he can ask what limits the party has placed upon artistic works. He can then ask why there should be any ideological limits or control over artistic expression, pointing out that the Westerner conceives of art as an activity in which the artist is constantly seeking new horizons. If he is not free to move in his chosen directions, the artist becomes atrophied and can no longer produce really creative works. He can ask why the writers and artists can sing only the praises of the communist system which the party seems to demand of them. He can point out that a true artist must be free to speak of the ideals as well as the iniquities of any society, to critize capitalism or communism, in short to say what he believes to be the truth. A number of American and European writers such as Steinback, John dos Pasos, Upton Sinclair, Sinclair Lewis, Sartre, Camus, Alberto Moravia, Stephen Spender, and others have criticized as well as defended various aspects of life in their home countries. In the last analysis this is all that the great artists such as Pasternak and Sholokhov have asked of the regime. To deny them the freedom to express their ideas and convictions is an admission of the regime's weakness and fear of the intelligentsia.

CS COPY

CONTINUATION OF DISPATCH	CLASSIFICATION ~~S-E-C-R-E-T~~	DISPATCH SYMBOL AND NO.

8. Soviets can be asked why they are not permitted to read Dr. Zhivago or any other literary work and judge its value for themselves. If the communist society is superior to any Western society, as its advocates claim, one may legitimately ask why it attempts to prevent the exchange of ideas whether they originate inside or outside the Soviet Union. Why, too, does the regime prohibit the import of most foreign journals and books? Surely after forty years of communism Soviet citizens should be mature enough to make up their own minds about what is good and bad art. In many cases answers to the above questions will be given according to the party line, but it may be worth posing them as a way of stimulating thought and raising doubts about the position of the intellectual in the communist society.

9. The above is not meant to be a diatribe on the subject of "Communism versus Freedom of Expression". It is obviously an over-simplification of an important but over-whelming theme. We include our thoughts here in the hope that they may be of some use in briefing travelers or officials who will have an opportunity to discuss Dr. Zhivago and the plight of the intellectuals with Soviets. We would appreciate any of the field's comments or suggestions for exploiting this subject. We would also like to know how many of the books have been given to Soviet citizens and their reactions to it.

27 March 1959

Enclosure: s/c
As stated above

Distribution:
3 -
2 -
2 -
1 - RI

CS COPY

FORM 10-57 53a (40)	USE PREVIOUS EDITION. REPLACES FORMS 51-28, 51-28A AND 51-29 WHICH ARE OBSOLETE.	CLASSIFICATION ~~S-E-C-R-E-T~~	CONTINUED	PAGE NO. 3

SECRET

ROUTING AND RECORD SHEET

FROM:

TO	ROOM NO.	DATE RECEIVED	DATE FORWARDED	OFFICER'S INITIALS	COMMENTS
1.			27 MAR 1959		
2.					
3.					
4.			MAR 30 1959		
5.					
6.					
7.					
8.		31 MAR 1959			
9.					
10.		1 APR 1959			
11.					
12.					
13. RI/D&P					
14. RI/AN					
15. RI/FI					
16.					
17.					
18.					"AC Dinosaur"

RECORD COPY

COORDINATING OFFICERS NAME	OFFICE
	SR/COP/PP
	WE/4

AUTHENICATING OFFICER NAME	TITLE
	C/SR/2

RELEASING OFFICER NAME	TITLE

ENCLOSURE	ABSTRACT	FILE NUMBER
Books	INDEX X	

DATE MICROFILMED	DOCUMENT DATE	DOCUMENT NUMBER
	1 APR 1959	

FORM 3-58 610b

SECRET

DISPATCH

CLASSIFICATION: ~~SECRET~~

DISPATCH SYMBOL AND NO.

HEADQUARTERS FILE NO.

TO

INFO

FROM: Chief, SR via Chief, WE

DATE: 1 APR 1959

RE: "43-3" — (CHECK "X" ONE)
MARKED FOR INDEXING
NO INDEXING REQUIRED
INDEXING CAN BE JUDGED BY QUALIFIED HQ. DESK ONLY

SUBJECT: Distribution and Exploitation of various Russian Editions of Dr. Zhivago

ACTION REQUIRED: Soviet reaction to reception of the book and comments on the significance of the Pasternak affair.

REFERENCE(S)

1. With the coming of the tourist season and the summer international fairs and festivals, we have been thinking about books which Soviet citizens would like to receive and which would, at the same time, produce a psychological impact upon them. We are acquiring a number of such books in Russian and English and these are available at Headquarters. The one book, however, which we feel will be of greatest interest to Soviet readers in 1959 is Pasternak's Dr. Zhivago. With this in mind we are forwarding by sea freight 5 copies of the Michigan edition of the book in Russian.

2. While the storm over the Pasternak affair has now subsided, the effect it has had upon Soviet writers, intellectuals and students continues to grow. The regime's outraged reaction to the rewarding of the Nobel Prize and the expulsion of Pasternak from the Writers' Union, demonstrated that Khrushchev's attitude toward the writers and intellectuals was not very different from Stalin's. The intelligentsia's reaction to the harsh treatment of Pasternak has been one of veiled and silent protest. The First Secretary of the Writers' Union, A. Surkov, admitted in his closing address to the Congress that the Pasternak affair had "disoriented progressive writers and put in their hearts some doubts about the rightness of our decision". A few of the better known writers such as Sholokhov and Ehrenburg have protested against the heavy-handed treatment given Pasternak and have let it be known that they do not believe that writers should be placed in a strait-jacket singing only the glories of the system. A number of the younger Soviet writers have attempted to separate themselves and their writings from any controversial issues. The great majority of writers seem to be confused as to just how far the artist can go within the boundaries of "socialist realism".

3. There is little doubt that Pasternak's position as a writer and poet has been enhanced by the regime's heavy-handed attempts to silence him and to prevent the public from reading his works. He has already become a symbol for every Soviet writer who wishes to express his own ideas and convictions. Even members of the "apparatus" who have officially condemned Pasternak have managed by ingenious means to read parts of Dr. Zhivago and have commented favorably upon its literary value. For many Soviet students he has become something of an intellectual hero: it is now a matter of intellectual pride to know as much as possible about the latest works of the forbidden poet. In spite of the personal risks involved, many students have been able to get clandestine copies of the controversial novel. Reports indicate that parts of Dr. Zhivago had been hand copies and are circulating among the students. Other reports state that clandestine copies of the book have been selling for one to two thousand rubles.

4. In view of this wide spread interest and demand for the book, we are attempting to make various editions of it available to Western travelers or officials who will have contact with Soviet citizens. Most of the 1,100 copies of the Mouton edition of Dr. Zhivago already have been passed to Soviets. We are, therefore, replacing this edition with the Michigan Russian edition of the book. Since this edition was published in the United States, it is particularly well suited for passage to Soviets

FORM 10-57 (40) 53 — USE PREVIOUS EDITION. REPLACES FORMS 51-28, 51-28A AND 51-29 WHICH ARE OBSOLETE.

CLASSIFICATION: ~~SECRET~~

[X] CONTINUED

PAGE NO.

RECORD COPY

RECORD COPY

c. I thereupon asked if someone could induce Feltrinelli to deal directly with [redacted] publishers on the rights question. [redacted] mentioned that he had been invited to a reception for Feltrinelli by Pantheon Books, Ind., Pasternak's American publishers, later in the afternoon of 1 April but was unable to go. Using this as an excuse for getting in touch with Kyrill Schabert, President of Pantheon, [redacted] telephoned to Schabert in New York. Gist of their conversation was: [redacted] asked Schabert to urge Feltrinelli to answer his mail, particularly from [redacted] publishers, because a lack of interest by Feltrinelli in [redacted] requests for rights would only encourage the theft of rights by irresponsible publishers there. Schabert promised to do what he could and would report back. When I checked with [redacted] today he said he had not heard back from Schabert, but added he would phone again. He also said he would ask Schabert if he considered a direct visit to Feltrinelli by the [redacted] publishers in New York would produce results. [redacted] hinted doubts about this approach, principally because Feltrinelli has told Schabert that his office had been handling requests for publishing rights, long before he left Italy. Even if he met [redacted] personally, Feltrinelli probably would not be able to remember the correspondence, and might not even be interested in pursuing the subject. Feltrinelli, [redacted] said he had been told, had an attitude of superiority of business details, especially as it concerned Dr. Zhivago, being more interested in "idealism." Upon my urging, however, [redacted] agreed to do everything possible along this line.

d. [redacted] confirmed that British Commonwealth rights in the English language, [redacted] have been conferred upon William Collins. Thus, anyone who wishes to publish Dr. Zhivago in English [redacted] must deal with Collins, whereas deals for other languages [redacted] may be made directly with Feltrinelli's office in Milan.

e. In the 1 April phone conversation Schabert reported he could not tell whether Feltrinelli was personally grateful to Schabert for having helped smooth the way for the American visa, but that he seemed to be enjoying himself. From [redacted] account, Schabert and others in contact with Feltrinelli in New York have found it difficult to get specific with him.

3. Dr. Zhivago. [redacted] learned at the same time that 596,000 copies of the Pantheon edition of Dr. Zhivago had been sold through book stores and an additional 250,000 through book clubs, for a total of nearly 850,000 as of 30 March 1959. By now Pasternak must have nearly $1,000,000 in royalties in Switzerland, [redacted] estimated.

Half of this is from the English-language editions, and most of the rest from French, German and Italian editions. He guessed that, of the American edition, probably not more than 200,000 had been read cover-to-cover.

6. Some 20 titles on the list of books recommended for exhibition in the Soviet Union this summer (Memo [redacted] dated 9 March 1959, subject "Books recommended for exhibition at Sokolniki Park and the Moscow Fair) were rejected, [redacted] informed me. These were publications of International Publishers, New York, and Citadel Press, New York. International Publishers is a Communist outfit and Citadel is at least fellow-traveling, and [redacted] understandably does not wish to sponsor the production of either, he said.

Distribution:
Orig - [redacted]
1 - [redacted] Attn: [redacted]
1 - O/S, Atten: [redacted]
1 - WE-4, Atten: [redacted]
1 - [redacted] Attn: [redacted]
1 - IO/1, Attn: [redacted]

2 April 1959

MEMORANDUM FOR THE RECORD

SUBJECT: Conference with [redacted]

1. On 1 April I visited [redacted] [redacted] in his office to discuss Publisher Giangiacomo Feltrinelli of Milan, Dr. Zhivago and other matters in the book field. We talked briefly on the same matters today, also at his office.

2. Feltrinelli.

a. [redacted] received from me a sterilized list of countries and languages in which Pasternak's novel had been published (taken from Memorandum for the Record, 23 March 1959, subject, "Editions of Dr. Zhivago"). I asked if there was some way to prod Feltrinelli himself on the subject of publishing editions in English [redacted].

b. [redacted] remarked the lack of [redacted] publishers on the list, and said he knew of [redacted] now in New York studying the American publishing business. All had written to Feltrinelli months ago asking for publication rights in their respective languages but had received no answer. Their names, and the languages for which they sought rights, follow:

Air

~~Secret~~

Info: Chief, WE
Chief, SR

REDWOOD/Psych

Purchase of Legal Edition of Dr. Zhivago

Action Required: None

Reference: , dated 3 March 1959

1. Upon receipt of reference, and order 15 copies of the legal edition of Dr. Zhivago. got in touch with Mouton and was told the book had not yet been published by them. Furthermore, they seemed unwilling to discuss the publication and evade questions about its eventual appearance on the market.

2. A couple of weeks were allowed to pass and called Mouton once again, only to receive the same treatment. We cannot explain Mouton's attitude but have made request for 15 copies a standing requirement for

Distribution:

15 April 1959:

~~Secret~~

CS COPY

CLASSIFIED MESSAGE

~~S-E-C-R-E-T~~

FILE NO.

DATE : 18 APR 59

TO : DIRECTOR

FROM :

ACTION: SR 6

INFO :

ROUTING: 1 SR/2, 2, 3, 4, 5, 6

RE Filing (check one):
No CS Record Value. Destroy.
RI file this copy as indicated ✓
Branch copy filed as indicated

APR 18 1417Z 59

ROUTINE

TO INFO DIR CITE

REDWOOD PSYCH

RE

MOUTON HAS BEEN POSTPONING PUBLICATION DOCTOR ZHIVAGO. UNCERTAIN IT WILL EVER BE PUBLISHED WILL ADVISE IF SITUATION CHANGES. RUSSIAN EDITION DOCTOR ZHIVAGO HAS BEEN PUBLISHED BY UNIVERSITY OF MICHIGAN PRESS.

END OF MESSAGE

RI COPY

ROUTING	INITIAL
RI/AN	
RI/TY	
~~DESTROY~~	
RI/FI	

~~S-E-C-R-E-T~~

FORM 4-58 1389 USE PREVIOUS EDITIONS

 Copy No. (35)

DISPATCH

CLASSIFICATION: ~~S E C R E T~~

DISPATCH SYMBOL AND NO.

TO: SR

HEADQUARTERS FILE NO.: Not known

FROM:

DATE: APR 23 1959

SUBJECT: REDWOOD/AEDINOSAUR
Request for Copies of Dr. Zhivago

RE: "43-3" — (CHECK "X" ONE)
- MARKED FOR INDEXING
- xx NO INDEXING REQUIRED
- INDEXING CAN BE JUDGED BY QUALIFIED HQ. DESK ONLY

ACTION REQUIRED: See below.

REFERENCE(S)

2. For the present, the previously reserved quantities of 50 copies of regular edition and 500 of the pocket-size seem adequate. We would appreciate your these in small quantities of 10 regular and 50 pocket-size each month.

/20 April 1959

Distribution:

Taking ... under AEDINOSAUR
Confirmed by phone on 14 May

23 apr 59

FORM 10-57 (40) 53b — USE PREVIOUS EDITION. REPLACES FORMS 51-28, 51-28A AND 51-29 WHICH ARE OBSOLETE.

CLASSIFICATION: ~~S-E-C-R-E-T~~

CONTINUED

HQ COPY

CLASSIFIED MESSAGE

S-E-C-R-E-T

FILE NO.

ROUTING

1	SR/2	4	
2		5	
3		6	

: 28 APR 59

TO : DIRECTOR

FROM :

ACTION: SR 6

INFO :

RE Filing (check one):
No CS Record Value. Destroy. ☐
RI file this copy as indicated ☑
Branch copy filed as indicated ☐

APR 29 0443Z 59

ROUTINE

TO INFO DIR CITE 7713

REDWOOD PSYCH

RE

1. NOW INDICATES 15 COPIES MOUTON RUSSIAN LANGUAGE EDITION DOCTOR ZHIVAGO WILL BE OBTAINED THIS WEEK AT COST APIECE.

2. CAN FORWARD AS SEES FIT. PLEASE ADVISE.

END OF MESSAGE

C/S COMMENT: *STATED MOUTON HAS BEEN POSTPONING PUBLICATION OF "DR. ZHIVAGO". UNCERTAIN WHETHER IT WILL EVER BE PUBLISHED. WOULD ADVISE IF SITUATION CHANGES.

ROUTING	INITIAL
RI/AN	
RI/TY	
~~DESTROY~~	
RI/FI	

S-E-C-R-E-T

16 July 1959

MEMORANDUM FOR: [redacted]

SUBJECT : Publication of the Miniature Edition of Dr. Zhivago

1. Nine thousand copies of the miniature Russian language edition of Dr. Zhivago have been sent to [redacted] for distribution to Soviets. The miniature edition will be distributed primarily by legal travelers going to the Soviet Union and by [redacted] [redacted] agents who have contact with Soviet tourists and officials in the West. Two thousand copies of the miniature edition have been made available for distribution to Soviet and East European students at the Vienna Youth Festival.

2. The miniature edition was produced at Headquarters from the original Russian language text of the Mouton edition. It [redacted] [redacted] appears in a one and two volume series. The book was designed so that it could be easily concealed and fits inside a man's suit or trouser pocket.

In addition to the above, Subject will bring a list of Soviet citizens to the late July briefing. This is a list of suggested contacts which [redacted] gave to Subject with the advice that these people will tell him what life is really like in the USSR. Subject states that [redacted] smuggled messages to Italy for Pasternac during the summer of 1957.

From [redacted] contact report dated 15 July 1959

24 September 1959

MEMORANDUM FOR: The Record

SUBJECT: Meeting on SR Division Project AEDINOSAUR,

2. met with before arrived so that could be given a little preliminary briefing on both the and positions in this matter. was told that was relying on to handle all the commercial and legal aspects of the arrangement and that their concern was that the whole matter be handled as simply as possible and that they wanted a long range commitment from .

3. When arrived the matter of publishing rights was first discussed. It was agreed that this matter should not be of too much concern on the first book, or on any other book which had already published in English, since in those instances should either already have the foreign language rights, or know how to get them, or not really be concerned about the matter. felt that probably does not really secure rights as such because they cannot be secured in most instances since most of the authors are behind the curtain. However, it was agreed by all persons present that as subsidy-purchasers we do not really have to be concerned with this problem.

5. was particularly concerned about the actual delivery of the books on each transaction. He wants them delivered,

SECRET

12. It was also agreed that we would make no attempt to participate in any royalties but that [redacted] would investigate the possibilities for getting a better contract price from [redacted] than the one originally proposed since we will be underwriting all the costs of publication and any books [redacted] sells will be "pure gravy" to him. Also the fact that we plan four or five deals each year should be further incentive for him to reduce the contract price.

Commercial Staff

if possible, in one package and at one spot.

8. also requested confirmation on the long-range commitment, ~~because SR is not interested in executing an agreement for the first book unless is willing to commit himself for the other activities SR has in mind.~~ He also is very concerned with timing because it is SR's position that they must have the first book, and any other books given to him this year, in published form by the spring of 1960 or the books would be of no value. They have to aim at the tourists each year and their distribution season is May through August. *erroneous per*

9. advised that he, of course, had not himself talked with but had to pass on to the attorney the information supplied by in his letter of 8 September 1959 and the attorney, in turn, discussed the matter with . Unfortunately the attorney did not get to spend much time with since was about to take off on an European trip. The information supplied by the attorney was principally concerned with the arrangements for the first publication, but assumed that had been approached on the long-range plan and had shown at least general interest in it. However said that he would, upon his return to New York, contact the attorney again and get more specific information from him. will be out of the country until the 19th of October and, therefore, any specific action with him will have to wait until then.

10. agreed to forward to the specific SR requirements, which SR had supplied, for his use in talking to the attorney.

11. Also during the interim period awaiting the return of agreed to work on a draft contract. has in its files a couple ~~subsidy-intervention~~ agreements which will make available to for guidance in this matter.

~~SECRET~~

~~SECRET~~
(WHEN FILLED IN)

PROJECT ACTION SHEET

I PROJECT CRYPTONYM	AEDINOSAUR		
	NEW PROJECT APPROVAL	DIVISION	SR
	AMENDMENT NO.	BRANCH	
XX	RENEWAL FY 1960	DESK	
	TERMINATION	CASE OFFICER	

II DIVISION CONCURRENCES

ORGANIZATIONAL ELEMENT	SIGNATURE TYPED & SIGNED	COPY NO.	DATE	MEMORANDUM ATTACHED YES	NO	DATE
SR/BF						
SR/SS						
SR/COP						
CSR						

III CONCURRENCES – OTHER DIVISIONS AND OFFICES

~~RR/RRD~~	~~XXXXXXXXXXXXXX~~	~~X~~				
A SSA-DD/S		2	9/24/59			
		1 & 3	22 Sept. '59			
		1	25 Sept 59			
	1) Funds programmed in operating budget					

IV APPROVAL

SUBJECT PROJECT ACTION IS APPROVED IN THE AMOUNT OF FOR FY 19 60
FUNDS TO SUPPORT THIS ACTION ARE AVAILABLE FROM WITHIN THE CURRENT ALLOCATIONS TO THE DIVISION. Single activities involving expenditures up to may be authorized Single activities involving expenditures up to may be authorized by Chief, SR Division.

Deputy Direc Plans)		25 Sept 59
APPROVING ORITY	SIGNATURE	DATE

Body-221

FORM 2-59 848 USE PRE EDITION (5)

~~SECRET~~

	FY 1959 Expend.	FY 1960 Estimates
TOTAL		
TOTAL		

4. Delegation of authority--Activities involving or less can be approved by

It is requested that Chief, SR Division be authorized to expend up to for a single D&TO activity. This level is suggested in view of the financial level of the project and the fact that this is the sole D&TO for SR Division.

SECRET

NOTIFICATION OF PROJECT APPROVAL

PROJECT: **AEDINOSAUR (D & TO)**

ACTION		AREA
	NEW PROJECT	DIVISION SR
	AMENDMENT NO.	
X	RENEWAL (FY 1960)	BRANCH
	TERMINATION	DESK
X	MEMO REQUEST Change in Authorization Level.	

AUTHORIZATION

APPROVING AUTHORITY	AMOUNT	FISCAL YEAR
DD/P 25 September 1959		1960

CONDITIONS OF APPROVAL

Renewal in the amount of [redacted] for FY 1960 approved. In addition, following authorization levels approved:

a. The [redacted] is authorized to approve expenditures not to exceed [redacted] for any single activity during the fiscal year.

b. The Chief, SR Division is authorized to approve expenditures not to exceed [redacted] for any single activity during the fiscal year.

c. Expenditures in excess of above will be coordinated with [redacted] and require approval of higher authority, as appropriate, under the Agency Approval System.

PP/PRD/PPB REF. NO.	SIGNATURE	DATE
		29 September 1959

DISTRIBUTION

1	DDP	1	SSA-DD/S	1	COVERT BUDGET BRANCH	1	OPERATING DIVISION CHIEF OF SUPPORT	1	PP/PRD	2	PP/PRD/PPB

Body-223

FORM 2-59 849 USE PREVIOUS EDITIONS.

SECRET

(5)

~~SECRET~~
(When Filled In)

6 Aug. 59

PROJECT FINANCIAL DATA *MAY NOT EXCEED SECRET CLASSIFICATION	PROJECT CRYPTONYM: AEDINOSAUR FISCAL PERIOD COVERED: 1 July 1959 THRU 30 JUNE 1960
RESPONSIBLE STAFF OR DIVISION: SR DIVISION	CASE OFFICER:

A. PERSONNEL REQUIREMENTS

Indicate number and type of personnel required and estimated total compensation for salary, allowances, travel and related employee benefits. Include everyone paid from project.

TYPE	NUMBER		ESTIMATED COMPENSATION		
	U. S. PERSONNEL	FOREIGN NATIONAL	BASE SALARY	ALL OTHER	TOTAL
STAFF EMPLOYEES					
STAFF AGENTS					
CAREER AGENTS					
CONTRACT AGENTS					
CONTRACT CONSULTANTS					
DETAILED PERSONNEL					
FIELD AGENTS					
MILITARY					
ALL OTHER					
TOTAL A.					

B. SUPPLIES, MATERIEL AND EQUIPMENT

Indicate amount required in applicable spaces. Attach complete supporting list for each.

COMMO	CHEMICAL	QUARTERMASTER SUPPLIES	OTHER SUPPLIES
$	$	$	$
MEDICAL	ORDNANCE	SPECIAL DEVICES	OTHER EQUIPMENT
$	$	$	$

TOTAL B.

C. OTHER OPERATIONAL EXPENSES

Indicate volume and nature of expenses such as (1) maintaince of two operational houses abroad (2) spot purchase of information, etc.

D&TO operational expenses.

TOTAL C.

D. SUBSIDY OR PROPRIETARY PAYMENTS

If funds are to be turned over to individuals or groups in large lump sums to be expended by the individuals or groups at their discretion to accomplish an agreed-upon objective, explain the type of financial accounts, factual verification or statements, if any, other than a receipt for the lump sum, which will be obtained.

TOTAL D.

TOTAL FUND REQUIREMENTS (A + B + C + D) $

FORM 7-57 756 USE PREVIOUS EDITION.

(1)

	FY 1959 Expend.	FY 1960 Estimates
TOTAL		

d. Anticipated Major Operations or Events

(1) Publication of ten to twelve books for USSR .

(2)

(3)

REQUEST FOR PROJECT RENEWAL

1. It is requested that Project AEDINOSAUR, the D&TO project for the SR Division, be renewed for FY 1960 in the amount of . The project was included in the FY 1960 Operational Program for the SR Division in the amount of (FY 1959, an extra) was obligated to) On 1 July 1959, responsibility as senior case officer for Project AEDINOSAUR was transferred from to

2. Funds approved and obligated by fiscal year since project initiation:

	Funds Approved	Funds Obligated
FY 1957	$	$
FY 1958		
FY 1959		

3. Summary of D&TO Activities:

	FY 1959 Expend.	FY 1960 Estimates
a. Development of Projects		
(1) Translation and publishing of (3000 copies).	$	$
(2) The publication of miniature editions of and (2500 copies of each).		
(3)		
(4)		

	FY 1959 Expend.	FY 1960 Estimates

b. Projects Submitted

(1) As a result of activities funded out of AEDINOSAUR, were approved in early 1959.

c. Target of Opportunity Activities

(1) $

(2) Exploitation of Dr. Zhivago.

(3) Purchase of hard-backed books, pocket books and phonograph records for USSR

(4)

(5)

(6)

purchase of materials for travellers to bring into the USSR.

(7)

(9) Misc.

TOTAL $

SECRET

14 October 1959

MEMORANDUM FOR: Commercial Staff

ATTENTION: [redacted]

SR Division

ATTENTION: [redacted]

SUBJECT : [redacted] Publication Project

Following our conference of today, I have drawn-up and attach hereto a paper I propose to leave both with [redacted] and the cleared attorney tomorrow with the request that the latter draw-up a draft agreement and furnish it to Ted for his and Headquarters' review. Please let me know if you have any suggestions.

Assistant General Counsel

Attachment
Distribution:
1 - [redacted]
1 - SR Division w/att.

SECRET

Requirements for [redacted] Contract

1. Translate book into Russian.

2. Print and publish in Russian.

3. Make available to us stated number of copies (2,000 to 3,000 normally) without charge.

4. Make available to us upon request additional copies at an agreed discount price.

5. Distribute the Russian language book through normal commercial channels and normal advertising media. Guarantee distribution in at least one Western Europe outlet and one New York outlet. Provide us with name and address of all outlets and date first shipment received by those outlets.

6. With respect to works, the copyright of which is not held by [redacted] copyright and royalty questions are [redacted] responsibility.

7. We will pay [redacted] __________ dollars for the foregoing (except amounts due under paragraph 4 above), __________ dollars on execution of this contract, __________ dollars on date required copies shipped to us and __________ dollars on date we notified of name, address and date of European outlet and date first shipment is to reach that outlet.

8. We will compensate [redacted] for any royalties he is required to pay with respect to works, the copyright of which is held by someone other than [redacted] provided the amount is approved by us prior to the date of [redacted] agreement with the owner of the copyright.

21 October 1959

MEMORANDUM FOR THE RECORD

SUBJECT: AEDINOSAUR

This is to record my understanding of the current situation and my participation in recent events concerning the proposal to have various novels published in the Russian language by

a. advises today that the senior Staff is contemplating a project to have novels published in several languages and there is a good possibility that the SR interest will be merged into the over-all project. Action is to halt pending decision on these points.

b. I talked yesterday with the cleared New York attorney. On my first visit with a few weeks ago I had said that I would furnish him with satisfactory identification of me as a CIA representative. went with me yesterday to see present his credentials, and thereby certify my identity. said he was glad to have this certification, but he had felt perfectly satisfied on that point. then left. I left with the attached statement of requirements for the contract which we had drawn up in Washington on October 19, and which and I modified somewhat just prior to my visit with , at my request, will prepare a draft contract to accomplish these requirements and send it to me in a few days for our review. It is our thought that this draft, modified as may be needed, will become the contract to be executed with for each of the several books.

c. I talked with again today. Following my visit with him yesterday he called who returned from Europe on Monday, and advised him that action is being held up pending further instructions from the client, including a possible instruction to publish another novel instead, and shall stand fast until further contact. further advised course it might be necessary to deliver some of the copies to a [redacted] warehouse or other delivery point which [redacted] would arrange, if desired.

SIGNED

Assistant General Counsel

Attachment

OGC/[redacted]
Distribution:
Orig. - AEDINOSAUR
1 - CI/[redacted]
1 - SR/[redacted]
1 - [redacted]
1 - [redacted]
1 - Chrono
1 - East

it is contemplated this may be the first of several publications. This point of course was made with the view to its effect on in setting his charge to us. indicated he was quite satisfied and would hold himself in readiness for further communication from I told I would be in touch with him shortly, I assumed early next week.

d. In New York, I told the present contemplation is that his client will be the name of which I would furnish him in due course, rather than "an undisclosed principle." At my earlier meeting with I had indicated that we expected he would bill us on an hourly basis, rather than a retainer. He advised on this occasion, upon my inquiry, that his hourly rate would be .

e. Before seeing I talked with Tuesday morning in New York. He suggested the following:

(1) With respect to the statement of requirements for the contract with , we should not undertake to compensate for royalties paid by him since should take this item into account in negotiating the amount to be paid him by us for publishing and distributing.

(2) We should require that at least a stated number of volumes be printed and published. This with the view to having copies available for commercial distribution and enabling to lower unit costs and presumably unit sales price.

(3) The contract should make clear that distribution and advertising costs are

(4) Probably the easiest, most normal way to handle this operation would be for to have little or no participation. There is really no business service required and if the cleared attorney, as is contemplated, is to function as our representative he can be in direct contact with his client (Headquarters) thereby removing one step in communications. did indicate that of

Requirements for [redacted] Contract

1. Translate book into Russian.

2. Print and publish in Russian stated number of copies.

3. Make available to us stated number of copies (2,000 to 3,000 normally) without charge.

4. Make available to us upon request additional copies at an agreed discount price.

5. Distribute the Russian language book, at publisher's expense, through normal commercial channels and normal advertising media. Guarantee distribution in at least one Western Europe outlet and one New York outlet. Provide us with name and address of all outlets and date first shipment received by those outlets.

6. Copyright and royalty questions are [redacted] responsibility.

7. We will pay [redacted] ___________ dollars for the foregoing (except amounts due under paragraphs 4 and 5 above), ___________ dollars on execution of this contract, ___________ dollars on date required copies shipped to us and ___________ dollars on date we notified of name, address and date of European outlet and date first shipment is to reach that outlet.

Approved for Release: 2014/04/07

артистическому и музыкальному миру, к которому принадлежали его родители.

Борис Пастернак приобрел большую известность, главным образом, как поэт и талантливый переводчик Шекспира и Гете.

"Доктор Живаго" - его первый большой роман, который, благодаря высокой художественности, яркости и глубине, обратил на себя внимание во всем мире.

Роман "Доктор Живаго" был опубликован в переводах на итальянском, английском и немецком языках. Настоящее издание является первым на русском языке. В Советском Союзе этот труд Пастернака до сих пор не издавался.

ОТ ИЗДАТЕЛЬСТВА

Автор этой книги, Борис Потернак, рассматривается знатоками русской литературы, как наиболее талантливый из современных мастеров слова в Советском Союзе.

По словам автора, этот роман является основным трудом всей его жизни. В монументальном произведении Пастернака отображена целая эпоха. Тут проявляется особое искусство автора, сумевшего перенестись от нарисования политических сдвигов данного исторического этапа к глубокому вниканию в вечные проблемы человеческой души.

В фокусе творчества писателя находятся люди, внешне захваченные событиями нашего века, но, до известной степени, стоящие в стороне от них. Герой Пастернака, доктор Живаго, хотя и принадлежит к советскому обществу, но связан с ним лишь постольку, поскольку ему было суждено в нем жить. Трагические потрясения, свидетелем которых был доктор Живаго, привлекают интерес автора в непосредственной связи с тем толкованием, которое им дает герой книги.

Борис Пастернак родился в 1890 году в Москве, в семье талантливого художника, проибретшего своими картинами мировую известность. Мать Пастернака была исключительно одаренной концертной пианисткой. Таким образом, с раннего детства Пастернак приобщился к тому высоко-культурному

Publisher's Note

Boris Pasternak is recognized by critics of Russian literature as the greatest living Soviet writer. Dr. Zhivago is the author's first long novel. Until now he has been acclaimed as a great poet rather than a novelist.

Born in 1890 in Moscow of an artistic family -- his father was a well known painter and his mother an accomplished pianist -- Pasternak first thought of becoming a musician. In his biography he writes that he "loved music more than anything else in the world....", but he soon decided to give up music to devote himself to philosophy because "life revealed the many abysses and terrifying discoveries of the unknown."

The force of imagery, the art of expressing himself in his own individualistic way and of creating profound visual impressions was evident in Pasternak's early poetry and has remained his particular gift ever since. He also has been recognized as one of the outstanding translators of Shakespeare and Goethe.

It is not known when Pasternak began writing Dr. Zhivago or what made him embark on this tremendous work; the author has only revealed that it is the work of his lifetime.

Like Tolstoy's War and Peace, Dr. Zhivago is a historical epic. Pasternak, however, is not concerned with any specific political events but with the role of the individual in history, with the contrast between the personal ambitions, hopes and fears of an individual and the "inhuman rationalism of history". Pasternak argues that in the last analysis it is only the moral and thinking individual who can build the humane and just society.

Dr. Zhivago was completed more than two years ago but it still has not been published in the Soviet Union. In the meantime, it has been published in Italian, English and German. It is now being published in the original Russian because it is considered to be a great work of art -- a work of lasting value.

ПРИМЕЧАНИЯ ИЗДАТЕЛЯ.

Автор настоящего романа, Борис Пастернак, рассматривается критиками русской литературы, как наиболее талантливый из современных советских писателей.

По словам автора этот роман является основным трудом всей его жизни. И, хотя в нем находят свое отображение события целой эпохи, однако, его отличительной чертой является глубокая проникновенность не в связанные с нею политические события эпохи, а в субъективную сущность тех эмоциональных переживаний, которые они вызывали в жизни описываемых им индивидуальностей.

В фокусе авторского интереса находятся люди, захваченные событиями эпохи, но до известной степени стоящими в стороне от них. Герой Пастернака, доктор Живаго, хотя и принадлежит к советскому обществу, но он связан с ним лишь эпизодически, постольку поскольку советское общество являлось тем окружением, той обстановкой, в которой проходила жизнь доктора Живаго. Те трагические события, свидетелями которых был доктор Живаго, интересуют автора лишь постольку, поскольку они находят оценку и субъективную интерпретацию со стороны его героя.

Борис Пастернак родился в 1890 году в Москве, в семье талантливого художника, приобревшего мировую известность своими картинами. Мать Пастернака была исключительно одаренной концертной пианисткой. Таким образом, с раннего детства Пастернак приобщился к тому высококультурному артистическому и музыкальному обществу, к которому принадлежали его родители.

В своей автобиографии Пастернак уделяет много места любви к музыке, которую он унаследовал от матери. Он даже хотел посвятить себя музыкальной карьере. По его словам "любовь к музыке была наисильнейшим стимулом в его жизни".

Пастернак приобрел литературную известность, главным образом, как поэт и как талантливый переводчик Шекспира и Гете.

"Доктор Живаго" является его первым большим романом, который благодаря его высокой художественности и яркости отображаемых им субъективных переживаний обратил на себя внимание всего мира.

Роман "Доктор Живаго" был опубликован на итальянском, английском и немецком языках и настоящее издание является первым на русском языке, так как в Советском Союзе он не был опубликован до сих пор.

Повествования романа начинаются с 1905 года и, таким образом, они отображают характерные эпизоды всей последующей эпохи, включая обе мировые войны, революцию и последовавшую за нею гражданскую войну.

July 8, 1958

AR 70-14

Enclosed is the publisher's note, together with a very rough translation thereof. I trust that the delay in my transmitting these papers will not unduly affect the timing on the plates.

Yours very truly,

AR 70-14

Encs.

www.ingramcontent.com/pod-product-compliance
Lightning Source LLC
Chambersburg PA
CBHW081134300726
48982CB00005B/967
* 9 7 8 1 6 0 8 8 8 3 1 0 3 *